"Oh, no." and laid her ear against his chest. The layers of clothes could've obscured the sound, but she didn't hear the beat of his heart.

Maybe she should've taken the CPR class Tristan had suggested.

Angeline leaned over Lincoln's all-too-still body and lowered her face to his. Just before she touched his jaw to pry open his mouth, Lincoln's eyelashes lifted. Mischief sparkled in his pale green eyes.

"Hello, Angel." His hand rose to cup the back of her neck while the other slid around her waist, pulling her on top of him.

His mouth, cold from the wind, captured her lips, muffling her surprise. A rush of desire followed on the heels of utter relief. Without meaning to do so, she relaxed in the warmth spreading through her.

Lincoln deepened the kiss, the taste of coffee and syrup still on his tongue. Probing gently, he explored her mouth, unleashing peals of excitement low in her belly.

Encouraging Lincoln's attention was reckless. He stirred up feelings no other man had since Tanner had left her. A feeling she wouldn't mind exploring with someone other than a Dogman.

So why didn't she want to resist his kiss?

Southern born and bred, **Kristal Hollis** holds a psychology degree and has spent her adulthood helping people and animals. When a family medical situation resulted in a work sabbatical, she began penning deliciously dark paranormal romances as an escape from the real-life drama. But when the crisis passed, her passion for writing love stories continued. A 2015 Golden Heart® Award finalist, Kristal lives with her husband and two rescued dogs at the edge of the enchanted forest that inspires her stories.

Books by Kristal Hollis

Harlequin Nocturne

Awakened by the Wolf
Rescued by the Wolf
Charmed by the Wolf
Captivated by the She-Wolf
Tamed by the She-Wolf

TAMED BY THE SHE-WOLF

—

KRISTAL HOLLIS

Recycling programs
for this product may
not exist in your area.

ISBN-13: 978-1-335-62969-2

Tamed by the She-Wolf

Copyright © 2018 by Kristal Hollis

Printed in U.S.A.

Dear Reader,

The opportunity to write Angeline and Lincoln's story came as a bit of a surprise. Not originally planned in the Wahyas of Walker's Run series, *Tamed by the She-Wolf* came into being after the announcement that the Harlequin Nocturne line would close. Though I was delighted to revisit the familiar characters and places of the Walker's Run world, I did experience a certain sadness as I wrote.

Nevertheless, I do love happy endings and I am excited to present to you the fifth story in the Wahyas of Walker's Run series. I hope you enjoy Angeline and Lincoln's adventure.

I love hearing from readers. To connect with me, visit www.kristalhollis.com.

Happy reading!

Kristal

To everyone on the Nocturne team, thank you
for not only making my dreams come true,
but also making them shine.

Chapter 1

"*D*ayax!"

Having shifted into his wolf form under cover of night, Lincoln Adams eased farther into the dilapidated two-story building, shot-up and abandoned long before he and his team had arrived in Taifa, a war-torn village in southern Somalia and home to the Yeeyi pack.

Wahyas, an ancient species of wolf shifters who were caught in the middle of escalating human conflicts, faced a greater likelihood of unintentional exposure. To minimize the risk, the Woelfesenat, the secretive international wolf council, developed elite Special Forces teams called Dogmen. Their primary function: safeguarding Wahyas in harm's way while aiding human allies in their worldwide peacekeeping endeavors.

Since their arrival in Taifa six months ago, Lincoln's Dogman team had been providing support to UN forces defending the area against militant insurgents and administering humanitarian aid.

Dayax, an orphaned wolfling who'd made himself somewhat of a daily pest at their base of operation, had disappeared from his village during the guerillas' morning raid.

Tonight, Lincoln's mission, though not officially sanctioned, nonetheless fell within the scope of his sworn duties. Still, he'd chosen to conduct the search and rescue alone.

Sensing movement behind him, Lincoln spun around, baring his teeth, and issued a low, threatening growl. Five dark, stealthy figures covertly closed in on the building.

Damn ass-wipes.

Affection flooded his wolfan body while he watched his team, in their human forms, fall into position as they had done on countless missions. Handgun drawn, Lila Raycen quietly and quickly entered the building, snapped a quick look around and then gave a hand signal to her teammates. Her gaze sweeping the street, she whispered, "Sorry, Cap'n. All for one and all that jazz."

Lincoln couldn't speak the words floating through his mind. Wahyas could only telepathically communicate with other Wahyas if both were in their wolfan forms. Unless, of course, they were mated, which he and Lila were not. Nor would they ever be.

Although grateful at the show of Lila's support, he growled to officially express displeasure at her disregard of his direct order for the team to remain on-base.

"You can thank me later—" she smirked "—with a fat, juicy steak."

She had a long wait. On deployment, Dogmen's diets consisted of water and rations—canned and freeze-dried. Lincoln couldn't remember the last time he'd eaten a real meal. But once this assignment ended and they returned to HQ, his first home-cooked meal would be fried, shredded beef empanadas. His weren't as good as the ones his mom made but she had the actual family recipe handed down from her *bisabuela*, while he had to make them from memory, since Dogmen weren't allowed contact with family or friends while in the Program.

One more team member entered the building; the remaining three set up watch outside.

"Are you sure this is the right place?" Damien Marquez asked. A member of Lincoln's team for less than a year and a royal pain in the ass, but the fresh-faced Dogman made a damn good soldier.

Lincoln nodded. Dayax had lived in the abandoned building ever since his parents died. On his first patrol of the village, Lincoln had discovered the wolfling scavenging in the streets. And Lincoln had been feeding him ever since.

He'd also notified his superiors of Dayax's plight, requesting an extraction and transport to a new pack. Their negative response didn't stop him from keeping an eye on Dayax or from planning to take the boy with him once the deployment ended. Screw HQ.

"All right," Lila said quietly. "Let's find the wolfling and get the hell out of here."

Using his snout, Lincoln motioned for Damien to stand watch at the entrance. Since he'd already searched the bottom floor, Lincoln signaled Lila to follow him upstairs. Remaining in his wolf form, he hoped the wolfling would either hear his telepathic calls or see his wolf and come out of hiding.

Lincoln bounded up the mostly intact stairwell. The bulletproof vest he wore, specially fitted for his wolf, chaffed despite a thick coat of fur.

Following close on his heels, Lila, his second-in-command, obeyed orders as well as she gave them. Except for tonight's excursion, she'd never disobeyed a direct command. But he wouldn't fault her for this one. Loyalty sometimes outweighed a crappy order.

Together for the last five years, he would miss her support and friendship when she got her own team. He knew she would because he had been the one to recommend her for promotion.

Lincoln continued reaching out telepathically to Dayax. Silence answered, time and time again.

The worry gnawing Lincoln's gut spread into his chest. As they carefully cleared the second floor, the probability that the wolfling had been injured in the earlier firefight or had been taken by the rebels became a clear and present concern.

"Más rápido!" Standing at the bottom of the stairs, Damien waved for them to hurry. "There's movement down the street and it isn't the Red Cross handing out lollipops and blankets."

Room by room they searched. The gnawing in Lincoln's stomach would eat through his chest before long. After seeing the cruel and evil side of man and wolf for so long, Lincoln had nearly lost hope in everything. Then Dayax came along. With his inquisitive mind, generous smile and trusting eyes, despite all he'd suffered, Dayax had renewed Lincoln's faith. If he lost the boy now, the last threads of his humanity would snap.

"Se acabó el tiempo!" Damien yelled.

"Almost done," Lila replied.

Lincoln exited the last room to the left of the stairs and returned to the corridor, shaking his head. He gazed out the large window into the empty alley below.

"Dayax, wherever you are, I will find you!" He sent the question telepathically in English and Somali, hoping the wolfling would receive the message and understand that Lincoln would not give up on him.

"Last one, Linc. Then we gotta scram." Lila stopped in front of the last door to the right of the stairs.

"All right, kid. Come out, come out, wherever you are," she said, turning the doorknob. "Hmm. Must be stuck."

Lincoln's stomach knotted and a horrible foreboding drove an icy knife into his gut. *"Lila, wait!"*

Unable to hear Lincoln's telepathic warning in her human form, she shoved her shoulder against the door. It swung innocently open and she darted into the room.

The breath stalled in Lincoln's chest continued on its path, though his heart still thundered.

"Vámonos!" Damien shouted, stomping up the stairs two at a time. *"Vámonos!"*

A flash of light accompanied a resounding boom. The percussive force slammed Lincoln against the window. Deafened from the explosion, he never heard the glass break. But the air swooshed around him and his stomach looped as he plunged downward.

He would be okay; his team would be okay. Dayax would be okay. The beautiful angel inside the thin silver case tucked in the pocket of his protective vest would make sure they were. She always did.

Nine weeks later

"I'm gonna wring his freaking neck!"

Angeline O'Brien glared at the man passed out on her brand-new leather couch, thrashing and yelling in his sleep.

She slammed the apartment door, envisioning her long fingers curling around Tristan Durrance's throat for giving his subletter the wrong key.

Friends since they were tweens, neighbors for nearly all of their adult lives, and both relationshipphobes, Tristan and Angeline had traded apartment keys with the understanding that they would look out for each other. Angeline had expected the arrangement to continue into their elder years.

Unfortunately for her, last summer Tristan had accidentally claimed a mate and subsequently fallen in love, breaking up their platonic cohesiveness. Angeline didn't begrudge Tristan's happiness, but she had felt a little lonely since he'd moved out of his apartment.

But not lonely enough to play nice with a *Dogman* who had found his way into the wrong apartment. Everyone in the Walker's Run pack had been anticipating the wolfan paramilitary man's arrival for weeks. Everyone except Angeline.

Turbulent emotions rose inside her. When her first and only love, Tanner Phillips, had chosen life as a Dogman over a mateship with her, Angeline had never wanted to hear the word *Dogman* again. Neither did she ever want to come face-to-face with one.

So instead of welcoming *this* Dogman like a hero, she had a mind to toss his ass outside into the cold and slam the door in his face. Next to the two empty beer bottles on the kitchen counter, she dropped her purse and the carry-out bag from Taylor's Roadhouse, her uncle's restaurant where she worked part-time.

"Hey!" she snapped. After being on her feet all night, Angeline wanted a hot shower to wash away the food odors from her body and to relax in the utter quiet and comfort of her home. Alone. The sooner she got the Dogman into the right apartment, the better. "Wake up!"

Curled on his side, face pressed against the duffel bag he used as a pillow, the man gave no indication that he'd heard her. Every muscle in his body remained tightly coiled. A muscle spasmed along his clenched jaw and the deep furrows creased his brow.

Angeline's irritation level dropped a few notches. "Are

you all right?" She touched him. An unexpected electric current caused her fingers to tighten on his bare shoulder when she should've let go.

His large hand cuffed her wrist as he sat up. "Who are you?" he snarled. His glaring silvery-green gaze appeared to be clouded and unfocused.

"The person who owns the couch you're sleeping on." Angeline yanked her captive arm against his hold. Instead of freeing herself, she became more entangled with him as he rolled off the couch and stood, leaning heavily on her.

"Where's my team?" A shag of black hair curtained his forehead, dark brows slashed angrily over his eyes and his naturally brown skin lightly glistened with sweat. "Where's Dayax?"

"Wherever you think you are, you aren't!" She grappled against his effort to restrain her. "This is my apartment, not Tristan's, and I want you to leave."

Angeline's heart pounded with a healthy dose of adrenaline, but not outright fear. She'd had to contend with two older brothers growing up. Wrestling over one thing or another had been a daily sport and they hadn't given her any slack just because of her gender.

She wiggled one arm free, sharpened her elbow and jammed it into his solar plexus. An audible gasp filled her ear. His hold loosened. Falling away, he snatched the tails of her sweater.

With a resounding oomph, he hit the carpeted floor, flat on his back with Angeline sprawling on top of him. Immediately, his meaty arms caged her, then rolling her beneath him, he pinned her with his weight.

"I can't breathe!" At least not all that well.

Hands flat against his muscled chest, damp from sweat, Angeline shoved hard but nothing happened. Pushing over a concrete wall might've been easier than getting the wolfan male to budge.

"Who are you?" Though he allowed her some wiggle room, the timbre of his growl gave grave warning.

"The woman who will unman you if you don't get the hell off me!" Angeline scraped her nails down his taut abdomen to the waistband of his boxers. Odd, considering wolfan males didn't care to wear men's underwear. But it was winter and she was grateful that his bare ass hadn't christened her new couch.

The undergarment, however, didn't prevent her from gripping his heavy sack in a manner any man would recognize as anything but playful.

A painful snarl parted his lips. Each time she squeezed, his lids shuttered and his gaze became more focused and alert. She knew the moment his brain recognized that he was crouched intimately above a female whose body was perfectly aligned with his.

"Think carefully about your next move, Dogman."

"Oh, I'm not moving, Angel," he said calmly. Clearly. Seductively. "Not until you let go of my balls."

"Good," she said, ignoring the flutter in her stomach that his deep, quiet Texas drawl had started to stir. "Now that you're awake, do you know where you are?"

A whisper of a smile curved his mouth. "In heaven." Eyes drifting closed, he lowered his face to hers and rubbed his cheek against her jaw, snuffling her hair. "God, you smell divine."

Despite the awkward circumstance, Angeline didn't sense any threat in his manner. The reverent way he breathed in her scent seemed almost like an act of worship.

His clean male musk invaded her senses, sparking a primal interest better left dormant.

"All right. The sniff feast is over." She squeezed his sack.

Once she had his full attention again, Angeline let go. He eased off her and she sat up, watching him hoist himself onto the couch. Only then did she realize that most of his left leg was missing. She also noticed the scattered scars on his arms and torso. Some new, others quite old.

Her heart pinched but she wouldn't allow sympathy to fester. She had no business feeling anything for a Dogman.

Leaning down, he picked up the blanket that had slid to the floor during their struggle and folded it. "Apologies for the intrusion, Angel."

"My name isn't Angel. It's Angeline." She sank into the oversize chair. "That was some nightmare you were having when I came home. Have those often?"

"Every time I fall asleep."

No wonder his eyes looked weary, and wary and sad.

"And why are you sleeping on my couch, *Dogman*?"

"I prefer Lincoln," he said quietly. "Tristan left the wrong key beneath the doormat. When I called, he said you wouldn't mind if I crashed here. Clearly, he made a mistake." He removed a nude-colored stocking from the oversize duffel bag. Grimacing, he began stretching it over his naturally bronze stump.

Angeline folded her arms over her chest, hoping he didn't notice her weakness, a traitorous heart that tweaked because of the traumatic loss he had suffered. "Tristan should've warned me."

If he had, she might've refused.

Watching Lincoln pull the state-of-the-art prosthetic leg from his duffel, guilt stabbed at her conscience. He would only be in town a few weeks. She could grit her teeth and be neighborly for that long, couldn't she?

Chapter 2

Half naked and legless wasn't how Lincoln had imagined meeting his guardian angel in the flesh. Angeline's long auburn hair framed a face Lincoln would have recognized even if he were a blind man with only his hands to feel the shape of her feminine brow, her high, angular cheeks and soft, full lips. God only knew how often he had traced every angle and plane of the woman in the worn photograph he'd carried with him for the better part of the last fifteen years. Now that he'd encountered the she-wolf in the flesh, his heart wouldn't stop fluttering and the tingly sensation in his stomach would make him sick if it didn't stop soon.

Attaching the prosthetic to his stump, Lincoln didn't dare take his gaze off Angeline, fearing she would disappear like she had so often in his dreams.

The old picture entrusted to him by the dying Dogman on Lincoln's first mission hadn't done Angeline justice because it had failed to capture her fire and strength of will. Unlike the fragile, ethereal female he'd envisioned, the real woman—strong, sassy, sexy—took him utterly by surprise.

"When is the last time you ate?" Despite the gentleness in her voice, Angeline's hard, no-nonsense gaze didn't soften.

"On the plane, somewhere over the ocean," he said over the loud rumblings of his stomach. Grabbing his camo pants, he stuffed his good leg into the pant leg and then slid the other pant leg over his prosthetic without embarrassment over his nearly nude state. For Wahyas, nudity was as natural as eating and breathing.

"I'm coming off a ten-hour flight from Munich. I got stuck in customs for over two hours in the Atlanta airport because the TSA agents had never seen the bionics used in my leg. Then I had a nearly three-hour drive to get here and all of the drive-throughs in town were closed."

He wouldn't starve, though. Inside his duffel were the rations he'd consumed for so long that he no longer remembered the taste of real food.

Wordlessly, Angeline stood and strolled into the kitchen. Lincoln quickly wiggled the pants over his boxers. He didn't particularly like the undergarments but had learned to tolerate them during his recovery when the friction from long pants made his stump feel as if it were on fire.

"Bon appetite," Angeline said, returning with a large foam box in her hands.

She opened the lid. The spicy scent of a mountain of buffalo chicken wings made his mouth water. His eyes might've, too, because she had offered him food. Actual everyday, take-for-granted, comfort food. Not canned or freeze-dried rations. Not bland, pasty mess hall slop or the airline's processed micro meals. Real, honest-to-goodness food, only mere inches from his face.

But, remembering the near-empty refrigerator and pantry, he waved away her offering. "Thanks. But no."

Times were tough and he didn't want to take advantage of her kindness.

Her nostrils flared slightly and her full, luscious lips flattened.

"I meant no offense," he said, pulling on a black sweatshirt. Wolfans took food seriously. Refusing food insulted the one offering it. "But I don't need your supper."

His stomach protested. Loudly.

"I'm not the one whose stomach is about to eat itself." She jabbed the box toward him. "Take them, they're yours."

"I saw the fridge." He gently pushed back the tempting container. "You need to eat those more than I do. I have rations that will hold me over. And I'll pay you for the beer." He dug a wallet from the duffel and held out a fifty-dollar bill.

Mouth open and shock rippling through her gaze, she stared at his hand. Suddenly, full-bellied feminine laughter shook her body.

Before the explosion, Lincoln had found a woman's laugh sexy. In his current circumstance, scarred and crippled, he felt belittled and hurt. He'd built up a fantasy about this woman. One where her kindness and gentleness had soothed and safe-guarded him. In reality, Angeline mocked him the same way the Program's bureaucrats had when Lincoln had insisted that he could still perform his sworn duties.

The money slipped through his fingers and drifted to the floor. Whether she used it or not, Lincoln didn't care.

He stood, steady and effortlessly. After a month of endless practice, he could stand, walk, run, jump and climb stairs with ease. Kneeling could be a bit tricky, but he managed. Shifting into his wolf form had proven to be the most challenging. No longer could he simply strip down and crouch before turning into his wolf. Now he had to carefully remove the artificial leg, otherwise it would turn to ash during the transformation.

As life changing as the loss had been, he was grateful to be alive. If he'd died instead of Lila, no one would go to the lengths Lincoln would to find his missing wolfling.

He slung the strap of the duffel bag over his shoulder then trudged toward the door.

"Where are you going?"

"To sleep in my truck until I can straighten this out with Tristan," he snapped, too exhausted to keep the frustration and anger from his voice.

"I wasn't laughing at you, Lincoln."

His hand froze on the doorknob.

"It's sweet of you to overpay for the beer to help me out with groceries, but I don't need it. The fridge is empty because I don't like to cook, not because I can't afford to buy food. That's why I laughed."

She eased behind him. "You see, I can take care of myself. And if I ever needed anything, my family and my pack would step up. That's how the Walker's Run Co-operative works."

A few years ago, while in Romania and assigned to a protective detail for the Woelfesenat's negotiator, Brice Walker, Lincoln had learned of the Walker's Run pack's co-operative. Consisting of wolfans and a handful of humans aware of the existence of Wahyas, the Co-op gave the Walker's Run pack a public, human face and a clever way to hide in plain sight among the unsuspecting townsfolk in Maico, a small Appalachian community in northeast Georgia where the pack resided.

Pivoting toward Angeline, Lincoln noticed the genuine concern etched on her face. Clearly, she hadn't meant to upset him and he felt like an idiot to have allowed a trivial misunderstanding to bruise his pride.

Nine weeks in the infirmary at Headquarters had turned him soft. Lincoln had hoped time away from HQ might help him regain his bearings. Now, he might need to reassess that decision.

How could he stay focused on increasing his stamina and sharpening his combat skills so he could return to Somalia and find Dayax when his guardian angel had escaped his dreams and lived only a few door down from where he would be staying?

"You can have this back." Slowly, her long, tapered fingers slid into his hip pocket to deposit the fifty. The ensuing jolt to his system rendered his entire body flaccid, except for his shaft, which instantly hardened.

"As I said before, bon appétit!" Moving her other hand from behind her back, Angeline presented him with the box of chicken wings. "And no there's no need to sleep in your truck. I have a key to Tristan's apartment."

"Why?" Lincoln wondered about the relationship between the two and why Tristan had failed to mention that tidbit during their brief call earlier.

"Neighbors look out for each other." She picked up a keyring from the kitchen counter, worked off a key and handed it to Lincoln. "Welcome to the neighborhood, Lincoln."

A key in one hand and food in the other, he should be happy to finally be getting into his temporary apartment. "I wouldn't mind some company for a while."

Her gaze slid down his torso to the erection his pants couldn't hide. Food and sex. A wolfan male's priorities.

"I gave you food. Now you need to take care of the rest on your own." She reached past him and opened the door. The biting February air gusted into the apartment and nipped his skin beneath the sweatshirt.

"Good night, Lincoln." Angeline patted his chest, urging him to leave.

He'd barely stepped outside when the door closed behind him and locked.

"Whew! That was close." Angeline's voice reached his ears despite the barrier.

Turning, he strolled down the open corridor to the corner apartment, a smile budding on his face even as a weight settled in his heart. He had a mission to complete. Until he found Dayax, Lincoln would do well to resist the devilish diversion of his angelic neighbor.

Heart thumping and holding her breath, Angeline leaned against the door. The jumble of feelings knotting inside her were a fluke. Lincoln was a Dogman. Period. She could be neighborly but absolutely nothing else.

She squinched her eyes to banish the vision of him watching her beneath long, dark lashes as his silvery-green gaze caressed her face with reverence and awe. The effort merely branded the image into her brain.

Inheriting her mother's model looks, Angeline had grown numb to people's ogles, waggles and even jealousy-filled glares.

But the way Lincoln looked at her when she'd laughed and he'd misunderstood had felt like an iron fist slamming into her stomach, hard and painful.

Pushing away from the door, she trudged to the couch, slouched against the leather cushions and pulled off her boots. Next she peeled out of the thick sweater she wore over the long-sleeved T-shirt and tossed it in the chair. Picking up the afghan Lincoln had carefully folded, she inhaled his earthy male musk. Instead of trotting outside to hang the afghan on the balcony in the cold night air to remove his scent, she shook it out and laid it across her lap. After all, she couldn't leave her favorite blanket out in the elements.

Too keyed up to sleep, Angeline visually searched for the television remote and didn't see it on either end table or the entertainment center. Slipping her hand between the cushions, she not only found the remote but also Lincoln's wallet.

At the thought of returning it to him, her heart picked up speed. The sudden acceleration caused her body to tingle and anticipation coiled low in her belly.

Perhaps a brisk walk would cool things down.

Tossing aside the blanket, she didn't bother with a sweater or shoes. It would only take a minute to return the wallet. She walked outside and scurried down the corridor overlooking the parking lot to the corner apartment.

"Lincoln, it's Angeline." Knocking on the door, her fingers were as cold as ice cubes.

Tristan had disconnected the doorbell years ago. Too many people pulling him in too many directions. Once he turned off his phone to sleep, he didn't want to be disturbed by someone showing up at his door and pressing the bell until he got up.

Sure would've been nice for him to have reconnected the bell before subletting his place.

Still holding Lincoln's wallet, she tucked her hands beneath her arms to warm them. "Hurry up! I'm freezing."

"What are you doing out here, Angel?"

Angeline spun around, doing a little jig that could either be described as a startled jump or a stealthy self-defense move.

She preferred the latter.

"Whoa!" Lincoln's hands lifted in surrender. "I didn't mean to scare you."

"You didn't." Angeline stood tall.

"Uh-huh." Lincoln's disbelieving grin raised her ire and suddenly she no longer felt cold.

"Why didn't I hear you coming up behind me?" Wah-yas had excellent hearing.

"You're not supposed to."

"Right. Because you're a Dogman."

Silent as a ninja, as deadly as one, too. Or so the rumors went. No one outside the Woelfesenat's militarized security force knew exactly what the Dogmen did, other than the generic job description of peacekeeping.

Considering the numerous scars on his body, whatever Lincoln had been doing, it wasn't so peaceable.

"You're right about one thing." Lincoln pivoted to block the gust of wind that caused her teeth to chatter and then reached around her to open the door. "You are freezing."

His broad hand heated the small of her back and he nudged her forward. Her mind mounted a protest but her feet didn't get the memo in time to keep her from crossing the threshold.

"What were you doing outside?"

"Cooling off." He tossed an odd-looking cell phone next to the take-out box on the asymmetrical coffee table. If he'd had the device in her apartment, she hadn't noticed it.

"Change your mind about sharing a snack?" Lincoln sat on the couch and opened the box of chicken wings.

"No." As a restaurant employee, she'd learned to eat only when truly hungry, otherwise she'd eat constantly and no amount of running in the woods would compensate for the extra calories. Ignoring the delicious scent taunting her stomach, Angeline held out Lincoln's wallet. "I found it between the couch cushions."

Mouth full of food, he gave a hand signal for her to leave it on the coffee table.

Angeline strolled around the living room. "This place is probably a culture shock for you. The furnishings are too modern for my taste. Tristan didn't like it much, either, but his mother is an interior designer and she loves this stuff."

Still eating, Lincoln watched her with the same quiet curiosity as he had in her apartment. And when she walked into the kitchen, his inquisitive gaze followed.

"You're in luck," she said, peeking into the refrigerator. "It's stocked with a few basics. At least you won't have to go grocery shopping on Sunday." Closing the refrigerator, she added, "Which technically is today, since it's after midnight, you know…in case your days are mixed up from traveling."

A chuckle accompanied Lincoln's slight head shake.

"You would think Sundays are good days to go to the grocery store." She sat on a stool at the bar rather than leaving. She and Tristan had their fair share of late-night chats. Being back in his apartment, it seemed natural to carry on tradition. Even though Lincoln was a Dogman, she could still be neighborly.

"Because everyone is either going to church or sleeping off Saturday night's good time. But actually, the early risers are buzzing around to get their shopping done to have the rest of the day free. Late-goers are trying to grab something on their way to wherever. And the rest are trying to find something to fix their hangovers."

"Good to know." Not one speck of sauce marred his mouth and very little dotted his fingers. An amazing feat considering most people who ate her uncle's wings required a plastic bib and a double stack of napkins.

And while looking at his mouth, Angeline couldn't help but notice the perfect shape of his masculine lips or how his straight nose balanced the angles of his cheeks. His black hair didn't conform to a human military's regulation cut but rather fell to his collar in soft waves. The muscles in his strong jaw, darkened by a shadow of stubble, worked in tandem as he chewed. When he swallowed, she watched the slow descent of his Adam's apple along his throat. The silver chain around the thick column of his neck held the dog tags hidden beneath his sweatshirt.

The thick dark slashes above his pale green eyes drew together as the curiosity in his gaze transitioned to something primal. "Angeline." He softly growled her name and it whispered across her skin, heightening her own awareness of him.

She shouldn't study him so intently. Wahyas' senses were acutely sharp and staring too long usually signaled a threat or sexual interest. Obviously, Lincoln wouldn't consider her a threat. He stood over six feet tall, while she only pushed upward of five-seven, and he out-massed her by at least seventy pounds.

However, underestimating her would be a mistake. Her brothers might not be quite as imposing as Lincoln, but they weren't pushovers. They'd never taken it easy on her and the skills she'd learned tangling with them had come in handy a few years ago when a hook-up had turned sour and she'd needed to escape the situation.

Like most wolfan males, Lincoln would misinterpret her interest as…well…*interest*. Which, of course, it wasn't. If she and a Dogman were the last Wahyas on Earth, she wouldn't be interested. Even if it meant the salvation of their race, it simply would not happen.

Too bad, thanks to a treacherous brain, her body had no troubling recalling the intimate heat of him crouched above her, while his fierce gaze mapped every inch of her soul. His light-colored eyes had presented a striking contrast to the rich brownness of his nearly naked body and thick black waves of hair. Unbidden desire curled inside her like wisps of steam rising from a cup of hot chocolate.

"Tuesdays," she said, throwing the brakes on primal instincts. Despite the close friendship with her former neighbor, Angeline had never experienced a sexual attraction toward Tristan. Considering her body's unexpected and wholly unappreciated reaction to Lincoln, she would not make a habit of being overly neighborly.

"Tuesdays?" Confusion clouded Lincoln's gaze.

"About midmorning." Angeline slid off the bar stool. "Trust me. It's the best time to go grocery shopping at Anne's Market."

"Appreciate the tip." From his neutral expression, Angeline couldn't discern if he truthfully did, or if he merely humored her.

"I should go."

Lincoln met her at the door. "Here." He tugged off his sweatshirt.

"Thanks." She kept focused on the faint scar below his eye rather than the short, dark hairs spread across the broad, chiseled expanse of his chest. "But I don't need it."

He slipped the sweatshirt over her head and onto her shoulders anyway. His clean, crisp, masculine scent immediately invaded her senses, and she obediently slid her arms into the sleeves.

The fabric still held his warmth, and she remained nice and toasty all the way to her apartment.

Standing watch from his doorway, bare-chested and unflinching against the icy wind winding through the corridor, Lincoln presented a striking image of a proud warrior. He reeked of confidence, but not the arrogance she had imagined to have infected all Dogmen.

Once inside, Angeline sighed against the locked door. Hugging Lincoln's sweatshirt to her body, she held the collar over her nose, breathing his scent and absorbing his warmth like a she-wolf showing more than a casual interest in a male—

Like cold water to the face, the realization shocked her senses and she couldn't get out of his clothes fast enough.

This was all Tristan's fault!

Leaving the sweatshirt in a puddle on the floor, she stomped to the kitchen bar, snatched open her purse, whipped out her cell phone and began furiously typing.

Chapter 3

"Dammit!" Angeline swiped the pick down the guitar strings, abruptly halting the sappy tune she'd been composing for the last hour.

Sitting in the middle of her unmade bed, she stared into her open closet at the numerous prestigious awards her love songs had won. Hidden away from all eyes but hers because no strong, self-respecting she-wolf would ever pine over a man who didn't want her. Neither would she write songs about the devastating experience. Especially not a she-wolf raised by Patrick O'Brien. He'd be appalled to learn that his daughter had been reduced to inconsolable tears by the man who'd broken her young heart.

However, Angeline had turned the heartbreak from Tanner's rejection and the heartache from his death into writing love-lost songs that country and pop recording artists fought over to record.

Of course, she had long moved past the actual events. But to write the music and lyrics people wanted, she had to tap into those old feelings, putting herself back into the maelstrom of all that pain. Lately, though, she had grown weary of the process.

Again, she blamed Tristan. His migration from her staunchest bachelor friend to happily mated had left her feeling off-kilter. A feeling magnified by her unusual reaction to Lincoln. Also, Tristan's fault. If he hadn't left Lincoln the wrong key, she wouldn't have his scent imprinted in her nose and lingering in the living room.

Obviously, she found the wolfan sexually appealing. Tall, broad-shouldered, with chiseled abs and sculpted pecs, and muscled limbs that proclaimed his strength without being ridiculously pretentious. The way he moved and carried himself proved he'd earned those muscles on the job rather than in the gym. But she was accustomed to physically fit wolfan males. Generally, they didn't stay on her mind.

But she couldn't stop thinking about Lincoln, whose commanding presence had not been diminished by the loss of his leg. The injury appeared to be fairly recent, considering the freshness of the scars on his stump and on the left side of his body.

However, it was the lost and lonely look in Lincoln's eyes that had haunted her all night and greatly interfered with her creativity today.

Sympathy infected her heart, causing it to ache for the Dogman. It shouldn't. Her heart should be cold and unfeeling toward them. They'd made their choices and should live with them. Why should anyone be sympathetic? Especially those they'd abandoned to pursue glory.

Growling, Angeline strummed the strings in frustration and set aside the guitar. She slipped off the bed, stretched and then padded out of the bedroom. The pounding at her front door halted her trip to the kitchen.

She opened the door to Tristan's famous grin.

"Hey there, Sassy."

"Hey there, Slick. Bite me."

Before she could close the door, Tristan thrust his arm through the opening, gripping a white paper bag. The scent of apples and cinnamon and sugar caused her nose to twitch. He nudged the door open a little wider and showed her the large coffee in his other hand. "I come bearing gifts," he said lightheartedly.

"Once upon a time that didn't work out so well for the Trojans." Regardless, Angeline lifted the coffee cup and bag of pastries from Tristan's hands. Ignoring him as he entered the apartment, she sat cross-legged on the couch and fished a bear claw with an apple filling from the bag.

Tristan closed the door and made himself at home in the overstuffed chair. "I'm not exactly sure what this means." He showed her the angry, emoji-filled text message she'd sent last night.

"Just delete it." Angeline wiped away the sugar sticking to her lips. "We're good now."

"I'm sorry that I didn't give you a heads-up about Lincoln." Tristan paused and suddenly the exhaustion he'd been hiding surfaced. "Nel and I were at the hospital most of the night."

"Is Nel all right? Did she have the baby?"

"False alarm. She's had Braxton Hicks pain on and off, but last night she got so uncomfortable, I took her in to be checked." Running his hand through his tousled blond hair, Tristan yawned.

Angeline did, too. Seemed they'd both had a long night.

"Lincoln called right as the nurse took Nel to an exam room. I meant to text you—"

"Forget it." She waved off Tristan's worry and he began to relax. "You're dealing with a lot. Seems to be your calling."

"I'm hoping to build a team to shoulder that burden."

Everyone's problem solver, Tristan—a former sheriff deputy, had recently been named the Walker's Run Co-op's chief of security. A huge undertaking considering the pack now had its own police force.

"Don't look at me. I like my life the way it is." In defiance of Tristan's pointed, disbelieving look, she shoved another pastry into her mouth.

"I'm talking about Lincoln," Tristan said. "Brice wants him to remain in Walker's Run."

Not surprisingly, the Alpha's son had a habit of keeping his friends close. "Good luck to him. Lincoln doesn't seem the type to walk away from the Program, even if he could."

"Apparently, he's being forced into a medical retirement."

"Whoa." The only utterable word able to form on Angeline's lips. A Dogman losing his career, much like a wolfan losing a mate, hurt to the soul.

She would not sympathize with Lincoln, though. Not about that.

"I have a favor to ask," Tristan said quietly.

Over the rim of her coffee cup, Angeline watched him squirm in his seat. The hot liquid heated her mouth and the warmth traveled all the way to her starting-to-clench stomach. "I'm not going to like it, am I?"

"I need you to keep an eye on him."

"No." Angeline cut her eyes at her oldest, dearest friend. He should know better than to ask such a thing. "I'm not spying on a Dogman."

"Just be neighborly." Tristan leaned forward, his elbows planted on his knees with his fingers laced. "Brice trusts him, but I don't know this guy. Dogmen are just this side of feral. I need to know sooner than later if he's on the verge of crossing the line. The pack has been through enough violence."

"Why me and not Shane? He's only a few doors down." And a legitimate pack sentinel.

"Shane doesn't have your assets," Tristan said good-naturedly. "Lincoln isn't likely to let his guard down around a male. But you?" Tristan's expression turned serious. "You could make a wolf lie down at your feet, roll over and purr, if you wanted him to."

"You know why I can't do this." Angeline swallowed another mouthful of coffee but the kinks in her stomach tightened rather than relaxed.

"Lincoln isn't Tanner. Don't judge him for Tanner's mistake." Tristan stood. "If Lincoln is the man Brice believes, when the realty of his medical retirement sets in, he's going to need help coping. It can be you or someone else, but I strongly feel you're the best person he could have in his corner because you know how it feels to lose the life you thought you were meant to have."

Quietly, Tristan closed the door as he left.

"Dammit!" Angeline slung a throw pillow after him. Harmlessly, it glanced off the door. She snatched it up and punched it. "Damn you, too, Tanner." She smacked the pillow again, then hugged it to her chest and schlepped to the couch, knowing she'd do just what Tristan had asked. Because she did know exactly how it felt to watch the future crumble. No one, not even a Dogman, deserved to face it alone.

Bracing against the cold, Lincoln knocked on the door to Brice Walker's residence, two miles up the mountain from the family-owned Walker's Run Resort. Used to the heat in Somalia, the lower temperatures in Northeast Georgia would be a welcomed change if his stump didn't ache.

The heavy wooden door opened to reveal a petite, human redhead. A smile warmed the porcelain tone of her skin and her cinnamon eyes shimmered.

"Hello, Cassie." Though they had never met, he knew her from the late-night chats he'd had with her mate during a mission in Romania several years ago.

"Lincoln! Please come in." She stepped aside, welcoming him into her home.

Gratefully, he shook off the cold.

"Thank you for keeping Brice safe so he could come back to me," she said, closing the door. "If you need anything, let me know. I'll make sure you get it."

"I appreciate your kindness." But what he wanted she couldn't give. Her husband, however, could be the Ace that Lincoln needed. After all, he had saved Brice's life. "I was just doing my job."

"You went beyond your job. You were a friend when Brice needed one the most."

Uh-oh.

Reading her body language and seeing the intent on her face, Lincoln leaned down so that her arms reached his neck in the full-on hug rather than banding around his middle, which would've appeared quite odd and a bit too personal to her mate. Lincoln didn't have a visual on Brice Walker yet, but his ears honed in on the slight thump of the man's limping gait inside the house.

A tawny-headed wolfan, not quite midtwenties, stepped into the hallway. On his shoulders sat a toddler.

"Shane—" Cassie grinned at the young man "—this is Lincoln Adams, Brice's friend from his time in Romania."

Lincoln hid his smile. Humans often identified a personal connection when introducing people. Wolfans pointed out their rank or benefit to the pack.

"Lincoln, this is Shane MacQuarrie. He's a close friend of ours."

Neither he nor Shane made an effort to observe the human custom of shaking hands. Instead, they greeted each other with a curt nod.

"I hear we're neighbors at the Chatuge View Apartments." Shane's wintry gaze didn't warm. Close to the age Lincoln had been when recruited for the Dogman program, the young wolf reeked of confidence, piss and vinegar. Lincoln liked him immediately.

"Good to know."

"And this is my daughter, Brenna," Cassie said.

The little girl's bright blue eyes targeted him with the same intensity Lincoln had seen in her father's gaze years ago. And although her hair wasn't red like her mother's curls, the blond ringlets held a tinge of fire.

Cassie held up her hands and Brenna practically launched into her mother's arms. "More monkey than wolf, I think."

Although the little girl's mother was human, her father was Wahya and wolfan genes were dominant. All Wahyan offspring were born with wolf-shifting abilities.

"Just brave and confident." Lincoln extended his hand in a nonthreatening greeting. "Nice to meet you, Brenna."

"Mmm…five!" Grinning, she smacked her palm against his open hand.

"That's not how we greet guests." Despite Cassie's frown, no true reprimand sharpened her voice. She turned to Lincoln. "Come. The others are in the family room."

Others?

Brice hadn't mentioned others when he'd invited Lincoln to Sunday supper.

Shane took a step back, allowing Lincoln to follow Cassie, but remained close enough to respond to any threat, should Lincoln become one.

"Lincoln!" Brice stepped forward as they entered the family room. "Good to see you, man."

Fairly equal in height, Lincoln didn't need to crouch for Brice's brotherly embrace and friendly pat on the back.

"Thanks for the invite."

"My parents." Brice waved his hand toward the more than middle-aged couple sitting in the love seat near the fireplace. "Gavin and Abby Walker."

The Alpha and Alphena of Walker's Run. Lincoln had expected to meet them eventually. Just not on his first venture out.

After a handshake from Gavin and a hug from Abby, Cassie hustled them into the dining room. Brenna insisted Lincoln sit next to her and he complied, despite Shane's obvious annoyance.

Throughout the delicious meal, Lincoln politely answered questions and listened to their security concerns. Although what they'd experienced over the last few years alarmed the quiet Appalachian pack, it couldn't compare to the violence Lincoln dealt with daily on deployment.

When finished with supper, everyone returned to the family room. Lincoln sat in an overstuffed rocking chair, leaving the couch and love seat to the mated pairs while Shane claimed the recliner. Conversation shifted to planning a spring gathering for the pack. For fifteen years, Lincoln had been isolated from first-world normalcy and he found the sudden reentrance jarring.

Brenna climbed into his lap with a book. Glad for the distraction, he read and reread the story until she fell asleep. Only then did he notice all the adults in the room silently watching him.

Thank you, Cassie mouthed, easing the child from his arms.

"I wouldn't have expected a Dogman to know how to handle children." In spite of Gavin's stony expression, his sharp blue eyes twinkled.

"Wherever I'm deployed, I see children impacted by the conflict around them. I do what I can to help them retain their childhood, in spite of the circumstance." The ache in Lincoln's heart grew stronger. Dayax had no one but him, and Lincoln was thousands of miles away. Safe, warm and well-fed. The lost little wolfling likely was none of those things.

"Sounds like you will be a great father one day," Abby said.

"Dogmen can't take mates," Lincoln replied gently. "We aren't meant to be fathers." Or mothers, or sons, daughters, brothers or sisters. The Program required absolute devotion. All ties with family and friends were severed upon joining.

"Aren't you ready to retire?" Shane's gaze dropped to Lincoln's left leg.

"Not anytime soon." Lincoln shifted his attention to Brice, who stood.

"I've got something to show you." Brice motioned for Lincoln to follow.

After closing the French doors to the home office, Brice sat behind a messy wooden desk, pulled a photo from the drawer and handed it to Lincoln.

He fingered the snapshot of them sitting by a campfire, laughing.

"Remember that night?" With one blue eye and one green, Brice's direct gaze could intimidate lesser men.

"Hard to forget." Especially since Lincoln still bore the scar from the bullet he'd caught protecting Brice less than an hour after the picture had been taken.

"When I talked to you a couple of weeks ago, I thought you were on board with the medical retirement."

"I only said that so the doctors would stop harping about adjustment issues. Yeah, I lost a leg, but I have more important things to worry about, which is why I need your help with something."

"Name it." Brice planted his elbows on the desk and steepled his fingers.

"I want to go back to Somalia."

To his credit, Brice didn't balk, blink or bat an eyelash.

"I was looking for a wolfling in an abandoned building when an explosion blasted me out of a two-story window." Lincoln fished out his wallet, removed a photo of him and Dayax and tossed it on the desk in front of Brice. "Insurgents took him. I want him back."

"I'm not a soldier, Lincoln. How do you think I can help?"

"Ask your friends at the Woelfesenat to grant me clearance to go back in." As the secretive international wolf council, the Woelfesenat not only had ruling authority over the packs but had executive power over the Dogman Program.

"I'm Dayax's only hope, Brice. I have to find him or die trying." Invisible fingers fisted around Lincoln's heart. His mission to rescue Dayax would be over before it began if Brice declined to help.

Brice glanced at the framed picture of his daughter on his desk. "I'll do what I can."

Lincoln managed to breathe again. "Thank you." Though grateful, he didn't allow himself even the smallest celebration. More than two months had passed since Dayax's disappearance. Finding him would take a miracle.

Chapter 4

"Have you met him yet?" Madelyn O'Brien, sister-in-law number one, nudged Angeline.

"Who?" She shoveled another spoonful of creamed corn into her mouth. The once-a-month family supper at her father's house provided Angeline with her only full-course home-cooked meal. Her brothers supplied the meat, their mates provided the sides, and Angeline always showed up with a healthy appetite and plastic containers to take home leftovers.

"The Dogman." Isobel O'Brien, sister-in-law number two and affectionately known as Izzie, flashed a conspiratorial grin. "Haven't you been listening?"

No. She'd tuned out at the first mention of "Dogman." Her brain needed the break.

"He was supposed to arrive yesterday," Garret, Angeline's oldest brother, said. "Did he meet up with anyone for dinner and drinks at Taylor's Roadhouse last night?"

"Nope," Angeline answered between bites.

"I bet he's handsome." Izzie grinned. "But not as good-looking as you." She kissed Connor—her mate and Angeline's other brother—on the cheek and his soft, disgruntled growl ceased.

So cute. Mated thirteen years and the father of two kids, Connor still got a little jealous when Izzie mentioned other men. He had nothing to worry about. Izzie loved him to the moon and back. Stinky feet and all.

"Angeline, what have you heard about this Dogman?" Patrick O'Brien clasped his hands over the dinner plate. Angeline's father might not like the idea of his daughter waiting tables for a living, but he certainly liked pumping her for the tidbits of gossip she frequently overheard.

"His name is Lincoln," she said. "He got in late last night, he's friends with Brice, and that's all I know." Not really, but it covered the basics.

"Have you actually met him?" Connor asked.

"He's subletting Tristan's apartment." Angeline speared the green bean bundle wrapped in bacon on her plate and chomped down so she wouldn't have to answer the barrage of her family's questions.

"Dogmen don't just come for a visit." Patrick O'Brien's statement quieted the table. "Why is he really here?"

All eyes turned on Angeline.

"How should I know?"

"You're tight with Tristan," Garret said.

"So?" She never disclosed the things Tristan revealed in confidence.

"Are you going to talk to him again?" Her father's narrowed gaze forced Angeline to swallow the food she'd just stuck in her mouth.

"Tristan? I talk to him a couple of times a week." Texts mostly, that way he could reply when he had the time.

"The Dogman," her dad growled. "Why are you being so evasive? Do you know more than you're telling us?"

"Actually, Dad, I don't." Angeline put down the food-laden fork in her hand. "Why is everyone so concerned about his business? He's just a guy that traveled a long way to get here. He arrived exhausted and hungry. I gave him the food I'd brought home from the restaurant and the key to Tristan's apartment, and then I sent him on his merry way."

"Are you going to see him again?" Connor asked.

"He's staying a few doors down from me. And I work at Taylor's." Most wolfans couldn't resist her uncle's fire-grilled steaks. "What do you think?"

Connor squinted, and she knew he wanted to stick his tongue out at her, like when they were kids, but they'd grown past that childish expression—in the presence of others.

"You only work part-time," her father said, always ready to seize an opportunity to hassle Angeline about her employment choice. "When are you going to get a real job?"

"You may not like than I'm a server, but it is a real job. And in three nights, what I make in tips is more than some people earn in a week."

"Your mother and I wanted you to be more than a wait-ress."

"Mom would've wanted me to pursue music. But when she died, you sold the piano and wouldn't allow me to bring any instruments home."

Her father's jaw tightened. "Someone had to teach you to be realistic about your future."

"Shouldn't *my* wants determine the reality of *my* future?" Angeline's chest tightened and with every beat of her heart she felt a sharp pain stab her eye.

"Not if your head is in the clouds," was what her father said. However, every time they had this argument, all Angeline heard was that her dad didn't want *her*—he merely wanted a version of her that she could never be.

"Dad, let it go," Garret said.

Angeline inhaled a few calming breaths, hoping to prevent a migraine.

Grumbling, their father stabbed his mashed potatoes and jabbed the fork into his mouth. Everyone else resumed eating in awkward silence, so everything had returned to normal.

After supper, Angeline collected the dishes and began loading the dishwasher.

Izzie leaned against the counter. "Your dad is worried about you."

"Worried that I might have a stroke from the spike in my blood pressure? Because that's what worries me."

"He's worried about what will happen to you—" Izzie lowered her voice "—after he's gone. You don't have a mate. Or a career. He thinks he failed you."

"No, not failed me," Angeline corrected. "Failed in raising me. I didn't turn out to be the daughter he wanted."

"Your dad loves you." Madelyn quietly joined them.

"I know." Angeline dropped the silverware into the utensils tray and closed the dishwasher. "But he doesn't understand me. All he wants is for me to fall in line with what he wants."

"Couldn't you give in, just a little?" Madelyn gave her a little shrug. "Maybe put your business degree to good use and help out your dad on one of your days off."

"No. He didn't teach me how to give in." Nor did she have a business degree, having chosen to secretly study music instead. Angeline dried her hands on the dish towel. "If you'll excuse me, I need to say good-night to the kids."

"Don't forget they're out of school for a teacher's workday on Thursday," Madelyn said.

"I have everything planned." Breakfast, sledding, watch-

ing a superhero movie on DVD while overloading on popcorn and hot chocolate.

"You haven't changed your mind about Sierra's birthday party, have you?" Mischief twinkled in Izzie's eyes.

"I'll be the one loaded with all the surprises." And Angeline couldn't wait to see the disapproving look on Patrick
O'Brien's face when forced to wear one of the fringed pas-
tel foil party hats she'd bought specially for the occasion.

Headlights briefly lit the dark stairwell. When they
blinked off, Lincoln glanced toward the parking lot and
stopped to watch Angeline slide out of her car.

Seeing him paused on the stairs, she waved but only a
faint smile touched her lips.

He waited, his heartbeat falling into an unusual rhythm,
pushing his blood more quickly through his veins.

"Hey," she said, climbing the steps behind him. "How
was your day?"

The question caused a little flutter in his chest. Other
than the nurses at the infirmary, Lincoln couldn't remember the last time someone had asked that question of him.

"Awkward," Lincoln said.

"Why?"

He remained one step behind Angeline as they continued up the stairs.

"Brice invited me to his home for supper. Didn't know
his parents would be there."

"Guess that would be awkward, especially not knowing them."

"What about you?" He'd seen the rigidness of her stride
walking to the stairs and could feel the tension radiating
from her now.

"Monthly family dinner. My dad uses the opportunity
to chide me about my life's choices. He's gravely disappointed that, at my age, I'm unmated and have no via-

ble career." Her entire body seemed to sigh. "If he only knew…"

"Knew what?"

They reached the third-floor landing.

"Doesn't matter." An artificial smile curved her tantalizing mouth.

Nearing his apartment, Lincoln bid Angeline goodnight. He fiddled with his keys, listening to the rhythmic thump of her boots retreating down the corridor.

"Lincoln?"

"Yeah?" He turned.

"Wanna come in for a drink?"

"Sure." Shoving the keys into his pocket, he walked down to her apartment.

She'd left the door partially open, so he entered and shut out the cold night air. Angeline had dropped her coat on the back of the couch and had headed straight for the kitchen.

"Beer, wine or Jack?"

"Your choice." He sat on the couch rather than the chair, giving room for Angeline to join him, if she chose.

After living in tents and barracks, sleeping on the ground, in cots, hammocks or in trees, Lincoln appreciated the upgrade to Tristan's modern-style apartment. But it lacked the cozy warmth of Angeline's place. Walking inside felt like coming home.

Or rather, what he imagined coming home would feel like, if he had one.

Calm, comfortable and filled with the enticing scent of a sexy, spirited she-wolf.

A fantasy. Nothing more than a fleeting dream the mind called forth in times of extreme stress just so he could get through the ordeal.

Each Dogman had just such a dream. They'd go feral without one.

Handing him a bottle, she plopped next to him on the

couch and kerplunked one furry-booted foot onto the coffee table, then the other.

"Cheers." Her bottle clinked against his, then she tipped back her head, exposing the slender column of her smooth, creamy neck, and took a long swig. His mouth parched with want of the taste of her skin despite the cold liquid sloshing down his own throat.

In all the years he'd carried Angeline's picture in his pocket, Lincoln never imagined he'd actually share a drink with his angel.

Oh, he'd tried to unravel the mystery of the woman in the photograph in the months following the death of the Dogman who'd entrusted him with the prized possession. But Lincoln had very little to go on. Only the name "Angel" had been written on the back of the picture and Tanner Phillip's next of kin had not known her identity.

In the beginning, Lincoln had reached for the photo when hurt, indecisive or just plain lonely. Later he'd spoken to her upon waking and just before going to sleep. Probably not the healthiest of habits, but his second-in-command, Lila, had said the rosary. By nature, Wahyas weren't religious. However, she had found comfort in the tradition and repetitiveness. And so had he.

They all needed something larger than themselves from which to seek guidance, absolution and everything else in between.

"What makes your family dinners stressful?" Lincoln asked, restarting the conversation they began on the stairs.

"Irreconcilable differences." Angeline took another drink. "It's insanity. My dad keeps picking the same fight, month after month, expecting that suddenly I'll conform to his expectations of a daughter." She snorted. "Not that he ever wanted one. After my mom died, he cut off my hair and dressed me in my brothers' hand-me-downs."

"You must've looked like your mother."

"I did." Angeline swirled her bottle. "Still do."

Lincoln took another swig of beer, unable to imagine the long auburn strands that fell below her shoulders stunted in a short bob. He much preferred the vision of her in masculine clothes…in particular, his sweatshirt enveloping her much smaller frame.

His thoughts drifted to the way the softness of her body had cushioned his when he'd rolled her beneath him while disoriented from a nightmare.

The mere memory of how perfectly their bodied aligned electrified his nerves, tingling and tantalizing his already sensitized skin.

"Everybody's curious about you," she said. "We've never had a Dogman in town." Her jaw tightened and her mouth pulled tight.

"Brice and I go back a few years. When he heard about my injury, he invited me here."

"Then why aren't you staying at his family's resort?"

"Not my style." Or in his comfort zone. He didn't need to be pampered or coddled. Besides, a couples retreat had been scheduled for Valentine's Day weekend and he definitely didn't want to be in the midst of a lovefest, especially during a full moon.

Wahyas were wired for sex. It regulated their wolfan hormones, keeping the primitive monster that lived inside them dormant. A full moon was the most critical time for Wahyas to have sex, but Dogmen had little time and opportunity to find willing partners every month.

So, Program scientists developed the hormone suppressor implanted into every Dogman before deployment. Only those involved in the Program knew of the implant's existence because of the known side effect of increased hostility.

Dogmen were highly trained to manage their aggressive impulses, whether naturally occurring or chemically induced. Unleashing the implant on the general Wahyan population could give rise to the very beasts that the drug had been created to suppress.

Removal of the implant proved just as challenging. After a wolfan's sexual instinct had been stifled for so long, some Dogmen found the deluge of natural hormones overwhelming.

Lincoln's implant had been removed after the last full moon. With less than a week until the next one, he needed to find a consenting sex partner. Soon.

He glanced sidelong at Angeline and his heart thudded all the way down to his groin. His wolf had declared his choice. Undeniably, Lincoln wanted to agree. But things could get oh, so complicated.

He liked simple.

And he knew one thing for sure. There was absolutely nothing simple about Angeline.

Chapter 5

"What is that god-awful noise?" It pounded in Angeline's head like a woodpecker drilling a tree for food.

Slowly and painfully, she opened her eyes. The shirt Lincoln had worn last night obscured her field of vision. Suddenly, the pillow her head rested upon moved.

"*Buenos días*, Angel." Lincoln's deep Texas drawl sounded thunderously close but at least the beep grating her nerves stopped.

The sluggish thoughts in her brain, however, kept going. Unfurling her legs, she sat up and rubbed her eyes. "Were you speaking Spanish?"

"Yeah. I grew up in a bilingual household. My maternal grandparents emigrated from Mexico to Texas when my mom was a child. But I also speak German, Tagalog and some Somali."

"Strange combo of languages."

"I learn whatever the Program tells me to." Lincoln began the process of putting on his prosthetic.

She remembered Lincoln asking if she was okay with him taking off his artificial leg because his stump hurt, but not much after he did.

"Um." She glanced at the coffee table littered with a Jack Daniel's decanter and likely every beer bottle she had in the fridge. All empty. "What happened last night?"

"You passed out and latched onto me in your sleep." He wiggled into his pants.

"I did not!" The screech in her voice made Angeline cringe.

"Oh, so it was a ploy to keep me here?" He cracked a smile. "Aw, Angel, all you had to do was ask."

She felt the weight of a frown on her jaw. "Tread lightly, I'm not a morning person."

Despite her warning, he laughed. "You certainly aren't. But you are quite adorable with your messy hair and grumpy face."

"You're not earning any brownie points, Dogman."

"That's not what you said last night." He had the nerve to wink.

"They only count if I remembering doling them out. Which I don't, so…" She massaged her temples.

"I'm not surprised." Lincoln stood, and Angeline felt woozy looking up at him. He began gathering the discarded bottles. "Most of these are yours."

"That can't be right," she said, trying to focus her fuzzy and somewhat incoherent memories. "I don't normally drink that much."

"Good to know," Lincoln said. "But I think your family dinners are more upsetting than you allow yourself to believe."

"Why? What did I say?" Angeline's heartbeat sped up, despite the sludge a night of drinking had deposited in her veins.

"Nothing that bears repeating." Lincoln dropped the bottles into the recycling bin underneath the sink.

"No, really. I need to know what I talked about."

"Tell me where the coffee is." Lincoln gave her an assessing look. "Then I'll give you a play-by-play of all the beans you spilled."

Angeline's stomach churned and it wasn't from the hangover. If her drunken self had told Lincoln about her music career…

"Check the pantry, third shelf. Coffee filters should be there, too."

While Lincoln busied himself in the kitchen, seemingly making as much noise as possible, Angeline dragged herself into the bathroom, soaked a washcloth in cold water and buried her face in it. This—the morning-after hangover—is why she didn't usually indulge in more than two drinks in one night.

Dampening the cloth, she glanced into the mirror and jumped back. Her bloodshot eyes were a little puffy, but her hair…yikes! What a tangled mess.

And Lincoln thought she looked adorable? Definitely, the man needed glasses.

At least nausea didn't accompany the hangover, but if she didn't take a painkiller for the pounding in her head, it might split open.

She fumbled through the medicine cabinet for ibuprofen and downed two caplets with a glass of water. After scrubbing her face and rinsing the funk from her mouth, she tackled combing her hair. Seriously, how did she get so many knots?

Emerging from the bathroom, Angeline looked much more presentable than when she'd gone in. Her nose twitched at the rich, robust aroma of fresh-brewed coffee, and she followed the scent all the way to the kitchen.

Lincoln handed her a big cup filled nearly to the rim.

"Thanks." Holding the ceramic mug between both hands, she took her first sip. The heat sloshed down her throat ahead of the flavor. The more she drank, the more the tightness in her body began to ease.

"I would've made breakfast, but your fridge is nearly empty and so is mine."

"I'm not usually up this early. On the occasion that I am, I grab a pastry from the bakery."

"Sweets for the sweet," Lincoln said. "I'll remember that."

"I'm not really sweet." She tried to glare at him over the rim of her coffee cup, but his sleepy eyes and soft smile were just so cute.

"Difference of opinion then." He poured a cup of coffee for himself and sat on the bar stool next to her.

"Okay," she said, swiveling toward him. "*You* spill the beans. I want to know every word I said to you."

"I don't have that much time. You became quite chatty after that third beer."

"Why did you let me keep drinking?"

"You have pretty, white teeth, Angel. And they looked very sharp when you snarled at me for trying to pry the bottle of Jack from your hand."

She-wolves didn't blush from embarrassment, but Angeline certainly felt mortified at her lack of self-control. "Why didn't you leave?"

"Clearly, you were upset. And drinking the way you did, I wasn't going to leave you alone. Something could've happened to you."

"Did anything happen?" They were both fully dressed when she woke up, but she really didn't remember much about last night.

"No," Lincoln said without hesitation and holding her gaze. "You drank, said a lot of nonsensical things, and then you fell asleep. I stayed in case you got sick." He lifted the coffee cup to his mouth to drink.

"You're a good guy, Lincoln. Thanks." Angeline swallowed another mouthful of coffee, too. "So what sort of stuff did I talk about?"

"Your mom. You miss her a lot."

True, Angeline did miss her mother. And she missed how differently her life would've been if her mother hadn't been murdered during a mugging.

"You also kept saying if I were Tristan, you would tell me a lot more." Curiosity edged around the uncertainty glimmering in his eyes. "Sounds like you and Tristan have been more than just friendly neighbors."

A subtle tension crept into Lincoln's body and his gaze left her face.

"No." Angeline shook her head. "It's not what you're thinking."

"It's okay," Lincoln said. "I don't need an explanation."

He might not, but Angeline's instinct pushed her to clarify. "Tristan is like a brother, but closer than my own. He knows things about me that my family and other friends don't."

"Maybe you should've called him last night instead of inviting me in." Lincoln carried his cup to the sink.

"Tristan has a mate now."

"So I've heard."

"I don't expect him to be my confidant anymore. It wouldn't be right."

Lincoln finished rinsing out his coffee cup. "I guess you're in search of a new one and I didn't cut the mustard."

"I barely know you." How could she trust him the way she trusted Tristan, who'd been there for her for most of their lives? "Is it true that you're retiring from the Program?"

"That's what people keep telling me."

Not exactly the answer she wanted to hear.

"Well, who knows?" She shrugged. "If you stick around long enough—" They might eventually become friends... good friends...really good friends with full moon benefits.

"I'm not planning on it," he said abruptly. "Neither should you."

Well, if that wasn't a door being slammed in her face...

"Thanks for playing watchdog last night." She walked to her front door and opened it. "But I'm in control of all my faculties now. Time for you to leave."

He dried his hands on the dish towel, walked to the door and stepped outside into the breaking dawn.

"Angeline." He turned around. Of the myriad of emotions flickering across his face, confusion, regret, loneliness—those were the ones that tugged her heart strings.

Damn, she was too soft.

"I have a really busy day," Angeline lied. She didn't have to be at the restaurant until the afternoon. "See you around."

Locking the door, she hoped her heart took notice. Lincoln was no different than Tanner. Dogmen lived for the Program. Nothing and no one else mattered. And she would never put herself through that turmoil ever again.

Lincoln stepped into the Walker's Run Resort and shook off the cold. A large fireplace in the rustic seating area crackled with flames, and red roses and hearts decorated the main lobby. A Happy Valentine's Day banner hung behind the guest services counter. Coming from a part of the world where conflict and violence had become commonplace, he found the commercialization of love off-putting.

Intentionally early for his meeting, Lincoln walked to a seating area near the fireplace and sat in a high-backed leather chair to watch everyone coming and going. Brice had invited him to meet the security team leaders and unofficially consult on the upgrade process of the pack's well-being. He'd also given Lincoln access to the resort's state-of-the-art gym, which he planned to use to continue his fitness training.

Two sentinels dressed as resort employees casually patrolled the lobby. Outside, Lincoln had noted at least three sentinels working valet and four handling bell service. Lincoln expected those numbers would increase, depending on the number of non-pack wolfans registered for rooms.

He turned his attention to the three offices with interior glass windows that faced the lobby. Two offices were dark, but the middle one had the blinds up and the light on. Cassie sat at a desk, her back straight and her fingers tapping on a computer keyboard.

Hands paused and she turned, looking directly at him.

He gave a slight nod as she waved.

A few minutes later, limping, Brice walked slowly out of the corridor. Cassie's attention turned to him.

Brice gave her a wink, which broadened her smile. Nearly an entity in and of itself, the palpable love bouncing between them was a phenomenon Lincoln had never witnessed.

His parents loved each other and loved him, in their own way. But their mateship, and their family life, had been centered on being the best of the best. Life was a competition to win and affection merely distracted one from the ultimate end goal.

If Lincoln had remembered what his family had taught, he wouldn't have allowed his emotions to lead him and his team into a trap. While in Walker's Run, he needed to stay focused on his mission and not be led astray by indulging in errant emotions and human customs, or he would screw up his chance to get back on active duty and lose the only opportunity he had to find Dayax.

"Tristan's office is on the third floor," Brice said, approaching.

Lincoln matched Brice's stride but remained a half

step behind him. As progressive as some wolfan packs were, a natural pecking order remained. Brice, the Alpha-in-waiting and a direct descendant of the first Alpha of Walker's Run, deserved his respect.

The Wahyas of Walker's Run had done well in choosing an Alpha family who, through the generations, had remained committed to serving the pack rather than accumulating wealth and power.

Not that the Alpha family didn't have both. The difference being that they shared the wealth and utilized the power for the benefit of the pack.

All able-bodied adult pack members were expected to work and contribute to the pack's finances—a tithe of sorts to the Walker's Run Co-operative that funded their health care, education, business start-ups and things for the pack's overall enjoyment. The Co-op's Family Park, for instance, included a baseball field, picnic pavilions and an entertainment stage. Unfortunately, the stage itself had been destroyed a few months back by a diversionary explosion in a domestic power struggle between a pack member and an outsider.

It might be easy for wolfan rogues to mistake the peace-loving Walker's Run pack as being ripe for a takeover. However, Lincoln had seen enough of the world to recognize that wolfans and humans who fought to defend their families and their ideals could become the deadliest forces on the planet.

They stopped at the brass elevators rather than continuing to the wide, curved hardwood stairs.

"I can make it up the steps," Lincoln said, trying to keep the strain from his voice. If he couldn't convince Brice of his fitness, he'd have no chance swaying the medical review board.

"Be my guest," Brice replied without censure. "But I can't. Cold weather wreaks havoc on my bad leg. It's a struggle to stand and walk today. Climbing the stairs will likely do me in."

Ding! The doors slid open and Brice stepped inside the elevator. Lincoln joined him.

"I meant what I said last night before you left." Brice held Lincoln's gaze as the elevator began to climb. "Regardless of when you retire, I hope you'll consider settling down in the Walker's Run territory."

"I appreciate the invitation," Lincoln said. "It's hard to look that far ahead when all I can think about is that scared wolfling waiting for me to keep my promise." A new pack, a new home, a new family to keep him safe: That was what Lincoln had vowed to find for Dayax. Until Lincoln fulfilled that oath, he couldn't begin to think of his own future.

The elevator doors opened. Instead of guest rooms, the third floor housed offices and conference rooms.

He followed Brice to an office with a large interior glass window looking into the corridor. No matter how civilized they became, wolfans didn't like being boxed in.

The wolfan sitting behind the desk and the one leaning next to him with his palm flat on the desk blotter studying the computer screen looked up as he and Brice entered.

"Lincoln, this is Tristan Durrance, our chief sentinel." Brice waved his hand toward the blond man behind the desk beginning to stand.

"Finally, a face to go with the voice." Grinning, Tristan extended his hand in the customary greeting that Wahyas who worked closely with humans had adopted. "Sorry about the mix-up with the key."

"No worries. Angeline got me oriented and I've settled in." Lincoln pocketed the key Tristan handed to him.

"Great." Tristan hiked his thumb toward the man beside him. "This is Reed Sumner, one of our lieutenants."

Like Shane, Reed greeted him with an obligatory nod

of acknowledgment rather than a handshake. After pleasantries were exchanged, they discussed the recent run-ins with illegal game poachers inside the pack's protected forest and a series of unrelated attacks by revenge-seeking wolfans. In Lincoln's experience, their concerns were generally consistent with what most first-world packs dealt with from time to time.

"It would be a great help if you ran through our security protocols and advised where and how to tighten our current measures," Tristan said.

Reed cut his eyes at Lincoln.

He needed to be careful to avoid stepping on the lieutenant's paws.

"Sounds like Reed has a good handle on things," Lincoln told Tristan, then turned his attention back to Reed. "But I'd love to stretch my legs if you don't mind a tagalong."

"I'd appreciate the company," Reed said, beginning to relax. "Is now too soon?"

"Not for me." Lincoln admired how their recent adversities had brought the Walker's Run pack closer together, making them stronger rather than tearing them apart. They were a united force working toward a common goal.

A team.

Something Lincoln no longer had.

His ribs seemed to fold in on his lungs. The immense sorrow he buried after realizing his team members had died because of their loyalty to him threatened to surface. If he gave in to the grief, it would simply consume him and their deaths would be in vain. He needed to keep a clear mind and a singular focus on finding Dayax.

Chapter 6

Five o'clock, and a few early birds were seated inside Taylor's Roadhouse. According to Reed, by eight the place would be packed and Lincoln wanted to be out before the crowd arrived.

Funny how masses of people had not bothered him while on active duty. However, a few days ago in the Munich airport surrounded by hundreds of people, he'd experienced the first panic attack in his life. Accelerated heart rate, shortness of breath, ringing in his ears, cold, clammy hands despite sweating profusely, had forced him to seek solace in the men's room. What an unwelcomed start to his first venture back into the civilian world. A splash of cold water on his face and a harsh internal dialogue had gotten him through the episode. And he'd sincerely hoped it would be the last.

However when Reed had invited him to meet up with some of the security team tonight, the same odd creepy-crawly sensation had tightened Lincoln's chest and he'd begged off with a rain check. Of course, that didn't mean he would deprive himself of "the best steaks in three counties." Nor did he want to miss a chance to talk to Angeline.

Last night, he'd made the right call not telling her about his connection to Tanner Phillips. But after the strained way they'd parted, she might not answer the door if he knocked. Clearly, he'd upset her, but the conversation was leading to a road he wasn't allowed to explore, no matter how much he might want to do so.

Visually, he searched the restaurant for her, but only spotted one server. A blonde a few inches shorter than Angeline, and human. Wahyas had an eerie sense that allowed them to recognize their own kind. And she did not set off any signals, wolfan or otherwise.

An older woman approached the hostess station. Silver threads glinted in her hair, the rich, robust color of chestnuts but her eyes matched the exact shade of Angeline's sapphire blues.

"Welcome to Taylor's." Her wide, genuine smile appeared all too human. "You must be Lincoln."

A prickle scaled his spine. "Yes, ma'am. And you are?"

"Miriam Taylor, Angeline's aunt," she said. "She's told me all about you."

Lincoln hoped otherwise.

"I'm surprised to see you this early. Angeline mentioned you were getting acquainted with the sentinels today. They don't usually come in until later."

"Jet lag." Lincoln used the same lie he'd given Reed. "I need to eat then crash for a while."

"We'll get your belly filled and then you'll sleep like a lazy pup until morning."

"Sounds nice, but I never sleep more than a few snatches at a time."

"I imagine out of necessity, considering your line of

work. But you're in Walker's Run, not a war zone. It's okay to relax and enjoy yourself."

"Yes, ma'am." Lincoln smiled, although he doubted there would ever come a time when he could drop his guard. "Is anyone joining you for supper?"

Only in spirit. "No, ma'am."

Miriam picked up one hard-bound menu. "Table or booth?"

Lincoln glanced around the cozy interior of the restaurant. The bar area had stools at the bar itself, booths along the wall and bistro tables of two and four. In the other section, booths were also along the wall with tables of four and six in the center. Larger parties probably used the huge round table in middle of the restaurant. A small stage sat in front of the dance floor and the kitchen had a long glass window in front of the grill so that patrons could watch their steaks being cooked. His mouth watered even though nothing had been placed on the grill.

"A small table in the bar is fine." He hoped the steaks tasted as good as his new friends had insisted they would. The ones he'd eaten in the Program's hospital in Germany had tasted like cardboard.

"It will be about twenty minutes before Jimmy starts putting steaks on the grill, so make sure to start with an appetizer, on the house." Miriam seated Lincoln at a bistro table and handed him a menu. "Would you like something to drink while looking over the menu?"

"Water, for now," he said, flipping through the three pages of alcoholic beverages listed at the back of the menu. It had been so long since he'd eaten in a restaurant like this, Lincoln had forgotten the variety of items to choose from.

"I'll send over Tessa when she's finished with them."

Tessa, Lincoln assumed, was the blonde server delivering drinks to a table of elderly wolfans.

"Is Angeline here?" he asked Miriam, internally volleying between the desire to see her again and the dread of needing to fulfill a promise to a dead Dogman, which would likely draw her censure.

"She's in the storeroom taking inventory." Locked on Lincoln, Miriam's gaze narrowed ever so slightly beneath the delicate arch of her brow. "I could ask her to come out."

"No." He pretended hunger caused the unpleasant tug in his gut. "I'll talk to her later."

"Angeline mentioned that you're staying in Tristan's apartment."

"For the next few weeks."

"Well, we're glad to have you here."

Once he told Angeline about Tanner Phillip's last words and the photograph he'd entrusted to Lincoln, he doubted she would share her aunt's sentiment.

At her departure, Lincoln closed the menu and pushed it aside. He didn't much care about what he drank and the plethora of options made him antsy.

Unease coiled inside his chest and his body tingled from the hairs rising on his skin, despite not being on any covert mission about to face untold danger. In fact, since joining the Dogman program, Lincoln had never touched a paw in a more peaceful place than Maico, the quaint little town at the center of the Walker's Run pack's territory.

Definitely, nothing like Taifa.

Lincoln dug into his pocket for the Program-issued satphone, a mobile device that connected to private satellites rather than cell towers on the ground, and dialed into a secure message line.

Nothing.

During his recovery at the hospital, Lincoln had been in contact with Colonel Llewellyn, the commander of the human forces in Somalia. Of course the colonel had promised to do all he could to find Dayax.

But sixty-three days had passed and the boy had not

been found. In his gut, Lincoln knew Dayax was alive and waiting. Waiting for Lincoln to bring him home.

"I'm Tessa." The bubbly blonde appeared table side, holding a round tray with a glass of ice water balanced in the center. "You must be new in town. I haven't seen you before, and everyone eventually makes their way into Taylor's." Her broad grin and sparkling green eyes didn't stir his senses the way Angeline's unamused frown and blue eyes darkened with irritation had.

"I rolled in Saturday night."

"Staying or passing through?" Tessa placed the glass of water on the table.

From the dilation of her pupils and the subtle way she inched closer to him, Lincoln got the feeling her questions were more for personal interest rather than the friendly banter the owners would typically ask their servers to provide to customers.

"A little of both. I'm doing some consulting for the Co-op for a couple of weeks." Unless Brice's contact in the Woelfesenat managed to get Lincoln's active duty status reinstated sooner.

"Well." Tessa laughed lightly. "They have a sneaky habit of keeping those they hire, so I expect to see you in here for a good, long time."

Lincoln didn't share Tessa's expectation.

"Ready to order?"

"A steak, rare."

"The Co-op steak?" She pulled a pad from her apron and slapped it on the tray hooked in her arm. "It's an eighteen-ounce porterhouse."

Suddenly, Lincoln remembered Lila, smirking at him and saying that he could thank her one day with a big, juicy steak.

"Make it two orders."

"You get two sides per platter."

Lincoln look at her and shrugged.

"Baked potato, sweet potato, steak fries, potato salad, Caesar salad, mac-and-cheese, green bean amandine, grilled asparagus—" Her words rolled into an incessant buzz.

"Surprise me," he said, swallowing the uncomfortable feeling scaling his throat.

Tessa jotted on her pad. "We have an extensive selection of domestic and imported beers."

Lincoln rubbed his hand along his jaw, stubbled with a day's worth of beard. "I'll have whatever Reed usually orders and make it two."

She stopped scribbling and slowly lifted her gaze. Her smile flat.

"You know him, right? He said he's in here a lot."

"Yeah, I know him," Tessa huffed. "It's a small town."

Her reaction suggested more, but Lincoln didn't care to ask.

"He drinks Little Red Cap."

"Never heard of it."

"It's domestic with limited distribution. We order it and a few other ales from Grimm Brothers Brewhouse in Colorado." She tapped her pen against the pad on the tray. "Is Reed joining you later?"

"Not tonight."

"You ordered two meals."

"I did." But Lincoln only planned to eat and drink one. The other he owed to Lila.

"As much as I appreciate you doing this," Jimmy Taylor said, accepting the weekly inventory sheets Angeline handed him, "I could get one of the full-timers to handle counting the supplies."

"I've been doing inventory since I was sixteen," Angeline replied. "It would be weird to hand over the job to someone else."

Her uncle smiled, but his eyes were filled with worry. "I don't want you to feel obligated."

"I don't," Angeline assured him. "I like working for you and Aunt Miriam." Mostly she liked having a routine that got her out of the apartment and gave her a chance to interact with people. Since she didn't work with a partner, songwriting was a solitary endeavor.

As pack-oriented creatures, Wahyas thrived on socialization and there was no better place for it than Taylor's Roadhouse. At least in their human forms.

The protected forest of the Co-op's wolf sanctuary allowed pack members to fraternize as wolves, especially during full moons. Although, when temperatures dropped below forty degrees at night, she preferred to run in the woods behind the apartment building. Afterward, she could walk straight into her toasty apartment, rather than waiting for the heater to warm her car on the drive back from the sanctuary.

"Do you like it well enough to take over the business one day?" Jimmy's gaze fell just shy of hers.

"What about Zach and Lucy?" Angeline's much younger cousins were Jimmy's true heirs.

"Zach has been talking to a Dogman recruiter again."

Icy fingers twisted Angeline's stomach. She certainly didn't want her cousin to end up like Tanner or Lincoln. She and Zach would have a frank discussion about the very real possibility of death and dismemberment.

"Lucy is considering transferring to a bigger college out of state." Jimmy sighed. "The more their mama and I try to keep them close, the more they can't want to scramble away."

"They need time to see that the world outside Walker's

Run isn't all they think it is." Angeline hugged her uncle. "They'll come home, just like I did."

"Still." He squeezed her tight before letting go. "You're the one who's put time into this place. Miriam and I would like for you to take over the restaurant when we retire."

"I'll consider it," Angeline said more to alleviate her uncle's concern than to suggest actual intent. "But I expect you to keep running this place for a long, long time."

Relief washed over Jimmy's face and his smile turned genuine. "Deal."

The daily grind of actually running the restaurant took more time than Angeline cared to invest, but she didn't mind giving Jimmy and Miriam some peace of mind while their children sowed their oats.

They walked out of the storage room into the kitchen. While one cook tended the large gas stove, the other dropped a basket of steak fries in to the fryer. Another cook and one more server would arrive shortly and stay through closing.

"Aunt Miriam," Angeline called to the woman entering the kitchen.

As a child, Angeline didn't think her aunt favored her mother very much. But as Miriam aged, not only had she grown to look more like her sister, she had developed some of the same mannerisms and quirks.

With Miriam, Angeline could almost imagine what it would've been like to have grown up with her mother. Her aunt had even encouraged Angeline's love of music and paid for her lessons when her own father refused to do so.

"I gave Uncle Jimmy the inventory list, but despite the numbers now, you might want to increase the meat order for more steaks and ground beef. The full moon and Valentine's Day is Friday."

"Thanks for the reminder." Miriam wiped her hand on the apron tied around her waist as she walked toward Angeline. "Did Jimmy talk to you?" she asked quietly, touching Angeline's arm.

"Of course I did." He brushed past them and headed to their office to thumbtack the inventory list to the bulletin board. More than once Angeline had suggested they modernize the books, but her aunt and uncle were old school and feared entrusting their tried-and-true manual accounting system to a computer program.

"Well?" Her mouth drawn in a pensive grimace, Miriam peered at Angeline with the same dark shade of blue she remembered seeing in her mother's eyes.

"I told Jimmy that I would consider his offer, but he had to promise not to retire anytime soon."

Miriam's eyes twinkled with tears, and she hugged Angeline. "Thank you for putting his mind at ease."

"It's the least I could do for all that you and Jimmy have done for me over the years." She stepped back from Miriam, willing her tears to stay deep in the wells. An O'Brien never showed weakness, a mantra her father had drilled into Angeline and her brothers after their mother's tragic and untimely death.

"I should get out there and help Tessa."

"Yes, you should. There's at least one customer anxiously waiting to see you." Miriam shooed her from the kitchen.

Angeline ducked into the employee room to put on her half apron and grab an order pad before walking into the dining room. Tessa finished taking an order at a table in Angeline's section then beelined for her.

"You have two orders in, plus this one." Tessa handed her an order ticket. "Table twenty should have their food coming out in a couple of minutes. Seventeen just went in. And have you met Lincoln, the new guy in town?"

Angeline followed Tessa's gaze to the bistro table for two in the bar where Lincoln nursed his beer. An untouched bottle sat on the placemat across from him. Curious, but definitely not jealous, despite the little kick in her gut, she couldn't help wondering who would be joining him.

"He's really hot, even if he does keep company with Reed—the rat bastard." Although Tessa had mumbled the last part beneath her breath, Angeline's wolfan ears had heard every word her recently dumped friend had uttered.

"Lincoln is my new neighbor," Angeline said, watching a kitchen helper deliver two steak platters to Lincoln's table.

"Lucky you." Tessa sighed dreamily.

"No. Not me," Angeline said, but Tessa had already walked away.

Over the next hour Angeline had a steady flow of customers and only managed to say "Hey" to Lincoln on her way to and from the bar with drink orders. The beer and food at the second place setting remained untouched throughout his entire meal.

Periodically, she'd felt him watching her. Perhaps he wanted an explanation for her behavior this morning. She wasn't quite sure herself. His warning that she should not expect him to become her new confidant shouldn't have bothered her. She knew better than to expect anything from a Dogman. Though Angeline felt no obligation to provide an explanation for her reaction, she did want to let him know that she wasn't angry at him.

Waiting for the bartender to fill a drink order, Angeline casually strolled to Lincoln's table. The beer for his guest remained untouched. "How was your day?"

"Informative." His eyes still looked tired and barely a fleeting smile dusted his lips. "I spent most of the time running the woods with Reed."

"He's a good guy. Smart. Loyal."

"Cynical," Lincoln added.

"He got shot by a poacher a few months ago."

Lincoln swung his left foot out. The hiking boot concealed the prosthetic within. "A bomb blasted me out of a two-story window."

"You still have nightmares."

"I imagine he does, too," Lincoln said easily. "Our failures haunt us far longer than our victories stay with us."

"He took a bullet for Shane. I wouldn't call that a failure."

"The failure is in believing we are invincible." Lincoln guzzled the last few swallows of his beer and slammed down the mug on the table. "And learning we aren't."

"You sound a bit cynical yourself."

Lincoln shook his head, avoiding her gaze. "Cynicism colors one's judgment and clouds the vision. What happened, happened. All I can do is adapt and keep going."

"Are you waiting for Reed?"

"No." Lincoln fiddled with the edge of his linen napkin. "I owe an old friend a steak dinner."

"You've been a while. Did he take a wrong turn somewhere?"

The muscle in Lincoln's jaw twitched. He lifted his sorrow filled gaze. "Died in the line of duty."

Angeline's stomach dropped, a sick feeling rose in her chest and her heart hurt as if it had broken all over again. Not for her loss but for all those who'd lost loved ones, living and dead, to the Program.

Dogmen turned their backs on everything and everyone they'd ever known. All communication with family and friends ceased. No one ever knew what became of their loved one unless they received a death notification or an injury forced the soldier into retirement, like Lincoln soon would be.

Long simmering anger ignited Angeline's tongue. "Instead of eating and drinking with the dead, maybe your sympathies should lie with those he abandoned when he became a Dogman. And, for what? To feed his ego and die who knows where without regard to those he left behind?"

"Angeline—" Lincoln began.

"Have you called your family? Do they know what happened to you? Do they know you're even alive?"

His guilty look answered for him.

"Unbelievable!" Angeline barely managed to keep the shriek out of her voice.

"They're better off not knowing."

"That's a lie Dogman tell themselves to keep their consciences clear. Speaking from experience, it's not better. It's far worse than any nightmare you've ever had."

Though angry and hurt by Tanner's rejection, Angeline didn't immediately stop loving him. Not knowing his whereabouts or his situation had been an unrelenting torture. Until one day when a sharp pain sliced all the way to her soul. In that moment, she knew Tanner was dead. He would never come home to her. He would never come home to anyone, except in a box.

Despite Lincoln's request for her not to leave, Angeline walked away and collected the drinks from the bar. Delivering the beverages to appropriate patrons, she caught a glimpse of Lincoln making his way to the exit.

Good riddance, she thought without truly meaning it. Neither Tanner's choices nor his fate were Lincoln's fault.

A deep part of herself compelled Angeline to apologize for her behavior. Another part of her refused.

As a Dogman, Lincoln represented the very ideal she hated. She'd lost her first love—her only love—to the Program, and it destroyed the life they should've had.

Lincoln slipped out of the restaurant and Angeline's heart clenched, a phantom ache that his ridiculous homage had resurrected. It had absolutely nothing to do with the devastated look on his face when she'd left his table.

And if she told herself that enough times, by the time she got off work she might actually believe it.

Chapter 7

"Lila!"

Lincoln wrenched himself awake before hitting the ground in his nightmare. In reality, he couldn't remember anything past those first moments of falling out the window. His mind remained blank until the moment he woke up, alone in the hospital at the Program's headquarters in Germany a week later, missing a leg.

Whenever he asked about his team, the medical staff would merely pat his shoulder and say that he needed to focus on his own recovery. The tight smiles and averted eyes that followed told him all he needed to know.

His team was dead. And he was to blame.

Lincoln threw aside the sheets and sat up. His breaths continued to come hard and fast and would likely continue until his heart stopped forcibly pounding from the dream-induced adrenaline rush.

Swinging his good leg over the side of the bed, he stared at his scarred stump. Life would never be the same but he refused to simply accept retirement and quietly fade into the background. Not until he finished what he started. For Dayax. And for his team, whose loyalty had been rewarded with death.

Heavy-handedly, Lincoln rubbed his stump, stinging with phantom sensations. The physical therapist had chided him for being too aggressive with the desensitizing massage. The doctors had said the same about his push for recovery. They didn't understand that the pain distracted him from the quagmire of self-pity and gave him a definitive obstacle to conquer.

He squirmed into his knee shorts and snatched the sleeve off the nightstand. Pulling on the elastic-like fabric, he smoothed out the wrinkles until the material gloved his stump like his own skin, except for the glaring pale color that was nowhere near his naturally brown skin tone. He reached for the bionic limb that had fallen to the floor and fitted the cup onto the remaining part of his leg.

Carefully standing, Lincoln rocked on the prosthetic, allowing his weight to push out the air while his stump slid securely into place. The first steps were tentative. By the time he reached the open bedroom door, his gait became as fluid as it could be walking on an artificial leg.

The lights were on in the living room and kitchen. Even though his wolfan vision allowed him to see clearly in the dark, he didn't want to take a chance of tripping over something he'd overlooked.

Staring into the refrigerator at the lunch meat and four bottles out of a six-pack of beer, Lincoln knew he'd have to get more substantial food soon. A creepy-crawly feeling spread across his chest. He shivered, shaking off the sensation that gave rise to a childhood memory he'd rather not revisit.

Lincoln grabbed a beer and closed the refrigerator door. Eating civilian food rather than rations and mess hall grub, and civilian life in general, felt odd. Especially since he didn't have his team alongside him. They had done everything together. And he missed them, more than he could ever express.

The satphone on the counter chimed and an unknown number flashed across the screen. His heart suddenly beat double-time.

Lincoln picked up the phone. "Adams."

"¿Que pasa, capitán?" The masculine voice shocked Lincoln's ear.

His heart stilled and the blood in his veins cooled. Without heat, his muscles froze up and yet his knees felt weak and rubbery.

Phone in hand and plastered against his ear, Lincoln leaned heavily against the kitchen counter. *"¿Quién eres tú?"*

"It's Damien," the man said. "Did the fallout of that two-story building screw up your brain?"

"Damien Marquez died over two months ago," Lincoln answered as his "screwed-up" brain tried to reconcile the familiar voice he heard to the belief that his team had perished in the explosion.

"I'm not dead, Linc," the man on the other end of the line continued. "In case you're wondering, neither are the others. Well, except for Lila. There wasn't even enough of her—"

"Shut the hell up, Marquez." The guy really had no tact.

"Now you sound like the guy I remember." Damien snorted.

"I don't see what's so funny."

"You never did." A stark pause hung between them.

"How did you make it out of the building before it collapsed?" Lincoln asked, not wanting to give in to a mounting sense of relief.

"The blast knocked me off the stairs and I landed on

the ground floor. Brax and Nico pulled me out." The dark emotion in Damien's voice as he spoke suggested he clearly remembered every horrifying moment. "Sam— she took care of you until the medics arrived."

All but one member of his team had survived. One of the worry knots in Lincoln's chest loosened.

"Honestly, I didn't know you'd made it until Colonel Llewellyn mentioned that you were dogging him to find that orphan kid."

"Dayax," Lincoln said beneath his breath. "The boy's name is Dayax."

"I guess you haven't heard from the rest of the team since you thought we were dead."

Was the relief in Damien's sigh real or imagined?

"If they weren't injured, protocol would be to reassign them after a debriefing." But why didn't his CO or some-one at HQ simply tell him that his team was alive?

Lincoln strolled into the living room and stretched out on the couch. "I take it you're not on active duty, or we wouldn't be having this conversation. Are you all right?"

"I had a dislocated shoulder, a torn meniscus in my knee, some shrapnel lacerations. Smacked my noggin pretty good but it didn't crack."

"Good thing you're hardheaded."

Damien laughed.

"Where are you, man?"

"Miami. Using up the last of my medical leave. I've been reassigned to a new team and we're scheduled to de-ploy to the Amazon. Does HQ not understand how much I hate the fucking humidity?"

"Command knows. They just don't give a shit."

In the eight months Damien had been on Lincoln's team, he'd never quite jelled with them. Of course, Lin-coln and the others had been together for considerably longer and he had fully expected that Damien would eventually find his groove.

Now he would have to start the process over with a new team.

"How about you, Linc? Were the HQ doctors able to fix your leg?"

"I got a new one."

"Damn." Damien's sigh crackled in Lincoln's phone. "How's that gonna work for you?"

"I'm still on medical leave. No new orders yet." A strange awareness prowled Lincoln's senses. "For now, I'm in Maico, Georgia, doing some security consulting for the Walker's Run pack."

Glancing at the clock—half past midnight—Lincoln stood, ambled to the door and looked through the peephole into the dimly lit, empty corridor.

"I may have some business in Atlanta," Damien said. "If you're close by, we should meet up."

"Tell me when and where, I'll be there."

A shadow moved up the wall. The click of boots echoed from the stairwell.

"I'll text you details as soon as my plans firm up," Damien said.

"Roger that." The line went silent.

Lincoln watched Angeline move lithely down the corridor. Then, she stopped and looked over her shoulder, casting a troubled gaze at his door.

Lincoln's heart thumped an unusual beat. His instinct said he'd be a fool to let her go to bed without clearing the air between them. Then again, the last time he'd trusted his instinct a dear friend had died.

Behind the condensation on the bathroom mirror, the reflection of a pissy she-wolf stared back at Angeline. A hot shower had not improved her disposition.

She knew what it felt like for a man to watch her every move. And she'd felt Lincoln's gaze on her the moment she'd stepped onto the third-floor landing.

Had he waited up for her? Why hadn't he opened the door when he'd seen her staring back, instead of letting her stand in the cold like a freaking idiot?

She finished towel-drying, dressed in her comfy clothes and wished her jumbled thoughts about the Dogman were as easily flushed away as the tissue she tossed in the toilet.

In the bedroom, she picked up her guitar and sat cross-legged on the unmade bed. After strumming a few chords, she tuned the strings and began again. Unfortunately, with her mind and fingers out of sync, everything she played sounded crummy.

The doorbell rang.

Pick between her fingers, her hand stilled over the strings. When Tristan lived down the hall, he would occasionally stop by for a chat when he got off work, knowing she would be up.

Maybe Lincoln wanted company, too.

Well, she had a mind to tell him a few things.

She laid the guitar on the bed and scrambled out of the bedroom, then nonchalantly walked through the living room. The doorbell rang again.

"I'm coming!" Agitation caused her to twist the dead bolt harder than normal and Angeline swung open the door with her chin tilted upward so she could glare into Lincoln's eyes.

Only, nothing but air looked back at her.

She dropped her gaze to the pizza delivery boy who barely looked old enough to shave.

"Fourteen ninety-nine." His gaze slid up and down her body and back up to her chest, which, in her braless state with cold air passing through the thin material of her long-sleeved T-shirt, clearly outlined her hardened nipples.

"Grow up!" She stepped back to shut the door.

"Hey!" He shoved the pizza box into the doorway, preventing the door from closing. "Pay up or I'm calling my supervisor."

"Call away. I didn't order anything. You have the wrong apartment."

"The ticket says Chatuge View Apartments, number twenty-one." He looked at her door proudly displaying the golden numerals two and one.

"Let me see." She snatched the ticket off the top of the box. Sure enough, the caller had given her address but the wrong name.

"This goes to Lincoln Adams," she said, waving the paper in front of the young man's face and pointing down the hallway. "He's in the corner apartment, number twenty-five."

"The delivery is for apartment twenty-one. Are you gonna pay up or what?"

Angeline matched the kid's exasperated huff. "Wait here."

Despite his protest, she shut the door. He retaliated by keeping his finger pressed against the doorbell until she returned with the cash and sent him on his way.

Glaring down the corridor, she thought about keeping the pizza. But wolfans took food seriously. Better to deal with Lincoln now rather than later, when he came looking for his food.

After closing the door behind her, Angeline beelined for apartment twenty-five. Taking a cue from the delivery boy, she pounded the door until Lincoln answered wearing only his boxers. With his dark hair in disarray and sleepy eyes narrowed at her, he loomed in the doorway.

"Here." She jabbed the pizza box into his chiseled abdomen. "Next time, give them the right apartment number."

He made no effort to claim the box. "It's not mine."

"Your name is on the ticket." Her teeth chattered as a cold wind blew through her.

"They delivered it to you."

"Because you gave them the wrong apartment number." Her nipples, definitely pointy after the last breeze, did not escape Lincoln's notice.

His entire body tensed and his Adam's apple prominently traveled down his throat. But when his gaze flickered back to her face, his eyes were clear. "It's not mine," he said again, then turned and walked away, leaving her standing in the doorway.

Since he hadn't shut her out, Angeline stepped inside to get out of the cold and closed the door.

"Sheesh! It's freezing in here."

Lincoln glanced at her from the kitchen. "Didn't notice." Opening the refrigerator, he pulled out two beers. "Grab a glass from the cabinet if you don't want to drink from the bottle," he said, strolling past her and into the living room.

First setting the beer on the coffee table, he eased onto the couch, grabbed the remote and muted the television. When she made no effort to join him, Lincoln's head slowly rotated in her direction. "I can resist a lot of things," he said as his gaze lifted from the box in Angeline's hands to her face. "Food isn't one of them. If you don't want to stay, leave the pizza on the counter. Otherwise…" He patted the seat cushion beside him.

A test, perhaps? To gauge her willingness to move past the kerfuffle at Taylor's.

"It's a little too frosty in here for me. I can almost see my breath." Angeline placed the pizza box on the kitchen counter.

Hand gripped on the couch arm, Lincoln hoisted himself up and went over to the thermostat.

"How about the fireplace?" Angeline opened the pantry

and snagged a handful of napkins. "The controller should be on the mantel."

For the first time, she noticed the quiet thump of Lincoln's artificial foot as he walked.

Lincoln picked up the small device and the gas fireplace came to life. "You know a lot about this place."

Napkins and pizza box in hand, Angeline strolled into the living room and placed the items on the coffee table. "Tristan and I have been close since we were kids. We've always looked after each other."

"Sounds like me and Lila," Lincoln said, joining Angeline on the couch. "For the last five years, she was my best friend."

"What happened?"

"She died on our last mission."

Angeline's stomach dropped. "Is she the soldier you bought the beer and steak for?"

"Yes." Lincoln's head bowed slightly and his eyes squinted shut before his hand swiped down his face. "One of the last things she said to me was that I owed her a nice, thick, juicy steak."

"I'm sorry for your loss," Angeline said quietly. "I understand what it feels like to lose someone close to you."

Wordlessly, he turned his head, glancing sidelong at her.

"I should not have been rude to you at Taylor's. It's not your fault that someone I loved chose to be a Dogman rather than have a mateship with me."

"No apology necessary, Angel." Lincoln flipped open the pizza box. Inside was a large heart-shaped pizza loaded with meats and cheese. Slowly, he turned to Angeline. One dark eyebrow rose in a question while an irritating smile spread across his masculine mouth.

"It's probably a special promotion. Valentine's Day is next week."

Still grinning, he placed a slice on a napkin and handed it to Angeline.

"I didn't order this pizza."

"And yet you paid for it and brought it to me," he teased. "How sweet."

"It would've been sweeter if you had paid for the pizza before the guy delivered it to me."

"But then you wouldn't have had a reason to come over." After grabbing a slice for himself, Lincoln leaned back on the couch, closed his eyes and took a giant bite. A sexy growl of satisfaction rumbled in his throat as he chewed. "I haven't had pizza since college."

"Really? Why?" Angeline wiped away the cheese that dribbled on her chin.

"No one delivers to the jungle, or the desert or the swamp. Or Antarctica."

"You went to the South Pole?"

"If I confirm or deny that question, I'll have to terminate you." He made the statement with lethal seriousness but his mouth quirked into a smile before he took the next bite of pizza.

She playfully bumped his shoulder and was rewarded with a soft, playful growl that flooded her senses with an awareness of his undeniable masculinity. Common sense dictated that she should leave immediately. But his apartment was warm and toasty now. Neither her body nor her stomach wanted to brave the crisp, cold night to scurry down to her home and an empty refrigerator.

Chapter 8

Stone-cold determination.

Lincoln faced each and every mission with stone-cold determination. This one would be no different.

Get in, get the objective, get out. That was the plan.

He'd followed the same plan when trying to locate Dayax. That mission hadn't turned out so well.

Midmorning on Tuesday, only a few cars were in the parking lot behind Anne's Market. Just as Angeline had predicted.

Lincoln shut off the truck engine and opened the door. Slinging his good leg out, he pivoted in the seat and grabbed the door handle for support. He climbed out and adjusted his balance until he felt steady on the artificial limb.

Slowly, Lincoln followed the sidewalk to the front of the long building, housing several businesses facing the one-way street framing Maico's quaint town square. Keeping focused on his agenda, he stared straight forward until he reached Anne's Market.

Inside, he glanced around to get his bearings. It was a small store with a decent produce section to the left, a small deli and refrigerated section to the right, canned and dry goods in the center and, according to the sign hanging from the ceiling, a meat section in the back.

First, he needed a cart. Unfortunately, the one he grabbed was jammed into another and wouldn't shake loose. He looked around to make sure no one was watching, then gripped the handle, lifted the wheels off the floor and slammed it down. It made a terrible noise but the force knocked the buggy loose and, heart pounding, he went on his less than merry way.

Though small, especially in comparison to the mega-size chain stores, the market seemed to have more than anyone could ever need. Aisles of canned goods lined the center of the store with so many selections that Lincoln simply did not know what to choose.

He headed to the outer sections filled with produce. How hard could it be to buy a tomato? Apparently a degree in agricultural science would've been beneficial. There were heirlooms, grape-size, Romas, organic, home-grown and imported. All he wanted was one to slice, salt and eat with a platter of scrambled eggs.

Closing his eyes, he picked one tomato then headed to the refrigerated section. Eggs were eggs, right? Apparently they came in half dozen, dozen, a dozen and a half, two dozen, three dozen and four dozen containers. He reached for the closest carton, noticing the slight tremor in his hand.

Seriously, he'd faced down terrorists and mercenaries. How could grocery shopping alone rattle his nerves?

He took a deep breath and slowly exhaled, which did nothing to ease the sound of his heart thumping in his ears or the crackle of electricity that raised the hair on his arms.

"Better check those eggs." Unexpectedly, Angeline's

Southern twang drifted over his shoulder. "You don't want to get home and find one cracked."

At the rate he was going, Lincoln would be lucky to get home with them at all.

She slid the carton from his death grip and opened it. "See?"

Two eggshells were broken, more than likely from the frustrated way he'd latched onto the carton.

Angeline set them aside.

"These are my favorites." Selecting a green foam container, she inspected the eighteen eggs inside, then set them in his cart.

Her handbasket crooked in her arm, Angeline continued on her way. Instinctively, Lincoln followed.

"I could use some good recommendations." He strolled beside her, the tightness in his chest easing. "It's been a long time since I've had so many things to choose from." He wasn't sure why anyone needed so many choices, especially when others in some parts of the world had none.

"You're going to need the basics, so let's start with the nonperishables."

"Lead the way." He waved his hand in an after-you gesture.

Wearing jeans tucked into her black, pointy-heeled boots and a long cardigan sweater, Angeline took the lead. If Lincoln wasn't careful, the mesmerizing sway of her hips might lead him to the edge of a cliff.

They stopped in the paper goods section.

"Do you like washing dishes?"

Lincoln shook his head.

"Neither do I." Angeline dropped a stack of paper plates into his cart. Followed by a roll of paper towels and a box of garbage bags.

The next stop, the personal hygiene aisle, displayed at least a dozen brands of soap—and that was just the bars that came in boxes. The body gels and foams took up nearly as much room on the shelves as did the shampoos.

He simply stared at all of them. The flutter in his heart started again and his stomach tightened.

Just pick one!

He reached for a small, rectangular box and envisioned the slippery bar sliding from his hand and dropping to the shower floor. Since he didn't want to spend half of his shower time hopping on one leg, trying to retrieve the soap, Lincoln grabbed the first bottle of body wash within reach.

"You should smell it," Angeline said.

Lincoln carefully unscrewed the cap and sniffed. It smelled like soap and flowers.

He lifted it toward Angeline for her to get a whiff. Instantly, her nose wrinkled.

Okay, not this one.

It really shouldn't matter which ones she liked, but he couldn't stop himself from seeking her opinion on every damn one of them. When her eyes closed and she took a second sniff of the woodsy-scented body wash with a hint of citrus and amber, a soft, sexy smile curved her mouth. Lincoln nabbed two bottles. The full moon was only a few days away and if she was looking for a partner for the evening, or any other evening, he definitely wanted her to have that same response if she scented him. And he hoped she did.

His libido had reawakened the night they'd met. At first he'd wondered if his reaction had simply been a response to his hormones righting the chemical balance in his body after years of suppression. But none of the other women he'd encountered over the last few days had sparked the same feeling.

The air seemed to charge whenever Angeline was near

and she pulled from him a need to protect and pleasure. A need that would intensify as the full moon drew near.

The way she turned and smiled made Lincoln feel as if she'd read his thoughts.

Silently, he laughed at the notion. In their wolf forms, Wahyas were telepathic with others also in their wolf form. The ability to mentally communicate did not transfer to their human forms, unless a mate-bond had formed. Not all wolfans in a mateship developed the ethereal connection, but those who did were synced mind and body, heart and soul.

Lincoln's heart and soul belonged to the Dogman program. His mind and body would do well to remember the commitment he'd made and not get used to Angeline's company. Despite pressure from his CO, Lincoln had no immediate plans to retire and settle down. But he was a long way from proving his readiness for active duty if he couldn't accomplish the simple task of grocery shopping on his own.

Humming the new tune that she was composing, Angeline drove into the parking lot of the Chatuge View Apartments. Admittedly, even if one climbed on top of the roof with a pair of binoculars, Lake Chatuge would be a distant blur. There was, however, a nearby retention pond the residents had jokingly named after the big lake.

She parked next to Lincoln's empty truck. Instead of following him to their apartment complex, Angeline had stopped by the gas station to top off her tank before coming home.

With one lightweight shopping bag in hand, she climbed out of the car. Rarely did she purchase more than she could eat in a week. Lincoln, however, had loaded up his cart. From the stress the activity seemed to cause him, Angeline figured he didn't want to return to the store anytime soon.

At first Lincoln had relaxed when she'd begun helping him find the things he wanted. But before they'd been ready to check out, a dark mood had settled over him. His side of the conversation had whittled down to grunts by the time they'd parted. Except for the harsh words he'd snarled when she'd asked if he wanted her assistance getting his groceries to the truck.

Angeline peered at the two bags left in the truck bed, wondering if she should risk a repeat. When Lincoln didn't appear after a full minute, she gathered his groceries with her own and headed upstairs.

His door had been left open and he stood in the kitchen guzzling a bottle of water. He turned as she walked into the apartment. The storm in his eyes had yet to subside. His gaze dropped to the bags in her hands. "What are you doing?"

"I saw these in the back of the truck. Since I was coming upstairs, I thought I'd save you a trip back down."

"Did you not understand what I said earlier?" An angry treble crisped his words. "I don't need anyone's help!"

"I'm just being neighborly." Angeline placed his bags on the kitchen counter. "I would've done it for anyone."

"I'm not *just* anyone." The underlying snarl was quiet, menacing, and absolutely pissed off Angeline.

"Because you're a big, bad Dogman," she snapped, stepping toward him. "Big freakin' deal!"

"It *is* a big deal." A tremor ran along his clenched jaw and his fingers tightened around the empty water bottle, crackling and collapsing it in his fist.

"Being a Dogman or accepting help?" Angeline stood close enough to feel warm puffs of air on her face as Lincoln's chest heaved. "You're in the real world now, Lincoln. And while you're here, you are part of the community. Part of the pack."

Giving him the *get-your-shit-together* look she reserved

for the babysitting times when her nieces and nephews got on her last nerve, Angeline raised on her toes. "Get used to people being neighborly and offering a helpful hand. It's who we are. It's what we do. And we aren't going to change for you—*Dogman*."

The corded muscles in his neck flexed as he swallowed.

After a glaring match that she refused to forfeit, primal interest flickered in his eyes, defusing the anger but whipping up emotions just as turbulent. His gaze drew back, as if taking in all of her face, which warmed with the visual caress. When he focused on her mouth, her lips tingled. Angeline could list a dozen or more reasons why she should walk away. Only one to stay.

Her instinct ruled in favor of the one.

Pressing her lips against his mouth, she gave him a chaste kiss. Eyes open and intently watching her, Lincoln laid his hands on her waist and urged her closer. As she snuggled against him, his arms wrapped around her, holding but not restraining. His eyelids slid closed and his lips parted.

Her eyes drifting closed, Angeline deepened the kiss. Gently, she probed his mouth, eliciting a soft, deep masculine growl. A shiver of satisfaction swept across her skin, warming her despite the cold breeze drifting in from the open door.

He took charge of the kiss, branding her mouth, claiming her breath and heating her to the very core. Usually she kept her head when kissing a man. Never allowing too much emotion or real feeling to emerge.

She'd lost her heart once to a Dogman. To do so again would be foolish. Dogmen were committed to the program every bit as much as true mates were to each other.

But that didn't mean she couldn't enjoy Lincoln's kisses or caresses, among other things.

The feel of his hands palming her curves and gliding up

her back to cradle her neck sent an electric tingle down her spine. He tilted back her head, comfortably resettling her from her tiptoes to the flats of her feet. She sighed against his mouth. Without breaking their kiss, he softly chuckled.

Whatever worries that had darkened Lincoln's mood, he seemed to have forgotten. Angeline sensed no more anger and frustration, only curiosity and desire.

"Am I interrupting?" Tristan's voice carried above the knock on the open door.

Angeline stepped back from the kiss. Despite the less than friendly look she aimed at Tristan, he responded with an irritating grin.

"We were, um…" Eyes still slightly hooded and a small smile upon his mouth, Lincoln cleared his throat. "She was helping me with the groceries."

"Never heard it called that, but okay." Tristan's grin broadened and a tease glinted in his dark eyes.

"Were we meeting up today?" Lincoln asked.

"Nah." Tristan waved his hand. "I was on my way to see Angeline and noticed your door was open."

Although Lincoln's expression and loose-limbed posture didn't change, Angeline sensed the tension creeping into his body. Could feel it, actually, tightening her muscles.

If she didn't know better, she would think Lincoln was a little jealous. More than likely, his heightened tension was due to Tristan's sudden appearance.

"Nel's baby shower is today," Angeline said. "I asked Tristan to pick up the gift."

"Not going to the party?" Lincoln asked.

"Not my thing." Nothing against Nel. Angeline didn't quite fit in with Nel's circle of human friends. And because Angeline and Tristan had been intimately close friends, she felt a little awkward around his pregnant mate.

"Well, thanks for being neighborly." Lincoln lifted a

couple of cans from the bag on the counter and stepped toward the small pantry.

Eyes narrowing ever so slightly, Tristan's gaze flickered to Lincoln and back to Angeline.

"Anytime." She snagged Tristan's elbow, tugging him along as she left.

"I'll catch up with you tomorrow," Tristan said to Lincoln, stopping to close the door.

Angeline hurried down the corridor to her apartment. Tristan followed at a leisurely stroll.

"So." He stepped inside and shut out the cold. "You and Lincoln seemed cozy."

"I don't do cozy." Angeline walked into the kitchen and put away her few groceries before gathering the gift basket in the bedroom. "Give Nel my best."

"I didn't do cozy, either, until I met Nel."

"Lincoln is a Dogman. No matter how strong of an attraction we might have, his heart will always belong to the Program." And Angeline wouldn't set herself up for another broken heart.

Chapter 9

The icy fingers of the crisp, Wednesday morning air pinched Lincoln's face. Standing near the edge of the ledge at Walker's Pointe, he gazed over the Walker's Run territory and down at the sleepy little town of Maico below. Calm, serene. Peaceful.

After all of the violence he'd seen and been required to do, Lincoln never expected to experience those feelings again. Yet, here he was, in the most idyllic place he would ever set his paw upon, daydreaming about accepting Brice's invitation to make Maico, the gentle town in the heart of the Walker's Run territory, his home.

But what would Lincoln do if he stayed?

A career soldier accustomed to watching tanks rolling past instead of ordinary trucks and cars and motorcycles, he lacked any useful civilian skills.

"This is my favorite place." Brice stepped beside Lincoln.

"I can see why." Lincoln deeply inhaled fresh, crisp mountain air. "It feels…"

"Like home?"

"Surreal. I'm not used to all this tranquility."

"It's not hard to adapt to Walker's Run. This place settles in your blood and roots in your soul. Makes it difficult for some wolfans to leave."

"I'm not here to settle down." Lincoln stuffed his hands into the pockets of the thick jacket he'd received in the shipment of clothes from headquarters.

"When we met in Romania, I saw the same restlessness and longing in your eyes that I had felt before returning home. Even then, you were growing tired of the Program. There's nothing wrong with wanting out."

"I don't want out." *Not yet.*

The news today from Colonel Llewellyn did not deviate from the script he'd given Lincoln every time he'd called. No one had seen or heard from Dayax, and his body had not been found.

This time, though, the Colonel had spoken the grim truth that the boy might never be found, alive or dead. Lincoln still had to try. "I can't help Dayax if I'm not a Dogman."

"My friends in the Woelfesenat agree."

Lincoln's entire body switched to running on silent mode. The breath stilled in his lungs. The steady thump of his heart quieted to a whisper. Even his thoughts paused as he watched and waited for Brice to continue.

"A new Dogman team will soon join the human forces in Taifa. When they deploy, so will you. Your only mission will be to find Dayax and the other missing children."

The tiny hairs at the base of Lincoln's neck began to rise. "I sense a *but* coming."

"You have to pass the readiness evaluation."

"Damn!" The test was a three-week assault of a recruit's senses, strength and willingness to die for the Program.

"Since you're already a Dogman, I convinced them to simply put you through the final physical obstacle course."

"Fair enough." As a weight lifted from Lincoln's shoulders, cold determination settled in his gut. Weeks of rehab had kept him physically fit, but he needed more practice shifting. No longer could he simply shuck off his clothes and go wolf. Now he had to carefully remove his leg or risk disintegrating the state-of-the-art prosthetic prototype the Program had entrusted to him.

"I bargained with the Woelfesenat to grant you one last mission, Linc. But I couldn't stop your mandatory medical retirement. Whether or not you come home with Dayax, your career as a Dogman will be over."

"I appreciate everything you've done." He was more than humbled by it, actually. Lincoln had seen the impact of Brice's hard-hitting negotiating skills in Romania. Brokering peace in the midst of pure, unadulterated hatred required more than talent. One needed divine favor.

Something Brice seemed to have in spades and wasn't stingy in dispensing.

"After you find him, what then?"

"Hadn't really thought much further than that."

"You need to, for yourself and Dayax."

Lincoln returned his gaze to the tranquil community below.

Home. The word pulsed through his mind.

Perhaps his pain medication had skewed his senses. Southwest Texas had been his home. And the Big Bend pack had always buzzed with activity and competition to be the best.

There was nothing inherently wrong with that mindset. It had propelled his mother forward in her career as a Texas Ranger and had kept his father alive as an undercover DEA agent. It had also formed the foundation of Lincoln's career. Unfortunately, no one could stay at the top forever. And his topple had caused his best friend her life.

"If the Woelfesenat allows me to bring Dayax to the States, would someone in Walker's Run be interested in fostering him?" Lincoln would be able to keep tabs on the boy if he was adopted into Brice's pack.

"What about yourself?"

"I'm not father material," Lincoln said. Dayax deserved so much more than a washed-up Dogman for a father.

"Are you sure about that?"

It was the one thing Lincoln had utter confidence in.

Angeline paused beside the babbling river, careful not to get her paws wet. A slight breeze ruffled her fur. The thick coat locked in her body heat against the cold night. A near full moon shimmered in the dark, velvety expanse of the sky.

There was a time when she'd eagerly anticipated the coming of a full moon. She never had to worry about finding a sex partner, full moon or otherwise. Usually she hooked up with a customer from the restaurant for a bit of fun.

A few years ago she'd picked the wrong man and narrowly avoided an unimaginable predicament. Still, the near miss caused her stomach to turn whenever she remembered the incident. Since then she'd toned down her flirtations and vowed never to have casual sex with a man she didn't know and trust.

That had become a complication in and of itself. Wolfan males could become possessive, especially of a female sex partner. However, some had managed to forge successful full moon partnerships. The caveat was that the male and female did not engage socially nor did they have human style sex. Their full moon rendezvous and romps were al-

ways in wolf form, thereby eliminating the development
of emotional attachments.

Angeline had yet to find such a partner.

It would probably help if she actually started looking
for one. Her throat grew tight. Lowering her head, Angeline stretched her neck to lap the water. The icy wetness
dislodged the lump of regret and sloshed it all the way
down into the pit of her stomach.

She had a good life. Maybe not the one she once wanted,
but good nevertheless.

Backing away from the stream, she padded along the
path worn by many sleepless nights. Though they had
experienced trouble in the recent past, the Walker's Run
territory was generally safe. Sentinels were never more
than a howl away, especially inside the wolf sanctuary.
But Angeline preferred to stick to the woods behind her
home. Easy access to a quiet place to shift and run at a
moment's notice was one reason some unmated Wahyas
resided at the Chatuge View Apartments.

Without any thought to time, Angeline meandered
along the winding trail, trying to sort out the mixed feelings Lincoln's arrival had caused.

For the period they had dated, not once had Tanner
mentioned his interest in the Program. When he'd broken
the news, Tanner had even admitted that, deep in his soul,
he believed Angeline to be his true mate. But he wanted
to be a Dogman more than he wanted her love.

Lincoln had also left behind everything he'd known and
loved to live the life Tanner had coveted. Facing mandatory retirement, Lincoln was forced to watch his dreams
slip through his fingers. Sometimes in his eyes Angeline
caught a glimpse of the horrified sadness of seeing all he'd
sacrificed for being so easily dismissed.

He seemed more disappointed than angry, which surprised her. She'd always imagined Dogmen to be selfish, arrogant adrenaline junkies.

Lincoln displayed none of those traits. It would be better for her if he had. Maybe she wouldn't have been so drawn to him if he'd acted like a pigheaded jerk.

Making the turn toward the apartments, Angeline lifted her nose. Lincoln's scent drifted on the currents. Sensing no advancement in her general direction, she presumed that he must be sitting on his balcony. He would see her coming home, and might even consider that it would be a good idea for them to run the woods together. It wouldn't be. Other than being neighborly, she should have no interest in the Dogman.

Her body disagreed. A solid mountain of muscles, Lincoln was as sexy as a wolfan male could be. With a full moon coming, she was tempted to give in to its aphrodisiac effects with him.

Even in her wolf form, Angeline's lips warmed and tingled. She'd had her fair share of kisses, but none had stayed with her the way Lincoln's kiss had.

The leisurely stroll quickly turned into a fast trot. Despite her mind's stern attempt to slow the pace, her paws maintained a steady rhythm. Only when she caught a flicker of movement through the bushes ahead did her canter ease to a stop.

Lincoln removed the long, slender tote slung across his shoulder, peeled off the cover and opened the folding chair. Slipping off his untied boots, he yanked the sweatshirt over his head and dropped it on the ground. The silvery shimmer of moonlight glanced off his sculpted chest. He shook off the cold and unzipped his pants, sliding them from his hips and allowing them to puddle at his bare feet. Or rather, actual bare foot and one artificial.

Protruding from a nest of dark hair, his long cock

bounced free and easy. Angeline's mouth watered for the salty, masculine taste of him. She could blame the lustful desire on the nearing full moon, but the accusation would be a lie.

Despite his career choice, she wanted him, even though she wished otherwise.

Careful to stay downwind, she watched him ease into the chair and begin the laborious process of removing his leg. His movements were slow and methodical, and it hurt her heart to understand that he would never be able to simply shuck his clothes and run free. Not if he wanted a leg to stand on when he returned.

With one hand, he lifted his thigh and carefully worked off the prosthetic cup. Each time he grimaced, Angeline did, too.

He laid the artificial limb on top of his clothes. Lincoln's naturally bronzed skin appeared several shades darker that the flesh-colored stocking covering his stump. Carefully, he began the tedious process of removing the protective sleeve.

A new ache rose in her heart at the independence he'd lost and sacrificed.

She wanted to go to him, to help so the task wouldn't be so difficult. Instead, she remained perfectly still. He'd resented her assistance with the groceries. How much more upset would he be if she tried to help him now?

The leg and sleeve wrapped in his clothes and stowed beneath the chair, Lincoln eased out of the chair and onto the ground. Balancing his weight on one knee and both hands, he shifted.

His wolf, black with glints of gold dust on the tips of his fur, looked as magnificent as the man. He took a few wobbly steps, but then his stride grew more confident. He lifted his snout and scented the air. Since she stayed downwind, he didn't pinpoint her current location but he quickly picked up her scent trail when she'd started her run. He stared in the direction she'd gone, then darted down the same path.

There could've been any number of reasons as to why he'd chosen to track Angeline. But that he did made her happier than it ever should have.

Chapter 10

Lincoln jarred awake, the deafening explosion still ringing in his ears. His heart pounded unmercifully and he struggled to breathe normally. The sweat coating his body seemed to burn his skin rather than cool it down.

Even with the glow of the television lighting the room, it still took a few seconds for him to realize that he was safe inside the apartment and not falling out of a two-story building. Shoving aside a lightweight blanket, Lincoln wiped the troubled sleep from his eyes and rubbed his hands along his jaw covered in several days' worth of stubble.

He'd dozed off on the couch again. The bed seemed too much a luxury to get used to sleeping on.

Muting the television didn't silence the noise. The rumble outside grew louder, chased by the tinkling sounds of laughter and giggles.

After putting on his leg and sweatpants, he stood slowly, shook off the sludge the nightmare had cast and limped to the door. The peephole gave him a perfect view down the corridor but not of the ruckus coming from the stairs.

He cracked open the door and leaned out for a quick peek. The flurry of activity storming the stairwell moved en masse to swarm him, firing questions and exclamations at him faster than a semiautomatic AK-47.

Angeline stepped up behind the crowd of children, their ages anywhere from six to sixteen. Despite the chaos ratcheting up his raw nerves, she appeared unflustered and unconcerned by the swirl of activity.

For a fleeting moment, Lincoln wished he would've caught up with her in the woods last night. He still needed to tell her about Tanner. After all, he had made a promise. But what if fulfilling that oath did more harm than good?

"Whoa! Whoa!" Angeline held up her hands. "Settle down, please."

The kids quieted, except for one. Obviously the youngest, she stepped forward. Her wide, rounded eyes were just as blue as Angeline's but her hair was a deep chestnut.

"Are you the...*Dogman*?" She whispered the last word. So adorable and brave.

"I am." He crouched to her level and flattened his palm over his heart. "Lincoln Adams, at your service."

A dazzling smile cracked the serious mask on the little girl's face, but it wasn't her brilliance that heated his skin. He slid his gaze to Angeline. The natural feminine curve of her mouth didn't waver. The heat he felt radiated from her eyes. All sparkly and bright, they warmed him to the depth of his soul.

The little girl's hand darted toward Lincoln.

"Sierra! No!" The oldest boy clamped a hand on her shoulder and pulled her back into the safety of their huddle.

Fear now filled the little girl's eyes.

Like a splash of ice water to the face, Lincoln regained his senses. Dogmen, though generally held in great esteem among Wahyas, were also feared for the awful things they had to do.

Peace came at a price. Dogmen were the ones who paid it.

Lincoln stretched to his full height and met each of the children's uncertain gazes. How brave Dayax must have been, alone and starving, to face a Dogman for the first time and ask for food.

"I hope we didn't wake you," Angeline said.

Lincoln checked his watch. Quarter past eight. "I needed to get up, anyway."

"Aunt Ange." The youngest boy spoke out of the side of his mouth. "Is he going to kill us?"

"Not if you study hard, finish your homework and don't talk back to your elders," Angeline said seriously.

"You said the same thing about getting presents from Santa Claus," the middle boy said.

"Who do you think Santa gives the naughty list to?" Lincoln stuffed his hands into his pockets.

The oldest girl, a teenager, rolled her eyes. "I'm hungry. What's for breakfast?"

"Well, that depends." Angeline stepped around the pack of children and stood in front of Lincoln. "Can we borrow some eggs?"

"And bacon!"

"No, sausage!"

"Bread! I want French toast."

Everyone shouted over each other, and Lincoln had difficulty determining who wanted what.

Angeline whistled, shrill and effective. The kids fell silent.

"Help yourself." Lincoln pushed open the door.

"We're going to need the kitchen, too," she whispered, ushering the kids inside.

"All right, then." He closed the door, watching them

file into the kitchen, each diverging into a specific area and setting up like a team of breakfast sprites.

"It's a teacher's workday at their schools." Angeline peeled off her coat and collected the ones the children had discarded on their way in. She laid them in a chair by the entertainment center. "And they always spend them with me. This—" she waved her hand toward the kitchen "—is tradition. We start the morning with a hearty breakfast."

"You don't cook."

"No, but Tristan does, so I always brought them here. Even after he moved in with Nel, we still came here because he has a larger kitchen." Angeline gave him a sidelong look. "We can gather everything and go to my place if we're disturbing you."

"What's in it for me if I let you stay?"

"Breakfast, and the kids clean up the dishes." Angeline's blue eyes sparkled and her mouth formed a pretty-please smile.

"Hard to say no to that."

"Hey! Mr. Dogman!" Sierra waved at him. "We're going sledding after we eat."

"You are?" Lincoln noticed an ebbing warmth deep inside. Had he made a different choice, he could've shared his life with a mate and a brood of kids.

"Yep. It's fun and then we drink hot chocolate." The little one gathered the silverware.

"Want to come?" Angeline asked.

"I probably shouldn't."

"Your loss. We always have a great time." The tempting smile curving her mouth wreaked all sorts of havoc on Lincoln's mind and body.

"I bet you do." Lincoln started toward the bathroom. "Don't let them burn down the place while I'm in the shower."

"I'll keep Aunt Ange out of the kitchen," the teenaged girl said. "She's more apt to start a fire than we are."

"Roslyn!" Angeline pointed a long, slender finger at her oldest niece. "Keep talking like that and no more driving lessons."

The carefree giggles and unrestrained laughter that filled the apartment were sounds like nothing Lincoln had every experienced. He dwelled in a world of strife and fear and desperation. He couldn't imagine adapting to civilian life, yet longing broke inside him.

After lumbering into the bathroom, Lincoln stripped off his clothes. Sitting on the shower chair, he removed the prosthetic leg and turned on the water, allowing the icy-cold stream to numb his skin. Too bad it couldn't do the same with his wayward thoughts.

Brice had asked what Lincoln planned to do after he found Dayax. "Bring him home" had been the only response Lincoln's heart would provide. But Lincoln had no home. No future, really. His entire life had been devoted to the Program. Watching Angeline with her nieces and nephews, he began to truly understand the tragedy of Tanner's choice. And now, possibly his own.

"We killed the Dogman!" Sierra shrieked.

Angeline's heart had not yet restarted after watching Lincoln's sled go airborne, flip twice and slam to the snow-covered ground with Lincoln tumbling behind. A thunderous howl had chased him down the hill.

"Everyone stay here!" She gave a look to Roslyn and Caleb, her teenaged niece and nephew. Immediately, they gathered Logan, Brent and Sierra closer and assured the younger kids that Dogmen were Wahyan superheroes, so they couldn't die from falling off a sled.

Angeline darted to the spot where Lincoln had landed.

The snow boots provided her feet with some traction, but she would have made faster progress in her wolf form. Seeing her shift on the fly would likely panic the children, who were already frightened and worried.

The muscles in her legs burned and tightened as she trudged through the snowdrift. The sunlight glinting off the stark white landscape caused her eyes to water, not the sight of the man, flat on his back, still as death.

"Lincoln!" Her breath steamed the air.

Don't be dead! Don't be dead!

Dropping to her knees, Angeline yanked off her mittens and brushed away the snow flurries dotting Lincoln's face. She didn't see any signs of blood, his body didn't appear twisted, and his neck wasn't crooked at an odd angle. "Hey, are you all right?"

His closed eyelids didn't flutter open, no sound escaped his slightly parted lips, and not one muscle twitched in response. Lightly, she pressed her hand to his nose and mouth. Not one puff of warm breath heated her palm.

"Oh, no." She yanked open his jacket and laid her ear against his chest. The layers of clothes could've obscured the sound, but she didn't hear the beat of his heart.

Maybe she should've taken the CPR class Tristan had suggested.

Angeline leaned over Lincoln's all too still body and lowered her face to his. Just before she touched his jaw to pry open his mouth, Lincoln's eyelashes lifted. Mischief sparkled in his pale green eyes.

"Hello, Angel." His hand rose to cup the back of her neck while the other slid around her waist, pulling her on top of him.

His mouth, cold from the wind, captured her lips, muffling her surprise. A rush of desire followed on the heels of utter relief. Without meaning to do so, she relaxed in the warmth spreading through her.

Lincoln deepened the kiss, the taste of coffee and syrup still on his tongue. Probing gently, he explored her mouth, unleashing peals of excitement low in her belly.

Encouraging Lincoln's attention was reckless. He stirred up feelings no other man had since Tanner had left her. A feeling she wouldn't mind exploring with someone other than a Dogman.

So why didn't she want to resist his kiss?

His hand slipped beneath her jacket. His hand branding her skin despite the layers of clothes.

"He *is* dead," Sierra yelled from the hilltop. "Aunt Ange is giving him air!"

"No, silly." Caleb's voice carried down the snow-covered slope. "They're kissing."

"Ewww!" a choir of voices chimed.

"Obviously, they have no idea what it's like to kiss an angel," Lincoln murmured against Angeline's lips.

She drew back and gave him her scrunched up I'm-not-impressed face. "Not funny, Dogman. Not funny at all."

"And yet I'm smiling."

Indeed he was. Mouth. Eyes. His entire face beamed.

"Are you all right?" Angeline kept her serious mask in place.

"Never better. But, I—um." Lincoln frowned. "I'm numb from the snow. Is my leg still on?"

"I think so." She patted the fleshy part of his left thigh.

Lincoln's head fell back and his chest rumbled with a deep groan that definitely had not come from a place of pain.

The sound sent a shock down her spine that spread through her body until it settled like a swirl of heat in her abdomen. Gritting her teeth, she danced her fingers lower until her fingertips felt the hard ridge of the prosthetic cup. "Yep. Leg in place."

The chatter of children drew closer.

"Can you take them back up the hill?" Lincoln sat up, his gaze falling to the artificial leg. "It might take me a while to get up."

"Nope," Angeline said. "It's tradition. After the first person falls, we all make snow angels."

She watched the kids' rosy faces as they made their way down the hill to her and Lincoln.

Sierra trudged up to Lincoln. Her small, mittened hands clutched his face. "I thought you were a goner."

"We all did. The way you flew through the air." Brent flopped onto the ground a few feet away. "It was spectacular."

"No," Angeline said. "It was a dangerous stunt and no one is going to repeat it."

"It wasn't dangerous." Lincoln pulled a wide-eyed Sierra into his lap. "No one was shooting at me." Mercilessly, he tickled her.

Her giggles of delight echoed around them.

Logan lobbed the first snowball and after tucking Sierra behind him, Lincoln returned the volley. Soon, all the kids had joined the fight.

Angeline no longer felt the cold in her fingers as unbidden affection warmed her inside and out. Lincoln truly knew how to connect with kids and that was the very reason why Angeline should not have invited him to come. The fastest way to her heart was the path carved by her nieces and nephews. And if he left them brokenhearted when he left, she just might kill him.

"How about those snow angels I heard about?" Lincoln said.

"It's easy." Sierra sat on the ground, lay on her back and spread her arms.

The others, including Angeline, joined her, plopping around Lincoln as if they'd known him their whole lives. And he gave each of them the attention and praise they craved.

Angeline's brothers loved their children, but like their father, had difficulty showering them with affection. And why she made a conscious effort to do so.

She hadn't expected that a Dogman would understand how much kids needed encouragement and acceptance. But there he lay, sprawled in the snow, giving time and attention to children he'd just met.

Snow angels made, they began getting up. Tension crept into Lincoln's body.

"All right, guys," Angeline said. "Lincoln is almost frozen solid, so let's get him up."

"Uh, no." Lincoln sat up, his face deadly serious.

Too late. The munchkins swarmed him and, despite the ferocious look Lincoln flashed her, he didn't speak one cross word to the kids.

Roslyn and Caleb each grabbed an arm. Brent and Logan pushed from behind and Sierra hugged his good leg. In no time, they had Lincoln up and standing.

Angeline sent the kids ahead, then grabbed Lincoln's arm. "Pull another stunt like that, don't bother playing dead. Because you will be, after I strangle you."

"Now why would you do that, Angel?"

"Because I don't want them trying to imitate you." She pointed at the kids.

"They won't." Lincoln draped his arm over Angeline's shoulders. "I'll talk to them."

"Thank you."

"And thank you." He squeezed her shoulder.

"For what?"

"Worrying about me." He smiled. "That was nice."

"Know what's nicer? Not doing something to make someone worry."

"Duly noted." He laughed softly and a feeling of contentment settled into Angeline's bones. And she started thinking that being neighborly to a retiring Dogman wasn't such a terrible thing after all.

Chapter 11

Ice-cold beer sloshed against the back of Lincoln's throat. His second, in what looked to be a very long evening. A full moon on Friday night and Taylor's Roadhouse was standing room only in the bar area and not a single empty table in the restaurant section.

The swollen crowd might've been overwhelming if he had time to focus on them. But he stayed occupied with keeping track of Angeline. As suspected, more than a few customers had gotten overly handsy with her. She, of course, had expertly handled the overzealous wolfans. Didn't make him want to break their thick necks any less.

He never should've gone sledding with her and the kids yesterday. A switch had clicked in his brain, moving her from the sexy next-door neighbor with whom he wanted to have a good time to a home-grown family woman who deserved so much more than a fast and furious tumble between the sheets.

Adored by her nieces and nephews, Angeline was as

kind and loving and encouraging as she was beautiful. And she deserved to be at home being loved by a mate instead of pawed and drooled over by horny males merely looking for a full-moon hookup. Lincoln included.

He'd wanted Angeline from the moment he'd met her in the flesh. And had hoped she would be the one he bedded on the full moon. But he had trouble reconciling the growing feelings complicating what should be nothing more than pure, unadulterated sex.

"Earth to Lincoln." Reed snapped his fingers in front of Lincoln's face.

He cut his eyes toward the younger man. "Do that again and I'll bite them off."

Reed smiled good-naturedly. "Coming from you, I'd believe it." He turned to the other sentinels gathered at the table. "On our first run together, I saw him catch a rattlesnake midstrike and chomp off its head."

Though there had been snow on the ground, the sun had been out, bright and warm. Likely the snake had surfaced from its den to bask in the sunshine and they had accidentally disturbed him. Normally, Lincoln left forest critters alone. But they'd been in the woods behind the Co-op's housing community and he hadn't wanted to risk a child getting bit.

"Good reflexes, huh?" one of the younger sentinels asked.

"Yeah," Lincoln said rather than going into detail about the extensive training he'd received to be able to dispatch a deadly threat with nothing more than his teeth.

The table buzzed with comparison stories, each trying to top the last.

"Are you all right? For a full moon night, you're awfully tense." Reed leaned across the table and lowered his voice. "There are a lot of single she-wolves here tonight. I can introduce you."

"Thanks, I'm good for now."

Angeline squeezed through the crowd and made her way to their table. "Hey, fellas. I'll be taking care of you tonight. Everyone want the usual?"

"Isn't this Tessa's section?" Reed asked.

"Trust me." She gave him a pointed look. "You don't want her near your food. She's still mad at you."

Conflicting emotions flashed across his face. He nodded but said nothing.

Everyone agreed to have the usual and Angeline jotted down their drink orders.

Reaching Lincoln, she looked up from her pad and smiled. "How about you? The usual or something else?"

"I haven't been around enough to know what the usual is."

"For these guys, it's a plate of ribs." Angeline leaned down and whispered in Lincoln's ear, "So messy, so not sexy."

"I'll have a burger, medium rare."

"Excellent choice." Her laugh zipped through him like a jolt of electricity. She leaned even closer. "See those ladies at the bar?"

Lincoln glanced at the trio of she-wolves wearing short skirts, spiked heels and low-cut tops. They were beautiful, maybe even sexy, but they didn't charge his senses the way Angeline did.

"They're dying for you to buy them drinks."

"I don't mind paying, but tell them they're from someone else."

"Not interested?"

"Not in them." He held Angeline's gaze and the wall holding back the blatant desire he had for her crumbled.

Satisfaction flickered in her eyes. "Good to know, Dogman."

She walked off, and Lincoln swore she put an extra dose of sass in the swing of her hips.

"You've got a thing for Angeline, don't you?" Reed's eyes narrowed on Lincoln.

"What's it to you?"

"Nothing." Using his thumb, Reed wiped the condensation beaded on the side of his beer bottle. "But she gets a lot of attention. Especially on a full moon."

"I've noticed."

"And I've noticed that you noticed." Reed shook his head. "Look, man. She doesn't do relationships."

"I'm not looking for one."

"You sure about that? Because you gotta look in your eyes and it's not the kind a wolfan gets when all he's after is a good time."

"Yeah?" Lincoln stared straight into Reed's eyes. "What's that look telling you now?"

Reed held up his hands. "Just offering a friendly piece of advice."

"I'll keep that in mind."

Reed rejoined the table conversation, and Lincoln kept up with it, as well. But he remained cognizant of Angeline's whereabouts. And it seemed whenever she sensed him watching, she'd lift her gaze and smile.

Never coy about sex or selecting partners, he could only guess that the hesitant gnaw in his gut had to do with Tanner. The man had entrusted him with his final words, yet Lincoln had not offered them to Angeline.

He needed to come clean about the man linked to both their pasts, but Lincoln didn't want to risk a chasm opening between them.

"Damn you, Tanner." Lincoln chugged his beer.

"Who's Tanner?" Reed asked.

"The first man to die in my arms."

The table fell silent.

"On my first deployment." Lincoln slammed the empty bottle on the table. "You never forget your first, boys." Or any of the ones who came after, and there were quite a few. Including Lila.

Lincoln left the table and headed into the men's room. After relieving himself, he bumped aside a few males preening at the sinks to wash his hands. One took issue, but one look from Lincoln and a clearly threatening growl, and the man backed away. Drying his hands, he suddenly had a sense of Angeline. Startled. Hurt. Angry.

Darting out of the restroom, he visually searched for her but the crowd obscured his view. He did, however, see Reed and two more sentinels making their way toward the bar.

"Excuse me," Lincoln said once, shouldering his way through the crowd to see Angeline bring her knee up sharply between a man's legs then smash her fist into his face.

Atta girl!

Another man stepped up. "You bitch!"

"Touch her and I'll rip off your arm and shoved it up your ass," Lincoln said, walking up behind the man.

"You and whose army?" The human male turned. His bloodshot eyes were filled with deadly anger and he reeked of liquor.

"Mister, I am an army."

"That bitch needs to pay for what she did to my brother."

"Looks like he needed to be taught some manners. Be thankful she served up the lesson and not me." Grabbing the man's shirt instead of his throat, Lincoln shoved him at Reed. Then he reached for the other guy, still doubled over.

"I'm going to make this simple for you." Lincoln smacked his palm against the man's forehead and tilted back his head to look him in the eyes. "She's off-limits. This establishment is off-limits. If you don't stay away, I'll snatch your balls off and feed them to the birds."

Fear flooded the man's eyes. Sometimes a healthy dose of it cured future problems.

Lincoln handed the man off to the sentinels.

"The show is over, folks. Go back to minding your own business." He turned to Angeline. "Are you hurt?"

"You can't go around threatening a man because he got a little handsy." The anger in her voice didn't quite reach her eyes.

"That's not an answer to my question. And for the record, I don't threaten. I explained the principle of action and reaction in terms he'd understand."

Angeline rolled her eyes. "I can handle myself. I don't need you to interfere."

She bumped past him and headed into the kitchen.

Lincoln rubbed his jaw. If she thought that was the end of it, she was oh, so wrong.

"Angeline?"

Coming through the kitchen doors, she narrowly avoided colliding with her uncle.

"What's wrong?" Jimmy's large hand gently cupped her shoulder.

"A couple of customers got rowdy when I refused to serve them liquor." Obviously intoxicated, they'd probably been cut off at the last stop on their bar hop and decided to come to Taylor's. "They're gone now." After giving his wrist a gentle squeeze, she headed to the ice machine.

"Are you all right?" Jimmy asked.

"I'm still waiting for an answer to that question, too." The double doors closed behind Lincoln.

"I'm fine." Angeline pushed up her long sleeve. Marks from the man's tight grip reddened her skin. She scooped a small amount of ice into a clean bar rag and pressed it against her arm. More to cool the notions running rampant inside her than to soothe her skin.

Lincoln's essence wrapped around Angeline seconds before his actual touch. "I should've kept a closer watch."

No, he shouldn't have. His searing gaze following her every move had kept Angeline distracted. Otherwise she would've been more alert and better able to defuse or deflect the drunk men's actions.

"I don't need a bodyguard. I've been handling drunks long before you came to town."

"You shouldn't have to," Jimmy said. "That's why we have sentinels here every night."

"Is it usually like this?" Lincoln coaxed the makeshift icepack from her fingers and gently inspected the bruises.

"No." Angeline closed her eyes, trying to ignoring the wild fluttering in her belly that his touch had sparked. "But it's Friday night and a full moon."

"It's also Valentine's Day," Jimmy added. "A triple whammy."

Lincoln's gaze caressed her face and raw passion heated his eyes. "She needs a break," he said to Jimmy.

"No, I don't." Angeline pulled down her sleeve.

"Got a place I can take her?" Lincoln continued. "Somewhere private?"

"The office. Miriam is in there, but she won't mind."

"I don't have time for a break. We're packed." Angeline looked hard at her uncle. "I'm fine, really."

Lincoln's low, soft growl grated her nerves as much as it stimulated.

"He's the one you need to convince," Jimmy said. "Besides, you haven't taken a break all shift and the others have had two each."

"Fine," she said, because Lincoln blocking the doorway would slow service and then they really would have a problem on their hands.

Angeline sensed rather than heard his steps behind

her. Awareness tingled her skin. Gritting her teeth, she knocked on the door of the office before opening it.

"Hi, Aunt Miriam. Mind if we use the office for a few minutes?"

"Everything all right, dear?" Miriam pulled off her glasses, her gaze shuttering between Angeline and Lincoln.

"Yes. Uncle Jimmy insisted that I take a break and Lincoln is making sure that I do."

The way Miriam looked at them made Angeline wonder if her aunt could see the energy bouncing between them. The full moon wasn't to blame. The current connecting them had begun well in advance of the lunar phase.

"Take all the time you need." Miriam turned the computer monitor off and pushed away from the desk. "I'll help with the hostess station for a while."

Lincoln closed the door behind Miriam as she left.

"How long do I have to—" she used air quotes *"—rest?"* Angeline perched on the edge of the desk. "I'm losing tips, you know."

Lincoln eased closer and she didn't stop him from entering her personal space.

"I know you are okay," he said quietly. "But I'm not sure that I am."

A storm raged in his eyes and a nearly imperceptible tremble shook his hands. "When I saw that guy's hands on you…" Lincoln's nostrils flared and his nose twitched. "I really did want to kill him."

"He was just drunk." A mean one, apparently.

"That's no excuse. For him or me." Lincoln cradled her cheek. The warmth of his palm sent a wave of heat through her body. "May I?"

Instinctively, Angeline knew he wanted to scent her. Warily, she nodded consent against her brain's instruction to the contrary.

Leaning in, Lincoln carefully planted his hands on top of the desk, caging her between his strong arms. His eyelids closed and he lightly grazed his stubbled cheek along her jaw. Goose bumps scattered across her skin, and she shivered.

He moved closer, drawing his hands up her hips.

Working her fingers up his chest to his shoulder, Angeline cozied into Lincoln as he nuzzled her neck on the way to the sweet spot behind her ear.

"God, you smell good." His hot breath puffed against her skin.

"So do you." She breathed in the heady scent of wolfan male musk. Desire threaded through her body like wisps of steam rising from a cup of hot chocolate.

If he was anything other than a Dogman, she wouldn't resist the pull between them. But tonight's full moon weakened her resolve and with his scent invading her being, she couldn't think of anything except coupling with him.

"Lincoln," she whispered against his ear.

He shifted ever so slightly to look at her. His masculine lips parted with a soft breath.

She kissed him and found his soft, firm mouth welcoming, drawing her in for a long, deep kiss. The taste of beer on his tongue wasn't overwhelming and she relaxed, knowing that he had full command of his senses. And so did she.

Her hands fell to Lincoln's waist and fumbled with his belt.

He broke the kiss. His eyes brilliant and branding her with their intensity, he cupped her face. "Are you sure I'm the one you want tonight?" he asked hoarsely.

"I wouldn't be unzipping your pants if I had any doubts." She wrapped her hand around his shaft. The hot, velvety hardness had her clenching with need.

Biology overrode any warning her brain may have signaled. She pulled off her shirt and slid off her bra.

Lincoln's soft growl of appreciation gave her a rush of feminine power. He yanked off his sweatshirt and pulled her tightly against him.

He dotted kisses down her throat, and she arched, allowing him more access. Gently, he kneaded her breasts. When he strummed his thumbs over her nipples, tiny bites of electricity sparked.

She grabbed his face, kissed him hard and insistently.

His hands palmed her back and slipped inside the waistband of her jeans. He slid them off her hips as she did the same to him.

Wet and wanting, she turned around. Lincoln wrapped her in his strength and warmth.

Closing her eyes, she luxuriated in the feel of his fingers sliding through her feminine folds.

He kissed her temple, gently bent her over the desk and nudged her legs apart. He entered her in a swift, deep thrust. The delicious shock caused a throaty rumble to erupt from within. His hands tightened on her hips, holding her steady as he rocked against her, harder and faster.

She loved the feel of him inside her and had no worries of pregnancy or disease. She-wolves could not get pregnant unless a male claimed her with his bite during intercourse. And her sharpened sense of smell would have warned her of sickness the moment she'd scented him.

Maddening tension balled in her lower belly, priming her entire body for climactic release, and Lincoln drove her right over the edge. Waves of pleasure buoyed her.

Behind her, Lincoln groaned in release and then stilled.

"You okay, Angel?" He eased out of her.

"Better than all right." She turned in his arms and he kissed her sweetly.

Normally she didn't engage in postcoital affection with

her full-moon partners. But the way Lincoln held her tight and rested his chin on her head felt nice.

A knock fell at the door.

"Angeline?" Jimmy called. "Everything all right, hon?"

"Couldn't be better." Angeline and Lincoln scrambled for their clothes and began dressing.

"If you need the rest of the night off—" Jimmy laughed.

"No. We'll, um, be out in a minute."

"Your shirt is on wrong," Lincoln whispered.

Groaning, Angeline readjusted her top. "How's this?" She held out her arms.

"I liked it better on the floor."

"You would." Angeline headed out of the office, her body humming. She glanced over her shoulder at Lincoln, one step behind her. He winked and the hope that now the itch had been scratched, the attraction between them would wane went up in flames.

Chapter 12

Lincoln stared at the shadows beneath his eyes and the lines feathering out from the corners. His brown skin had weathered from years of exposure, responsibility and the weight of the things he'd done. And he could use a good shave and haircut.

He didn't look quite like a vagabond, but neither would his face grace the cover of *GQ* magazine. Not that he cared.

Before joining the Program, he'd been popular with the ladies. They'd said he had a devilish smile and was easy on the eyes.

In recent years he hadn't had a lot to smile about and his once charming manner had become more than a little rough around the edges. After all he'd seen and done, who could blame him?

Well, Angeline did. Or had when they'd first met.

He wondered how she now saw him. As a man or Dog-man?

Foregoing the shave, he reached for the crutches and

turned from the bathroom mirror to make his way into the bedroom. He'd left the prosthetic on the bed, his stump slightly sore from the friction caused by the sexcapade with Angeline a few hours ago.

Given the chance, he'd do it again.

And again…

Despite a good, long run in the woods behind the apartments and a cold shower, he couldn't shake the desire for more.

Vivacious and independent, for Angeline their encounter had been all in good fun. However, it would've been damn impossible for him to have stayed at Taylor's without his fist connecting with a face whenever someone got too friendly with her. He felt far too protective and possessive of her for their own good.

A full moon encounter shouldn't generate feelings of any kind. Jealousy was a dangerous emotion for Dogmen and Lincoln wasn't proud to be infected with it. Angeline was simply his first full moon partner in a very long time. There could be nothing between them and yet when they coupled, Lincoln had been filled with a comforting sense of home.

Strange, because his real home had been less than cozy. His parents were strict, career-focused and had the highest expectations. They were disappointed with anything less than perfection.

He picked up the photo Tanner had entrusted to him. Thankfully, the picture had been tucked safely inside a thin silver case when he fell from the second-story window. The moment Lincoln had lost consciousness, he'd shifted back into his human form. The shift energy would've destroyed the photo without the protection of the silver case.

He stared at the worn, familiar image of Angeline that had been his lifeline too many times to count.

Mine!

"No," he sighed, tracing the angelic face of the woman in the picture. "She's not."

Lincoln's jumbled emotions were simply a confusion of
instinct. For years he'd studied Angeline's picture, mem-
orizing every detail, imbuing it with the belief she was
his guardian angel, and treating it as if it were a living,
breathing entity. As a result, his instinct had forged a bond
with the figment of his imagination. Now his wolf didn't
understand the difference between fantasy and reality.

Yes, he'd had sex with Angeline. But full moon sex was
nothing more than the quenching of a biological necessity.

He needed to keep his distance until his body, his brain
and his wolfan instinct understood that Angeline was not
the fantasy he'd concocted to get him through some really bad times.

A flesh-and-blood woman, she had feelings and a heart
that had already been broken by a Dogman. Considering
Lincoln had one last do-or-die mission to complete, he
couldn't encourage anything to develop between them.
To do so wouldn't be fair to either of them or to Dayax,
who was depending on Lincoln to find him.

From the dresser drawer he pulled out a clean pair of
boxers and a T-shirt then sat on the bed to get dressed.
Barely 10:00 p.m. and too keyed up to sleep, he used the
crutches to hobble out of the bedroom.

The satphone he'd left on the kitchen counter had not
received any messages while he was in the shower, which
meant no news on Dayax's whereabouts. He scrolled to the
only picture stored in the phone's memory: Dayax hugging him. Lincoln had just given the wolfling some beef
jerky. The sheer pleasure on the kid's face always made
Lincoln smile.

He tossed the phone onto the kitchen counter and made
his way into the living room. Laying the crutches on the
floor, he stretched out on the couch. Nothing caught his
interest on the television but he left it on, hoping the light
and sound would keep the nightmares away. At the very

least, it would mask Angeline's footfalls as she came up the stairs. She didn't have heavy steps, but somehow he always heard her coming home.

Barely had his eyes closed before his stomach started gurgling. He'd skipped supper, ducking out of Taylor's before being served. Deli meats and condiments were in the fridge, but preparing a sandwich would be cumbersome on crutches and he simply lacked the motivation to get up.

Knowing how to ignore hunger, he grabbed the blanket off the back of the couch and settled into a comfortable position beneath it. The crawly feeling spread into his chest and a pricking sensation ran up his spine.

Someone pounded on the door.

"Lincoln."

He sat up, his heart beginning to rev.

"Lincoln, are you home?" There was a slight pause. "Sheesh! It's freezing out here!"

He reached for the crutches despite his brain's warning to not answer.

Maybe if Angeline saw him this way, she would start avoiding him, saving him the trouble.

Halfway to the door, he saw it swing open.

"Oh!" The downward curl of her mouth slid into a vivacious smile. "You're home."

"What are you doing here?" The gruffness in his voice didn't deter her from coming inside and toeing the door closed behind her.

"You left without eating." She waggled the carryout bags in her hands.

"Since when does Taylor's deliver?" His fingers tightened around the hand grips on the crutches.

"It's a perk of being my neighbor." She waltzed past him, dropped the food on the coffee table and stared at the pillow and rumpled blanket on the couch. "Still sleeping on couches?"

"Aren't you supposed to be working?"

"I got off early. It's a tradition." She went into the kitchen and opened the refrigerator. "Before Tristan met Nel, he and I always hung out on Valentine's Day. Strictly platonic. We'd eat and watch a movie." Holding a couple of bottles of water, she returned to the living room and sat on the couch. "Since you're here, I thought…" Her voice trailed off.

If Lincoln intended to turn her away, he needed to do it now.

Taking a deep breath, he joined her. She didn't flinch or grimace watching him come toward her, legless and crutch dependent.

"What do you usually watch?" He eased down beside her.

"Anything non-romantic." When she opened the bags, the delicious scent of saucy chicken wings made his mouth water. "Tristan likes all the comic book movies. Great special effects, over-the-top action."

"All right." He tried not to tense, thinking of the epic battles and explosions.

Looking over her shoulder, she gave him a pensive look. "I prefer something with less drama tonight."

"Be my guest." He handed her the television remote.

Her fingers grazed his hand and warmth ebbed beneath her touch. She pulled up a pay-per-view channel then finished unpacking the food and handed him a container filled with chicken wings.

"Thanks." He loved the soft smile she gave him.

"So." Settling next to him, she stole one of his wings. "Does your prosthetic always make your leg red?"

"No," he said. "It's a friction burn."

"Is it because we…you know." She bit into the wing.

"Probably." Not sensing pity, he began to relax. "My stump is still a little tender from everything that happened."

"I didn't realize that it bothered you."

"I do exercises to help desensitize the nerves, but I'm still getting used to my new..." He couldn't bring himself to say "limits."

"Way of life?" Genuine understanding shimmered in Angeline's eyes.

"Yeah." One that he began to think could be better than he'd ever imagined.

Angeline inhaled Lincoln's clean masculine scent. The warmth spreading through her had little to do with the blanket she snuggled beneath. She smiled, despite herself.

"Hey, Dogman." She elbowed the lump next to her. "What time did the movie end?"

When he didn't answer, she sat up, opening her eyes, a little disoriented with the darkened living room.

"Lincoln?" Even as she called out for him, Angeline knew he wouldn't answer. The apartment felt too empty for him to be there.

Uncurling her legs, she tossed aside the blanket. Normally, she'd leave it where it landed. But she noticed Lincoln had removed the take-out containers filled with chicken bones and dirty napkins from the coffee table, folded her jacket across the chair and placed her boots near the door. He seemed to like things neat, so she smoothed the blanket over the back of the couch.

"All righty." She clasped her hands between her knees. "Guess I should go."

Normally, she didn't do sleepovers. Watching a comedy with Lincoln last night had been fun and relaxing. She hadn't meant to fall asleep and apparently her staying all night had freaked out Lincoln so much that he'd left. Pulling her phone from her purse, she checked the time.

Nearly ten in the morning, she might as well get to work on that song niggling her brain. Maybe she could figure out the bothersome last refrain and come up with some lyrics that didn't churn her stomach with their sappiness.

Slinging her purse over her shoulder, Angeline collected her coat and boots and padded to the door. She felt sad leaving this way, but clearly understood Lincoln's hesitation about facing her the morning after.

Their full-moon coupling wasn't meant to be anything more. But coming over last night didn't have anything to do with it. She and Tristan really did have a V-day tradition and she didn't want to spend it alone. It had been a mistake to assume Lincoln had felt the same.

So much for being neighborly.

Turning to leave, she heard footfalls nearing Lincoln's apartment. Her heartbeat picked up speed.

After quickly finger-combing her hair, she opened the door. "Hey, I was— Oh!"

"I'll be damned." A man a few inches shorter than Lincoln, with a short crop of dark brown hair and a jagged scar slicing across his handsome face, slowly removed his mirrored sunglasses. The accompanying smile lacked real warmth. "What's your name, sweetheart?"

"Not *sweetheart*."

His laughter rang hollow.

"Are you lost?" She knew every resident in the small apartment complex and this wolfan was not one of them.

"Definitely not." He adjusted the shoulder strap of his duffel bag that looked an awful lot like the one Lincoln had.

"You're a Dogman, aren't you," Angeline said, flatly. She'd gotten used to Lincoln because he didn't resemble what she'd imagined a Dogman to be.

"I am." Now the stranger's broad smile turned genuine and arrogant and expectant. "Is Adams up? Or sleeping off a long full moon night?"

"I didn't catch your name," she said instead of slamming the door in his leering face.

"Marquez." Lincoln's voice drifted up the stairwell.

Angeline's heart began that fast-paced *tha-dump* again.

Reaching the landing, carrying two large coffees and a small white bag, he smiled at Angeline. "I picked up breakfast." His gaze shifted to the man. "Should've told me you were coming."

"My business in Atlanta ended sooner than expected. Didn't think you would mind if I dropped in."

Lincoln's stoic look gave no hint as to whether or not he was glad to see Marquez. However, his eyes twinkled when he handed her the paper bag.

Angeline wasted no time checking the contents. "Oo-ooh, raspberry éclairs. I haven't tried these yet."

Instead of grabbing one and dashing home in the cold, she dumped her things in the chair and made herself comfortable on the couch. Lincoln set the drinks on the coffee table.

Marquez closed the door and dropped the duffel bag on the floor next to the entertainment center. "Are you going to introduce me?"

Sitting next to Angeline as she took her first bite of the delicious pastry, Lincoln tipped his head toward her. "Angeline O'Brien, Damien Marquez."

A mouth full of food saved her from expressing the sentiment that it was a pleasure to meet him. It wasn't. She could manage dealing with one Dogman, but two?

"Nice place you have," Damien said, glancing around the apartment.

"It isn't mine." Lincoln sipped his coffee.

Damien's gaze darted to Angeline. Instead of answering the man's silent question, she turned to Lincoln. "These are really good."

"Glad you like them." He wiped away a dot of

raspberry-cream filing from her mouth and sucked the confection off his thumb.

"So." Damien looked at the chair filled with Angeline's coat, purse and boots. "You two are—?"

"Neighbors," she and Lincoln said in unison.

"Right." Damien grabbed a chair from the round table in the dining area off the kitchen, turned it around and straddled the seat.

"You two worked together?" Angeline asked Lincoln.

"He's my captain." Damien shrugged. "Was, anyway. I'm going to a new unit. I guess Linc will be going into retirement."

A subtle tension crept into Lincoln's body, and Angeline noticed a gleam of satisfaction in Damien's eyes. Instinctively, she'd disliked the man upon opening the door. His standing hadn't improved in the last few minutes.

Angeline finished off the éclair and picked up her coffee as she stood. "I should get home."

Disappointment flashed in his eyes as Lincoln pushed to his feet. "Thanks for stopping by last night," he said softly.

"It was fun, wasn't it?"

"Especially when you started snoring," Lincoln said, walking her to the door.

"I do not snore."

"Yeah, you did." He smiled. "Until I let you hog the blanket and you curled up in my lap."

"No, I didn't."

The truth in his pale, wistful eyes convinced her otherwise.

She gathered her things and he walked her to the door.

"See ya later." She meant to give him a quick peck on the cheek but he responded with a soft nuzzle that had her curling into his warmth.

"Stop by anytime."

She nodded then hurried down the corridor to her apartment. Tucked safely inside, she headed into the bedroom to get her guitar. She needed to write down the notes of the new tune running through her mind.

Chapter 13

"**Y**ou lying bastard." Damien's short laugh raised Lincoln's hackles. "I never understood your obsession with a stranger in a photo, but you've known who she is all along. And now you're up close and personal with her."

"I didn't lie." Lincoln closed the door after Angeline disappeared inside her apartment. "I accepted an invitation to finish out my medical leave here rather than in the infirmary at Headquarters. Finding Angeline, nothing more than a coincidence."

"No such thing. Isn't that what you always said?" Damien migrated from the dining table chair to the leather one in the living room.

"Apparently, I was wrong." Lincoln returned to the couch, popped the lid of his coffee cup and swallowed the hot drink. All the while his mind spun with ideas.

Ideas of the quickening that brought together true mates. Dangerous ideas with a promise of a future he wasn't entitled to have.

"What did she say when you told her how long you've been carrying around her picture?"

"I haven't mentioned it." Lincoln didn't want to risk her rejection, even if they were nothing more than friendly neighbors. He fished out the éclair Angeline had left for him and bit into it. "I would offer you breakfast, but I didn't know you were coming."

"I grabbed a sandwich on the way up from Atlanta this morning. Good thing I hooked up with a flight attendant last night. If I hadn't, I might've interrupted your sleepover."

Lincoln's skin prickled, but he dismissed the errant warning because the peculiar smile on Damien's face was likely caused by the deep scar running down the side of his face.

"That picture of her must be pretty damn lucky," Damien continued. "No one would know that you were knocked out of a two-story window. Not one damn scratch as far as I can see."

"I lost my leg." Lincoln hiked his pant leg, revealing the prosthetic. "I'd say that's more than a scratch."

"At least the Program gave you a new leg." Damien traced the long, deep, jagged scar down his cheek. "They wouldn't give me a new face. Apparently cosmetic reconstruction isn't worth their time."

Young and more than a little cocky about his looks, of course Damien considered the Program's refusal to erase the scar to be a deeply personal affront.

"Sorry, man," Lincoln said regretfully. If Lila hadn't convinced the team to follow him, she would be alive and Damien would still have his perfect face.

He waved off Lincoln's concern. "The ladies still love me. I've been told I look dangerous and sexy." Damien grinned. "Damn right I am."

Lincoln laughed, glad that Damien had taken what had

happened in stride, but it tweaked his heart that he'd never get the chance to talk it out with Lila.

"It's good to see you, but what are you doing here?"

"I have some time to kill before my next deployment." Due to the Program's restrictions, a Dogman's social circles consisted entirely of other Dogmen. "Is there a hotel in this flea-sized town?"

"A resort, but they're hosting a couples retreat."

"Just my luck." Damien frowned.

"You can bunk here. You can even take the bed. I'm partial to the couch."

"What about your neighbor?"

"She's off-limits," Lincoln said a bit too abruptly.

"How about passing along her picture? I could use a good-luck charm."

"It's not mine to give away." Before he left Walker's Run, Lincoln would return the photo to Angeline and give her the message he had sworn to deliver.

Damien shrugged. "It was worth a try."

"If you're going to stay awhile, you'll need a key." Lincoln stood and went to the door. "Help yourself to the fridge, the shower, whatever you need. I'll be back with a key in a few minutes."

"She has the key, doesn't she?"

"Her name is Angeline and, yeah, she has the spare." Lincoln stepped into the corridor. The cold air nipped his face and hands. Memories of Angeline snuggling against him in her sleep heated his blood. He could've woken her up after the movie ended, but he was comfortable, she was comfortable and he simply didn't see the need to disturb either of them. And for the first time since waking up in the Program's hospital, he'd had a peaceful night's sleep.

The faint sound of music touched his ears just before he rapped on Angeline's door. "Hey, Angel, it's me."

The music stopped. A funny feeling tickled his stomach right before she opened the door.

"Tired of your company already?" She stepped back to allow him to enter.

"Well, he's not you."

That earned him a stellar smile and put an extra sparkle in her deep blue eyes.

Lincoln saw the guitar on the couch and sheets of music spread over the coffee table.

"Planning on joining the band at Taylor's?"

"Keeping up my skills. In college, I majored in music, but don't mention it to my family. They think I have a business degree."

"Why would it matter to them?"

"The family business is handcrafted cabinets and furniture. My dad and brothers are carpenters. They expected me to handle the administrative and financial tasks." The shimmer in her eyes faded. "It never mattered to them what I wanted."

"What do you want?"

"Neighbors who aren't so nosy."

"I guess asking you to play a tune for me is overstepping my welcome." Lincoln shoved his hands into his hip pockets.

Instead of answering, Angeline moved the guitar off the couch and sat, tucking her bare feet beneath her legs. "Is there something I can help you with, Lincoln?"

Apparently he'd unintentionally exposed a nerve.

"Damien is staying for a few days and since I don't want to be stuck with him 24/7, I need the spare key."

"Oh!" Shock then disappointment registered on her face. "Sure. No problem."

She reached for the large purse lying on its side on the floor. After digging through the contents, she worked a key off a key ring and held it up. "All yours."

Electricity sparked in his fingertips as he grazed her fingers retrieving the key. "As soon as Damien leaves, it will be yours again."

"Why?"

"Are you kidding? You bring me food, make me watch movies that put you to sleep, but mostly because I enjoy your company."

Her smile reappeared.

Lincoln turned to leave.

"Hey, Dogman," Angeline called after him. "I like being your neighbor, too."

Walking back to his apartment, Lincoln barely registered the cold because of the warm, fuzzy feeling bubbling in his chest.

"Have a hot Valentine's date?" Tessa stowed her purse and jacket in the locker. "You ducked out pretty early last night."

"No." Angeline tucked an order pad in her half apron. "Just keeping to tradition."

"With Tristan?"

"Of course not. He and I were always just friends. Besides, he's madly in love with Nel and their baby is due any day."

"So what did you do?"

"Stuffed my face and watched a movie." Snuggling with Lincoln on the couch. "Pretty boring."

"Then why are you smiling?"

"No reason." No, really. She had no reason to be smiling. Her new neighbor might possibly evolve into a friend. But that was the extent of things.

While Brice might want Lincoln to make Walker's Run his permanent home, Lincoln had not once mentioned retirement. He often seemed preoccupied and checked his service-issued phone frequently. Regardless of his injury, he belonged to the Dogman program and as long as he did, Angeline couldn't develop feelings for him and be made the fool twice in a lifetime.

"I think Reed wanted to talk to you last night." Angeline glanced at Tessa, sympathizing with her human friend's heartache. After all, Angeline had been the one to introduce Tessa to Reed.

"I thought I'd have a lot to say when I saw him again, but I realized I don't want to be with someone who doesn't light up when I walk into a room, the way Lincoln does with you."

"Um, Lincoln isn't interested in me."

"You really should get your eyes checked." Tessa smiled. "It's so cute the way he watches you. And last night, the way he handled those drunks messing with you..."

"I handled the drunks."

"He's so protective." Tessa didn't seem to be listening.

"I didn't need protecting."

"And he's so sexy."

On that matter, Angeline would be hard-pressed to argue.

Incredibly attractive, tall, muscular and, even missing a leg, he had an air of strength and grace that she found irresistible.

"Is he coming in tonight?"

"No. One of his buddies dropped by unexpectedly and they're off doing guy things." Actually, Lincoln took Damien to meet Brice and Tristan. Afterward the two Dogmen would likely run the woods, swim in the icy river and race to the top of Walker's Pointe to see who would leap off first.

Wolfan males, in general, were competitive. Dogmen took the competition to a whole new level.

"Angeline?" Miriam walked into the employee room. "Will you be at Sierra's party tomorrow?"

"Have I ever missed one of my nieces' or nephews' birthdays?"

"What about Lincoln?"

"He told Sierra that he would come, but one of his buddies just arrived and I'm not sure what his plans are now."

"Could you give him a call? I'd like a final head count so I know how much food to prepare."

Angeline reached into her locker for her cell and autodialed Lincoln's number.

"Hello, Angel," he said soft and low before the third ring.

"Hey." Even Angeline heard the breathiness in her voice. Cringing, she glanced at Tessa, her brow arched and her hand cocked on her hip. "Um, Aunt Miriam needs a final head count for Sierra's party tomorrow." Angeline turned her back on Tessa and dropped her voice. "It's okay if you can't go."

"A promise is a promise."

"What about Damien?"

"I don't think a little girl's birthday party is up his alley."

"But you're okay with going?"

"I never go back on my word."

"Okay, then. I'll see you tomorrow."

"Not tonight?"

Despite her initial reservations, she didn't mind spending time with Lincoln. But Damien put her on edge.

"I'm working until closing and I have some things to finish up."

"If you change your mind, I'll be up."

"I won't be home until after two." Her heart skipped a beat. "Are you planning to wait up for me?"

"Being a good neighbor doesn't stop at five p.m."

A feeling of warmth wrapped around her like a big, generous hug.

"I guess it doesn't." She felt the smile stretching her mouth.

"'Bye, Angel."

"'Bye." The breathiness returned, accompanied by a certain giddiness.

"I've never seen you googly over a guy," Tessa said. "There really is something between you and Lincoln, isn't there?"

"We're neighbors like Tristan and I used to do."

"You never got dreamy-eyed over Tristan."

"I'm not dreamy-eyed. Tristan knew I could take care of myself. I think it's sweet that Lincoln thinks he's looking out for me."

"See…protective." Tessa unfolded her crossed arms. "This might be a game changer for you."

"What do you mean?"

"You can kick ass with the best of them."

"Thanks to my dad and brothers."

"Yes, but you didn't seem to mind him stepping in with those two drunks. I heard Lincoln threatened bodily harm before tossing them out, then he went to check on you."

"He didn't toss them out. Reed did."

"You were off the floor for quite a while. When you and Lincoln came back out, you both looked quite rosy."

"Jimmy forced me to take a break and Lincoln made sure that I didn't sneak back before my time was up."

"Uh-huh." Tessa touched Angeline's arm. "There's nothing wrong with *liking* him."

Oh, but there was. Lincoln's heart belonged to the Program. As long as it did, Angeline would not risk hers.

Chapter 14

"Lincoln!"

Nothing rivaled the delighted squeal of a little girl on her birthday.

"You came!" The pure joy on Sierra's face nearly caused Angeline's heart to burst.

Lincoln picked up the newly turned six-year-old. "A Dogman always keeps his promise."

In the living room sat Izzie and Connor and Angeline's dad. Their mouths fell open when Lincoln strolled in like an ordinary man, carrying the birthday girl on his shoulders. Obviously, he wasn't what they'd been expecting, and she liked that about him.

"I told you he would come," Sierra announced triumphantly, then promptly stuck her tongue out at her brother, Logan.

Angeline introduced Lincoln to Sierra's parents, Connor and Izzie.

"Thanks for coming." Connor nodded at Lincoln in greeting.

"We're so happy you're here." Izzie hugged Lincoln's neck. "Sierra's been talking about you coming to her party for days."

Sierra looked around the room devoid of birthday decorations. "It doesn't look like a party because Pawpa doesn't like froufrou."

"Pawpa would be my father, Patrick." Angeline casually flicked her hand in his direction.

The two men silently regarded one another for a moment. Angeline's father pursed his lips the way he always did before a lecture.

"No froufrou, huh?" Lincoln lifted Sierra from his shoulders and gently set her feet on the floor. He leaned down to her eye level. "A close friend once told me that a little froufrou was absolutely necessary in the right circumstances."

"Sounds like something Angeline would say," Patrick scoffed.

"Actually, her name was Lila." Lincoln's attention remained focused on the little girl. "She died on our last mission."

"She was a Dogman?" Sierra's eyes and mouth rounded.

"Yes, and she loved parties. Froufrou and all."

Despite the harsh look from her father, Angeline couldn't tone down the ridiculously big smile staked on her face.

"Sierra, why don't you and Logan play upstairs?" Angeline's father said. "I'm sure Lincoln would rather talk with the adults."

"Actually, I wouldn't." Lincoln's smile didn't quite mask the subtle, not-so-friendly undertone in his voice. "I'm here for Sierra."

"Let's have a tea party." Sierra's small hand clasped Lincoln's large one.

"Lead the way, princess."

Angeline could almost hear her father's teeth grinding.

Midway up the stairs, Sierra turned. "Coming, Aunt Ange?"

"I need to help your mom, first."

When Lincoln, Sierra and Logan disappeared upstairs, Angeline faced her family. "So." She held up a bag. "I brought some decorations."

"Of course you did." Angeline's father frowned.

"This is a fabulous idea, Ange. A surprise party at the party. Sierra doesn't suspect a thing." The happiness in Izzie's eyes matched her radiant grin and it was easy to see which parent Sierra took after the most.

"Good! Lincoln is in on the surprise. He will keep her occupied until I get them."

"He's a Dogman, not a babysitter." Patrick O'Brien's disapproving look might've worked when Angeline was a child, but now she simply ignored it.

"Lincoln is a man who knows how to make a little girl happy on her birthday." Angeline placed a shiny, pointy hat on her father's head. "And so do I."

"Keep your father occupied while Angeline and I get the decorations up." Izzie gave Connor a sparkly party hat. "I expect both of you to wear them during the party."

Angeline caught a glimpse of her father's stunned face before her brother whisked him into the home office.

"We'd better get started." Angeline pulled the ladder from the laundry room and began hanging streamers in the family room.

Shortly after, Garret and Madelyn arrived with their three kids—Rosalyn, Caleb and Brent—to help. By the time Angeline tied the last balloon, Jimmy and Miriam, along with their daughter, Lucy, and their son, Zach, came in with platters of food.

Angeline followed them to the kitchen and once Zach's hands were free of the large platter, she pulled him into a corner.

"Is he here?" The golden flecks in Zach's brown eyes glittered. "Mom said the Dogman was coming."

"Let's get a few things straight," Angeline said. "One, this is Sierra's party and Lincoln is her guest. You will not talk to him about the Program. Got it?"

Some of the enthusiasm faded from Zach's expression.

"Two, you're not going into the Program."

"Ange, I'm almost twenty-three. I can make my own decision."

"This isn't up for debate, Zach." She rested her hand on his shoulder. "I can't explain tonight, but there are things I want you to know about being a Dogman that you don't fully understand."

"Wouldn't it be better for me to talk to Lincoln? An actual Dogman?"

"I'll ask him to meet with you, but first you need to hear what I have to say. Deal?"

"Do I have a choice?"

"No. We'll do lunch tomorrow."

"I have classes at the college tomorrow, but I could swing by your place around seven." His eyes narrowed. "In the morning."

Ack! A morning person she wasn't.

But if she could get up early to take her nieces and nephews sledding, Angeline could get up early to talk her younger cousin out of signing his life over to an organization that would rip him away from everyone who loved him. "I'll need sugar and caffeine."

"Spot me a twenty and I'll pick up an assortment of

pastries and a couple of large coffees to-go from Morning Glories."

"Deal." Angeline squeezed Zach tightly, remembering when he had reached the age when he thought himself too cool for affectionate expression. Thankfully, he'd outgrown the phase and freely returned the hug.

"It's time to get the birthday girl!" Izzie said when Angeline and Zach walked into the living room.

"On it!" Angeline's steps quickened on the stairs and she tiptoed to the playroom.

Lincoln, Sierra, Logan and their cousin Brent were sitting in a circle on the floor. The Dogman tossed a card onto the stack in the middle of their circle.

"No, silly." Sierra giggled. "That's the wrong one."

"Are you sure?" He gave her a dubious look. "I think someone is changing the rules."

"It's called cheating," Logan said.

"Nuh-uh!" Sierra's bottom lip protruded.

"Did you know that on a little girl's sixth birthday, she gets to make up the rules on all the games she plays?" Lincoln said to the trio.

"No way," Logan and Brent exclaimed in unison.

"Really?" Sierra squealed.

Lincoln held up two fingers. "Dogman's honor."

"He's a natural." Miriam's soft whisper startled Angeline. She had been so focused on the scene in the bedroom, she hadn't heard her aunt coming up the stairs.

"Yeah, he is." A bubbly feeling filled Angeline and she wasn't as resistant to it as she should be to her growing fondness for Lincoln.

"In case you haven't noticed, he's good with you, too."

Oh, she'd noticed.

Miriam squeezed Angeline's shoulder then slipped away quietly.

Sierra tossed down a card and threw her hands in the air. "I won!"

"The game isn't even over." Brent pouted.

"The birthday girl always wins on her birthday." Lincoln gathered the cards.

"Well, everything is going back to normal tomorrow." Logan huffed.

"Hey, you guys." Angeline stepped into the room. "Everyone is here and the food is ready."

Sierra stood and held out her hand. "Come on, Lincoln."

"Give me a sec." He straightened his prosthetic leg. Flattening his palms on the floor slightly behind his hips, he drew up his good leg and pushed from a squat to stand. The flawless motion made Angeline wonder how long he'd practiced those moves for it to look so effortless.

She admired his tenacity and persistence. He also had a calm, steady manner that she more than appreciated, especially in the company of her family.

Sierra stopped her brother from getting ahead of her exiting the room. "Birthday girl first."

"I can't wait until this day is over." Logan rolled his eyes.

The birthday girl snuggled up to Lincoln when they reached the stairs. "Why is it dark down there?"

"Maybe the power breaker blew," Angeline said. "I think they're coming back on, right now."

Right on cue, light flooded the house to the chorus of "Happy Birthday!" Balloons and streamers decorated the living room filled with family.

"It's a party!" Sierra squealed. "For me!"

She darted down the stairs, her brother and cousin following behind.

"Everything looks great," Lincoln said. "Well done."

"Kudos to you, too." Angeline took his hand as they

slowly descended the stairs. "We couldn't have pulled off if you hadn't kept Sierra busy. She adores you."

At the bottom of the landing, Lincoln drew Angeline whisper-close. She loved his scent. Clean, masculine and woodsy, the smell made her feel grounded.

"I wish her aunt could be as easily enchanted." His understated smile wrapped around Angeline's heart.

"Maybe I am." She kissed his warm cheek, and the contact caused her lips to tingle.

"Only in my dreams."

"Lincoln!" Sierra waved madly across the room.

"See? You have a new best friend."

"I hope so." Lincoln's hand trailed down Angeline's arm and brushed her fingers. Reluctance filled his eyes. Still, he obeyed the birthday girl's summons, treating her like the princess he'd professed her to be.

An undeniable fondness welled inside Angeline.

"He really knows how to handle kids." Madelyn walked over to Angeline. "Not what I expected from a Dogman."

Nor what Angeline had presumed, either. A Dogman's likelihood of stealing her heart rivaled a snowball's chance of surviving the gas fireplace in Lincoln's apartment that she coveted. But if she wasn't careful, a man who played games with children, made them laugh and gave them his undivided attention just might beat the odds.

Angeline's scent filled the truck. Each breath, her essence, invaded Lincoln's senses, drawing him deeper into a life he coveted but could not yet claim.

"You're really good with kids," she said, gazing out the window.

"I've had a lot of experience. During my down time on deployment, I gave out treats and played games with any kids I found."

"That's so sweet." Angeline laid her hand on his thigh.

Suddenly, he didn't need the heat blowing out of the air vents.

"It's actually pretty sad." The gravity of what many of the kids faced had a profound effect on Lincoln. "Their world was falling apart. I just wanted to give them something that resembled a normal childhood. At least, what I thought might be normal."

"What do you mean?"

"I'm an only child and my parents never gave me treats or played games with me. For them, life is a competition. They placed a lot of pressure on me to be the best."

"So you never got to be a kid." Angeline's tone mirrored the heaviness he felt when remembering his childhood.

"I guess not."

"My mom died when I was six." She stared straight ahead. Her hands clenched in her lap. "My dad chopped off my hair, threw out my dolls and dresses, and I had to wear my brothers' hand-me-downs. He also sold our piano even though I begged him to keep it. Mom had been teaching me to play. She loved music. I do, too."

"He didn't want any reminders of her?"

"He didn't want me to be weak." Angeline anchored her arms over her chest, her fingers digging into the sleeves of her green sweater. "A mugger killed my mother. She was human and my Dad thought if she'd been Wahya, she would've scented the danger and would've had a better chance of defending herself. So he became a drill sergeant instead of simply being our father."

"He didn't want to lose you, too." Lincoln couldn't imagine the depths of a father's fear. Dayax wasn't his son, yet sometimes the uncertainty of the wolfling's safety and well-being nearly ate him up inside.

"I worry that my brothers will become like him." Angeline looked at Lincoln. "So I make sure their kids get plenty of fun time with me."

Slowing to stop at the red light, Lincoln squeezed her hand. "Your nieces and nephews are lucky to have you in their lives."

"You were great with them. Tonight and when we went sledding." She offered him a small smile. "I'm lucky to have you as a neighbor."

"Really?" He snickered. "When I arrived, you weren't exactly thrilled."

"I only saw you as a Dogman, then." She hesitated. "In college, I had a bad experience with one."

"Did he hurt you?" If he did, Lincoln would go to his grave without revealing Tanner Phillip's last words.

"No, no. We were really good together." Angeline's voice cracked.

The sadness that suddenly enveloped her hurt Lincoln's heart.

"He simply chose to be a Dogman," she continued, "rather than become my mate."

"Angeline—"

"Don't." She waved off further discussion. "Ancient history."

The light turned green and Lincoln continued driving. Amicable silence filled the space between them. Though he sensed no real tension from Angeline, she appeared lost in her thoughts.

Lincoln teetered with the decision to tell Angeline the truth about her Dogman. But what would the man's final words of longing and regret do to her? Rip out her heart all over again?

Lincoln wouldn't do that to her.

She'd called the relationship ancient history. Maybe Lincoln shouldn't resurrect ghosts while dealing with his own present demons.

Dayax remained unaccounted for and it could be an-other week or more before Lincoln returned to Munich to take the readiness test for active duty. He missed the wolfling terribly. Lila had warned him about becoming emotionally attached to the young orphan, but Dayax had burrowed into Lincoln's heart and he simply couldn't rest until the wolfling was safe.

Once he'd located and retrieved Dayax, Lincoln had no idea what would happen next. Brice had suggested that Lincoln adopt the orphan wolfling. After all, once the mission was completed, Lincoln would no longer be a Dogman.

Having been a soldier for the last fifteen years, he would have a hard enough time learning to cope long-term in the civilized world. Unmated and with no place to call home, how could he even think of raising a young boy?

Still, the time spent with Angeline and her family had brought his longing for family sharply into focus. Angeline had a natural ability in handling the kids. She listened. She supported him. And she responsibly indulged their needs to simply be kids. She would be great with Dayax, too.

But Lincoln had no business making that leap. Not even in his dreams.

"It's still early," Angeline said as he parked. "Do you have plans with Damien?"

"No." Although Lincoln had been the team leader, he and Damien weren't exactly friends. They had different ideas of fun and had very little in common. "Why?"

"I need to burn off the calories from those cupcakes." Angeline opened the passenger door, climbed out and waited for him at the front of the truck.

"What do you have in mind?"

"It's a beautiful night." The sinking sun tinged the cloudless sky with streaks of red and orange. Although the temperatures had warmed to the midsixties, it would come down a few degrees after nightfall.

"There is a nice trail in the woods behind the apartments," she continued. "Care to join me?"

She-wolves didn't run with just any male. The moments of nudity and the vulnerability of the smaller female wolf in the presence of a larger, more dominant male required a lot of respect and a great deal of trust.

"I'd love to," Lincoln said.

Their fur would keep them warm once they shifted, but their human forms would be subjected to the chill while they stripped down. The thought of seeing Angeline naked again caused his breathing to go wonky.

Following her into the woods behind the apartment building might not be the smartest decision, but Lincoln did it all the same.

She led him to a thick patch of evergreen bushes that provided some privacy in case someone looked out of an apartment window. Turning his back to her, Lincoln tried to concentrate on something other than the zipper sliding down her boots and the rustle of her jeans.

Leaning against a tree, Lincoln removed the boot and sock from his good leg. Despite the lack of new snow, the ground felt ice-cold against his bared foot. His sweatshirt and T-shirt came off together. He shoved his jeans down his legs to his ankles and stepped out of them.

No breeze wafted through the trees. Still, the crisp, chilled air nipped his bare skin. He sat on the ground, his buttocks clenching in protest at the cold, hard earth. Carefully, he removed the prosthetic and wrapped his clothes around the artificial limb to protect it. Then he peeled off the protective sleeve covering his stump.

Completely naked, he maneuvered into an on-all-fours position. Well, except for him, it was on-all-three since he no longer had his left knee.

He looked over at Angeline. Crouched in a ready position, she gave him a soft smile.

"Ready?"

"I'll give you a head start."

"What?"

"You wanted a run, so run!" He growled the last word as he shifted.

Angeline didn't shift quite as quickly, so Lincoln watched her transform. Though the process took only a second, he glimpsed the soft, silvery glow engulfing her body before she turned into a beautiful wolf. Her fur remained the same rich auburn as her hair, and her eyes were just as strikingly blue. She had a tuft of white beneath her chin and down her slender neck, and white cuffs around her paws that looked like socks.

Without hesitation, she launched from her perch and disappeared into the woods.

Mine!

The declaration drummed in his mind.

It wasn't the first time he'd heard it in Angeline's presence. Nor did he expect it would be the last.

He'd connected with the real woman as easily as he had fallen for her photograph. But until he came clean about the past that linked them together, they couldn't be anything more than friends.

Lincoln also decided not to tell Angeline about his reinstatement to active duty. She'd said not knowing Tanner's whereabouts or whether he was safe had been the worst kind of torture. Lincoln wouldn't put her through the turmoil again.

Once he returned from Somalia, then and only then would he tell her everything.

Chapter 15

Heart pounding, Angeline bounded down the mile-long trail. Her paws barely touched the cold, hard ground before propelling her forward again.

Dogmen were competitive by nature and conditioning. Winning was held in the highest regard. If racing against a fully able-bodied Dogman, she would lose without a substantial head start. Lincoln, with only three legs, had still given her the lead. Any other she-wolf might've foolishly believed the race would be easily won.

Angeline doubled her efforts. Though she couldn't hear Lincoln coming, she sensed him closing the distance.

Her instinct had become highly attuned to Lincoln's presence. And her thoughts often either dwelled on moments they had shared or obsessed about when she would see him again.

There were a lot of reasons as to why they often sought out each other's company. Only one frightened her—the possibility that they were true mates.

She had loved Tanner with all of her being and his rejection had nearly broken her. Never had she imagined the possibility of wanting to bond so intimately with another again.

With Tristan, Angeline had felt a kinship to him closer than the one she had with her brothers. He had actually understood her and encouraged her to nurture the things important to her.

Lincoln also seemed to sense the layers no one else saw in her. She hadn't told him about her secret career as a songwriter yet, but she wanted him to know.

Ever since Tristan had claimed a mate, Angeline had scaled back the more personal aspects of their friendship. That had left a big, gaping hole in her life. One that in a very short time, Lincoln had filled.

Except with him, her feelings had quickly spread beyond the plateau of platonic friendship to become more emotionally intimate than she had anticipated.

Now she had to figure out what to do about it.

Following the well-worn path, she cut sharply to the left. The chilly air ruffled through her fur, invigorating her senses. Lincoln's scent grew stronger. Anticipation tightened her stomach as she wondered when and where he'd finally catch her.

Angeline glimpsed movement between the thickets of trees ahead, but Lincoln's scent remained behind her. Ordinarily someone else running the woods at the same time wouldn't have bothered Angeline. Tonight, however, she wanted an exclusive run with Lincoln and an interloper would spoil the moment.

"Angeline, stop!" Lincoln's calm command echoed through her mind.

Immediately, she halted. Although she didn't detect any alarm in his telepathic communication, Angeline doubted he would use a ploy to win a race.

"Don't move."

Standing absolutely still, she felt the sudden rush of Lincoln's essence pour into her. Strong, masculine, protective. A second later his sleek, powerful, sable-color wolf form soared over her. He landed about five feet in front of her, his front legs absorbing the impact of the landing before he touched down his hind right foot.

Magnificent, she mused silently. Even missing a leg, Lincoln's wolf form commanded respect.

His soft chuckle tickled her mind. *"Thanks, Angel."*

Uh-oh. She needed to keep a better handle on her thoughts. *"What's going on?"*

"We've got company."

About fifty feet ahead, a large brindle-colored wolf emerged from the shadows and blocked their path. Angeline didn't immediately recognize the male wolfan, which meant he didn't belong to the Walker's Run pack.

The unknown wolf trotted toward them, and she sensed a subtle tension creeping into Lincoln's body.

"What are you doing here, Damien?"

"Same as you. Getting fresh air and exercise."

Damien stopped in front of Lincoln. The moonlight cast grotesque shadows on Damien's face, distorting and exaggerating the appearance of the jagged scar down his cheek.

"Angeline?" The look he gave her made the skin beneath her fur crawl. *"You are absolutely stunning."*

Angeline didn't reply with the customary "thank you" since his compliment gave her an icky feeling that she wanted to wash off.

Lincoln sidestepped, blocking Damien's view of her.

"Why don't we go out and get a drink?" Damien continued to stare.

"I'll pass." Working three nights a week at Taylor's Roadhouse, Angeline didn't want to spend her time off hanging out in a bar.

"Rain check," Lincoln confirmed.

"Any suggestions on what I can do tonight? I've had a royally boring day." There might've been an undertone of resentment in Damien's response, but since Angeline didn't know the man, she dismissed the thought.

"Maico is pretty tame on Sundays." And every other day, mostly.

"I should've stayed in Miami." Damien shook his head. *"I'm gonna die of boredom here."*

"I told you that I had plans with Angeline today." Lincoln's matter-of-fact tone held no sympathy for Damien's little pity party. *"Tomorrow, I'll introduce you to some of the sentinels. I'm sure they can plug you into all the exciting things Maico has to offer."*

"Tomorrow it is, then." Damien bumped past Lincoln.

Not wanting Damien to do the same with her and spread his scent along her fur, Angeline stepped aside to let him pass. He continued on his way at a leisurely trot.

"I feel a little bad for him." Angeline stepped next to Lincoln. *"He came to see you and I've been hogging your attention."*

"Do not feel bad. I prefer your company to his." Lincoln's gaze remained fixed on the path behind them. *"I'm not sure why Damien came to see me."*

"Obviously, to spend time with you." A brisk wind sifted through Angeline's fur.

"We weren't close."

"Maybe the explosion changed things."

Both Lincoln and Damien had been injured and lost a colleague, although Lincoln likely felt the loss more sharply.

He turned his muzzle toward Angeline, and the hard look in his eyes softened. *"It certainly did."*

Her heart fluttered and a flood of awareness caused her to shiver.

"Cold?" Cautiously, he stepped closer and lowered his snout.

"Maybe." Angeline leaned in, encouraging Lincoln to nuzzle her.

His heat wrapped around her, sheltering her from the chill, and the gentle way he scented her made Angeline feel cherished. Burying her snout in the thick fur of his neck, she slowly and deeply inhaled his clean, woodsy scent, drawing part of him inside her with each breath. She missed this closeness, the ethereal connectedness of two souls merging.

Before Lincoln, Angeline considered herself a smart woman. The inability to race back to her apartment and lock Lincoln out for good suggested a significant problem with her common sense.

"We should head back." Lincoln's thoughts nudged her mind.

He was right, of course, which made a little piece of her heart inexplicably sad.

"I'll race you," she told him and then darted down the path toward the apartment building.

No longer sensing him behind her, Angeline looked back to see Lincoln headed in the opposite direction.

Boy, had she misread his signals.

Setting her sights ahead, Angeline bolted home.

"You look awful." Standing in the kitchen, squinty-eyed and sporting dark shadows beneath his lashes, Damien lifted one of the two large coffees from the cardboard drink holder in Lincoln's hand.

"Seen a mirror lately?" Lincoln dropped the bag filled with breakfast sandwiches and pastries onto the counter, popped the lid off his foam cup and swallowed a large gulp of dark, rich coffee.

After the night he'd had, one cup would not be enough.

Too bad he'd canceled the order for Angeline's coffee. A late riser, she probably wouldn't have been happy if he woke her, especially after he'd intentionally ditched her.

Plucking an egg, cheese and bacon croissant from the bag, Damien straddled the kitchen bar stool. "I take it things didn't go well with your *angel* after I left."

Damien was not wrong.

Instead of accompanying Angeline home, Lincoln had chosen to finish his run alone. And he'd sensed the awful moment when Angeline had slammed the door on their growing closeness.

Even though he'd never been in love, Lincoln suspected the reason his instinct kept drawing him to Angeline was that the ethereal ties of the mate-bond were at work. However, now was not a good time to delve into the possibility of a mateship with Angeline.

Dayax remained his priority. Once he and the wolfling were safely reunited and Lincoln officially retired from the Program, then he would be free to indulge in his feelings for Angeline.

Until then he expected a lot more sleepless nights.

"It's complicated." Lincoln popped the lid off the drink container and swallowed a mouthful of coffee.

"You don't do complicated." Damien's inquisitive gaze tracked Lincoln's every move.

"That's why I look like this," he said, pointing his index fingers at himself. "What's your excuse?"

Damien shrugged, taking his time chewing his food.

Lincoln hazarded a guess as to the young Dogman's sleeplessness. "Nightmares?"

"How did you know?"

"I have them, too." Post-traumatic stress syndrome, the psych doctor at Headquarters had called it. Then he'd prescribed Lincoln medication and assigned him to a therapy group.

But the pills fogged his brain and listening to stories about someone else's traumatic experience didn't help Lincoln deal with his own. It merely made him angry.

"Does it get better?" Damien stared at Lincoln over the rim of his coffee cup.

"God, I hope so." Lincoln held the young man's gaze. "I'm sorry, Damien. I never intended to involve the team in my search for Dayax."

Damien's eyes glazed and he seemed to be watching a memory play out in his mind. Methodically working his tight jaw, he slowly shook his head. "*No es tu culpa*, Cap'n. You ordered us to stay put." A dark look briefly drew his thick brows together. A moment later his expression lightened. "We all liked that little scamp."

In the long weeks of separation, Lincoln was beginning to realize that he didn't simply like Dayax. He loved that Somali wolfling as his own.

Nudging aside the cherry turnover in the bag, Lincoln lifted a bear claw and bit into the sticky-sweet deliciousness. If he wanted to pass the physical readiness test, he needed less junk food and more exercise.

"I haven't been the greatest host since you arrived." He gave Damien a half shoulder shrug apology.

"Word of advice," Damien replied lightheartedly. "Don't consider B and B operator as your next career. You have absolutely no hospitality skills."

"You have a comfortable bed and running water. Plus, I brought you food that's actually edible." Lincoln lifted his cup in a mock salute. "What else do you need?"

"A mint on the pillow would be a nice touch."

"I'm not a PEZ dispenser."

"Good one, *Capitán*." Smirking, Damien returned the coffee cup salute.

Fresh out of training when assigned to Lincoln's unit, Damien had been a royal pain in the ass to command.

Cocky, self-centered and a self-important know-it-all who really didn't know anything about an actual deployment, he had not been any different than any other Program graduate who believed himself to be invincible.

Damien had found out sooner than most that he wasn't.

"When are you headed to the Amazon?" Lincoln finished devouring the pastry and licked the sugar from his fingers, making a mental note to put in an extra hour at the resort gym later.

"What?" Damien squinted at Lincoln.

"How long before you meet up with your new team?"

"Oh." Damien shook his head. "HQ put the brakes on that deployment. I'm awaiting new orders. Why?"

"I'm being stepped up to active duty—"

"How the fuck did you manage that?" Damien leaned toward Lincoln, curiosity glinting in his eyes.

"I called in a favor from a friend in tight with the Woelfesenat," Lincoln said.

"Of course you did."

"They're allowing me to go back to Somalia. And I'm going to track down Dayax."

"How do you know the kid is still alive?"

"He's scrappy, smart, resourceful and managed to stay alive six months on his own before we arrived. He's doing whatever it takes to survive. I made a promise and I *will* find him." Failure was not an option.

Damien absently scratched his stubbled jaw. "Does your sexy guardian angel know what you're planning?"

Lowering his gaze, Lincoln shook his head. How could he tell Angeline that he planned to go on a suicide mission to save a child no one really believed was still alive?

But Lincoln knew. He could feel the truth gnawing at his gut. Dayax was waiting, and watching and wondering if Lincoln would come for him.

"Yeah, well, you better tell her," Damien huffed. "You're

going to need all the divine intervention you can get, or else you might lose more than a leg." Damien pushed aside his coffee cup and half-eaten sandwich, then shoved off the bar stool and headed for the bedroom.

"Wait," Lincoln called after him. "You're here for some R & R, so no more Program talk. Come with me to the resort. I'll introduce you to the pack's security team. Maybe you can tag along with the sentinels on their patrols."

"Beats doing nothing." Damien's demeanor lightened. "I could give them pointers on perimeter surveillance and bringing down interlopers."

"I suppose you could," Lincoln told him. Although young and brash, Damien had elite military training. If they listened, the sentinels probably would learn a thing or two from him.

"Are you going to run with the sentinels, too?"

"Not today. The resort has a gym and I need to buckle down for some serious workouts. Before I'm certified for active duty, I have to take the readiness test."

"Oh, man." Damien scrunched his face. "There is nothing that would make me go through those three days of hell ever again."

If—no, *when* Lincoln got Dayax back, everything he endured would all be worth it.

Chapter 16

"Having a rough..." Lincoln checked his utility watch. "I would say night, but it's not yet six o'clock."

Angeline slammed the office door shut. "This is all your fault." She snatched the bag from his hand and dumped the contents onto Miriam's desk.

"I was nowhere around when that happened." Flashing an insufferable grin, he zigzagged his index finger in her general direction.

So far, a pitcher of beer had spilled down her leg, someone's kid had slung mac-and-cheese at her ass, and her favorite sweater got splattered with barbecue sauce from the platter of ribs in her hands when she'd collided with Tessa.

"Turn around," she said, clenching her teeth.

"I've already seen you naked."

Angeline shook her finger. "Full moons don't count."

Still smiling, Lincoln turned his back to her and stuck his hands into his hip pockets. "What's got you agitated, Angel?"

"You!" Angeline toed off her shoes, then peeled off her jeans.

Last night, things had been going so well until Damien had showed up and Lincoln had suddenly decided he needed to get far, far away from Angeline. Despite her resolve to write him off, she'd barely slept. Her mind had kept trying to figure out how she'd misread the signals while her instincts argued that she hadn't.

Then, after a sleepless night, she'd had to get up early to talk to Zach. She'd told him about Tanner but it was hard to gauge if anything she said got through to him. But he had promised to speak with Lincoln, as well, and she had already texted him Zach's number.

"Is this about last night?" Lincoln glanced over his shoulder.

"Eyes facing the door or this stapler is going to land right between them."

Lincoln complied, and Angeline was grateful he didn't call her bluff.

"I needed to clear my head. For both our sakes."

"You could've said something to me." Angeline stuffed her legs in the clean jeans and then yanked off her top to put on the soft blue sweater Lincoln had brought her. "When I looked back and saw you hightailing it in the opposite direction—"

She balled up the dirty clothes and dropped them into the bag. "I would have understood. I can see how you might've been weirded out by spending the afternoon with my family and then me asking you to go running."

Having Lincoln at Sierra's party had felt natural and the get-together had turned out better than most of the family events she'd attended. "I wanted to run with you because I sensed a connection that I haven't felt in long time. If I'm wrong, I would rather know up front."

Lincoln's posture stiffened. Of course his body language affirmed that she had made a grave mistake.

"Just forget it." She slipped on her shoes and combed her fingers through her hair. "Being around my family puts me a little off-kilter."

"I can't forget it." Slowly, Lincoln turned around. "I feel it, too, Angel. From the moment I first saw you."

"Oh?" Angeline's heart thumped faster, then seemed to drop straight into her stomach. She leaned against the edge of the desk. "Is it a mate-bond I'm sensing between us?"

Although Lincoln nodded, he didn't look happy.

Having been in this situation before, Angeline's own concerns doubled. "We have to stop interacting. You don't come to my place, I won't go to yours. And definitely no more invites to family functions."

A mate-bond could be circumvented if one or both parties resisted the ethereal connection.

"It's not okay." Closing the distance between them, Lincoln opened his hand for her to take.

She did and static electricity snapped at the contact. Before she could pull away, Lincoln's fingers closed around her hand. Immediately, she sensed his essence infiltrate her being.

Pulling her close, Lincoln nuzzled her neck. "Only a fool wouldn't want this with you."

The sincerity in his voice and touch couldn't mask the conflict she sensed deep within him.

"I'm being forced out of the Program," he said softly. "Mandatory medical retirement."

Understanding how difficult the circumstance must be for Lincoln, Angeline pressed her cheek against his chest. Although unable to hear his heart thumping beneath the thick pullover, she sensed the strong, steady beat pulsing alongside her own.

"But I have final orders to complete before my papers are processed."

"Final orders? That doesn't sound good." Angeline's stomach tightened.

"A formality, mostly. Just a few loose ends that I need to tie up. Nothing to worry about, I promise."

"How long will your final orders take?" Angeline searched Lincoln's face, wondering if he could or would hide the truth from her as Tanner had done.

"Not long, I hope."

"When will you leave?"

"Whenever they call me up."

Angeline's entire body tensed. She'd have no time to prepare. One minute Lincoln would be here, the next he wouldn't. Just like Tanner.

"Hey." Lincoln hands slid up and down her back. "I won't be gone any longer than absolutely necessary."

Angeline wanted to believe him, but she refused to set herself up for another heartbreak. A lot could happen before Lincoln came home. *If* he came home.

"I'll be fine."

"You're already reading my thoughts?" When connected by a mate-bond, a couple could communicate telepathically in their human forms.

"Body language." With both hands, Lincoln cradled her face. Then, using his thumbs, he pushed up the corners of her mouth. "Much better."

He brushed her lips with a feather-soft kiss.

Suddenly, everything did seem better.

Wrapping her arms around his shoulders, she pressed against his body. Lincoln slipped one hand behind her neck, tilting her head to the perfect angle for a long, deep kiss. All the while, his other hand trailed down her arm then migrated to the small of her back.

He was holding on rather than pushing her away.

Hope sparked in her heart despite the reservation that Dogmen seldom, if ever, went quietly into retirement.

Lincoln broke the kiss and pressed his forehead to hers. "I must not be doing this right if I can't get you to stop thinking about all the things that could go wrong."

"I wasn't…" Angeline stopped talking because Lincoln's gaze became so intense that she knew he could see straight into her soul.

"I never make a promise that I can't keep," Lincoln said. "I will come back." He sealed the oath with a kiss. The softness of the previous one dissipated. This possessive and all-consuming kiss stole her breath and branded every inch of her mouth. His essence flooded her senses, claiming the very core of her being.

She would be frightened of the developing bond if she hadn't watched Lincoln playing with her nieces and nephews. Every time he'd made Sierra giggle, every word of encouragement he'd given to Brent and Logan and the way he'd listened to Roslyn and Caleb revealed Lincoln's longing for family. From what she sensed, Lincoln Adams was ready to make a *home*.

"Angeline? Tessa said you had an accident." Miriam entered the office. "Oh, oh! I didn't mean to intrude."

"Busted." Lincoln smiled against Angeline's mouth before taking a step back.

"I'm fine, Aunt Miriam." Angeline brushed her lips with the back of her hand. "I asked Lincoln to bring me a change of clothes. I couldn't work feeling like I went swimming in the garbage can."

"Thank you, Lincoln. For helping my niece—" Miriam gave an exaggerated wink "—clean up."

"My pleasure." Smiling good-naturedly, Lincoln touched Angeline's hand. Her nerves lit up. "I should go."

"Stay for supper," Miriam said. "It's on the house."

"I'd love to, but I made plans with Damien to shoot pool

with Reed and some of the sentinels." Lincoln edged toward the door. "Call me if you need…anything, Angel."

Angeline finger-waved as he left.

"I've never seen such a huge smile on your face." Miriam said. "I think Lincoln coming to town has been good for you."

"Yeah, I think so, too." But Angeline couldn't help wondering what would happen when he left.

"Something's changed." Damien tipped another beer bottle to his lips and took a long swallow. "You scored with Angeline, didn't you?"

All the chatter around the pool table ceased. The young blond man about to break the balls in an opening shot froze midstrike.

Slowly, Shane straightened, the cue stick sliding through his fingers until the rubber bumper touched the floor and his hand tightened around the tapered shaft. "What did you say?" His steely gaze cut from Damien to Lincoln.

"His neighbor is really hot," Damien said to Shane, then turned to Lincoln. "Caught up with her for an afternooner, didn't you? Must've been really good to have loosened that stick up your ass."

"Angeline is my neighbor, too," Shane said with lethal softness. "A packmate and a friend."

The air charged with the energy of pack mentality. The other sentinels quietly and effortlessly moved to close ranks. If Shane pounced, the rest would follow.

Except for Reed. Holding his position across the pool table, he slowly laid his cue stick on the felt top. A lead sentinel, he merely observed and assessed the situation without falling victim to an emotional reaction. When he acted, it would be swift and calculated.

Lincoln didn't consider any of them a viable threat. He

wouldn't have lasted long as a Dogman if a few pissed-off wolfans could bring him down.

Not nearly as drunk as he appeared, Damien seemed to enjoy the heightened tension. Lincoln suspected the younger Dogman wanted to intentionally provoke the hometown sentinels.

"What Angeline does or doesn't do with me or anyone else is not your business," Lincoln said to Damien, then swung his gaze to Shane. "Or yours."

"It is when someone disrespects her." Shane made no effort to back down, and Lincoln admired his grit.

"Damien, apologize."

"For what?" He dropped the empty beer bottle onto the table.

Lincoln slowly turned his head and gave Damien a look that meant he expected the order to be followed. It didn't matter if they were both on medical leave. Lincoln was a superior officer and it would be an outright act of insubordination if Damien failed to comply.

Defiance flashed in Damien's eyes. Hot-tempered and reactionary, he needed a lot of seasoning that only time and experience would provide. At least some of his training had taken root because he shook off the attitude and presented a sincere face. "I meant no offense to Angeline."

"Shane, are you going to break or should I?" Reed picked up his cue stick.

The young sentinel studied Damien for a few seconds longer then gave a nearly imperceptible nod to Damien. "I won the toss." Shane turned back to the pool table. "I'm not giving up my advantage."

As if a switch had been flipped, the tension around them dissipated. Apparently, among these wolfans, once an understanding was reached, everyone simply moved past whatever hurdle had tripped them.

Kara, their server, stopped by the table and collected Damien's empty bottle.

"Keep 'em coming, *bomboncita*."

"You got it, sugar." Kara placed her hand on Damien's shoulder and glanced at Lincoln. "Anything for you?"

"Nix his beer for now. We'll both have water."

"Gotcha." As she left, Kara flashed a bright smile and interest glittered in her hazel eyes.

"You're the one nursing a single beer," Damien said. "I know how to hold my liquor."

"Apparently not tonight," Lincoln said. "What's going on?"

"There's not much to do in this town. I'm getting antsy doing nothing."

"Didn't you join the sentinels on patrol today?"

"Yep." Damien rolled his eyes and slumped back in his chair. "Buh-orr-ing."

After a lifetime of being on guard against bullets, incendiary devices, poisons and knifings, the threat of torture upon capture, Lincoln appreciated the calm, slow pace he'd discovered in Walker's Run. But he understood Damien's restlessness.

The Program's training taught recruits to thrive on extreme levels of adrenaline for extended periods. It kept them sharp, quick and deadly.

"How are you not crawling out of your skin?" His face so young and earnest, Damien looked at Lincoln.

"Who says I'm not?" Lincoln watched the surprise flicker in Damien's eyes. "I need to get back in the field. It's eating me up to be here, knowing Dayax is still missing."

"Huh." Damien scratched his ear. "You don't look bothered."

"It's all about focus. I'm still on a mission. The first part is to prove readiness for deployment. If I'm melting down over a little R & R, HQ will pull the plug on the second part." Lincoln paused. "If you can't handle the downtime, they will do the same to you."

"I'm not having a meltdown," Damien shot back.

"Inside, you feel jittery. Your mind is racing. The tightness in your chest makes it hard to breathe. Everything is closing in, you feel trapped. Desperate. Angry," he said, watching Damien's hands curl into fists. "You're in withdrawal."

Dangerous and habit-forming, high levels of adrenaline enhanced the Dogmen's natural abilities and often kept them alive in extreme circumstances. The downside was that when the levels returned to normal, a Dogman's body protested significantly.

The best way to mitigate the side effects was to create an adrenaline rush.

"I'm not in withdrawal," Damien snapped. "But I am angry."

"Do tell." Lincoln opened his hands. "I'm all ears."

Damien glanced toward the pool table. Absorbed in the game, the sentinels appeared relaxed and unconcerned with the two Dogmen in their company. Except for Reed, who kept a friendly watch as any good leader would.

"I don't want to be here." Hands balled, Damien rested his arms on the table and leaned toward Lincoln, beginning to bare his teeth. "I didn't become a Dogman to trot the expanse of some lame territory. I should be out there—" he pointed in no particular direction "—making a difference. Not stuck here with you."

"You came to me. And you can leave at any time," Lincoln said.

"Where should I go? I can't go home. You know the rules."

All too well. It was one reason Lincoln hadn't called his parents. The other being that they would consider what had happened to be a failure. See him as one, too. After all, his leadership had cost him a leg, a friend's life, a recruit's face and the young wolfling he meant to find was still missing.

"I thought you'd want to get out of here," Damien said. "We could go anywhere. Do anything."

"I want to get to know Angeline better."

"You are so twisted, you know that?" Damien shook his head. "Obsessed with a photo and now finding the actual woman… It's creepy."

"I think it's fate."

"Unbelievable." Damien's short laugh sounded harsh and hollow. "You really are sick."

"Never felt better."

"Well, yippee ki-yay for you." Damien stood. "I feel like shit."

"And it's my fault."

"Damn straight, it is." Damien's knuckles thudded against the table. His elbows and shoulders locked as he leaned forward. "We wouldn't be here if—"

"If I hadn't gone looking for Dayax."

Damien's glare focused on Lincoln.

"Then Lila wouldn't have convinced everyone to follow and none of us would've been caught in that explosion. Is that it?"

"You should've been looking out for *us*." Frustration and bitterness laced Damien's soft-spoken words.

Lincoln had. That was why he'd ordered Lila not to come after him.

"Are you a Dogman or a toddler?" Lincoln stood.

Damien's face darkened, turning his scar a purplish-black. "You know damn well what I am."

"Prove it." Lincoln intentionally kept his body loose. "Outside. I'm not paying for damages inside the bar."

"Are you serious?" Some of the anger in Damien's expression faded. Extremely competitive, a Dogman could no more turn down a challenge than a steak when starving.

"We need some fresh air," Lincoln said to Reed. "We'll be back in ten."

"Ten?" Damien scoffed, following him to the door. "I can take you in five."

Lincoln hid his smile. Ten was merely a generous time allotment to spike Damien's adrenaline and ease his withdrawal. Otherwise, he'd take down the kid in less than one.

Chapter 17

"Nothing below the waist. And no leg kicks or sweeps."
In an empty area of the bar's back parking lot, Lincoln
raised his arms, held his fists in front of his face and stood
with his feet shoulder-width apart. "Upper body only.
Break my prosthetic and you'll get the bill for a replacement."

"Are you sure you want to do this, *old man*?" From the
unnecessary display of twinkle-toed footwork, to the pre-
emptive air jabs and all the way up to his single-minded
gaze, Damien reeked of arrogance.

Lincoln preferred the young Dogman figure out how
to handle the downside of adrenaline withdrawal without turning himself into a punching bag. But he'd been
in Damien's shoes before and had had a mentor do the
same for him.

"Have at it, *pup*." Lincoln punctuated the intentional
slur with a broad grin and achieved the exact response
he wanted.

Damien jabbed a right hook that Lincoln could've blocked with his eyes closed. Instead, he let the punch connect. It rattled his teeth, but he didn't taste blood, so he shook it off.

"Is that all you got?" He watched Damien, fists close to his face and rocking from one foot to the other. "Don't see how you ever made it out of Basic with those weak-ass hands."

"I'm just warming up." Damien shuffled back and forth in a half-circle perimeter, periodically quick-punching the air to see if Lincoln would take the bait.

"Is this a fight or a dance?" Lincoln taunted. "Because if it's a dance, I'm going to find a prettier partner."

"Hey!" Shane called out. Most of the sentinels seemed to have come along with him. "What's going on?"

Damien took advantage of the momentary distraction and threw a punch that would've landed dead center of the solar plexus if Lincoln hadn't turned in time. The blow glanced his ribs. He drew a sharp breath, but was other-wise okay.

"This is what we do for fun." Lincoln shoved Damien away and eyeballed Reed, who stood to the side of the small posse with his arms crossed high on his chest. "Stay out of this or someone will get hurt and it won't be us."

"You heard the Dogman," Reed said. "Look but don't touch. Anyone who intervenes forfeits their spot on the security team." Despite the grumbles, all took a healthy step back.

Emboldened by the audience, Damien launched a full attack. Lincoln absorbed each punch with only a few forcing him to take a step back. Sentinels shouted, some cheering for Damien, whom they viewed as the under-dog. Others yelled warnings to Lincoln in misguided at-tempts to be helpful. By the time Damien's fist slammed into his body, Lincoln had already calculated where the next would land.

Damien's punches grew more aggressive and his friendly banter turned surly. An uppercut to the jaw caused Lincoln to bite down on his cheek. He spit out the blood, and a feral gleam lit Damien's eyes.

"You've had enough adrenaline tonight."

"Are you conceding? 'Cuz I'm just getting started." Damien threw a right jab, followed by a right cross and then a left hook. But he left himself open, and Lincoln responded with a power-packed, one-two counterpunch and finished the combination with a right hook to the jaw.

Damien sprawled to the ground.

The sentinels fell silent.

Lincoln crouched over his opponent. The young man's eyes were glassy and an odd smile distorted his face. "Are you all right?"

When he didn't answer, Lincoln snapped his fingers. "I asked you a question, Dogman."

Damien blinked rapidly and the glaze cleared from his vacant gaze. "Yes, sir. I'm fine, sir."

"Feel better?"

Damien sat up and spit, then wiped his mouth on his sleeve and grimaced. "I would, except I think you broke my jaw."

"It's not broken." Lincoln offered him a hand up. "Put some ice on it to help with the swelling."

The sentinels swarmed the younger Dogman with accolades of his putting up a good fight and advice on how to have a better fight next time. Escorting him back into the bar, the group promised he wouldn't have to buy another drink tonight because each of them would buy him a round.

"You could've ended this before he took his first swing."

Reed hadn't moved from his position. "Why did you let him get in all those hits?"

"He needed the rush." Lincoln rubbed his jaw, tender and swollen from Damien's last punch. "Better for him to unload on someone who could handle it."

"You don't think me and my guys could?"

"This isn't personal, Reed." Lincoln liked the guy and didn't want to make an enemy unnecessarily. "Damien is a Dogman, plain and simple. Pit him against someone who lacks that level of training and Damien will likely kill them, albeit unintentionally. He's still green and nearly died on his first deployment. There's a lot of chaos whirling inside him right now. I know how to help him deal with it in a constructive way."

"Getting your ass kicked is constructive?" Ever-so-serious Reed cracked a smile.

"My ass is fine." His jaw, chest and ribs, however, hurt like hell. He needed to get home and soak in ice if he wanted to be able to get out of bed tomorrow. "Come on. I'll buy you a drink."

"I'll take a raincheck and let Damien bask in his new-found fame with your sentinels."

"Are you and Damien good?" Reed asked. "There seemed to be a lot of anger in those punches."

Lincoln had noticed that, too. But after what had happened in Somalia, he couldn't blame Damien for harboring some resentment.

"We're good. He just needed to get it out of his system."

"I hope he got it all out," Reed said. "I don't like the idea of him going off like that on someone else."

"He won't." Lincoln would make sure of it.

"You let him hit you?" Angeline stared at Lincoln. Beneath his darkened eye and bruised cheek, an arrogant grin split his face. Thankfully, he didn't seem to be missing any teeth. "On purpose?"

"Last night, it seemed like a good thing." Lincoln picked up the plastic-covered breakfast menu the waitress had left on the table.

At Mabel's Diner—a staple in Maico's town square for more than thirty years—the fare was always the same. Good, ol' fashioned, Southern-style cooking. Anything that couldn't be loaded down in butter was deep-fried in lard. Just a whiff of the delicious scents wafting from the kitchen could harden the patrons' arteries.

But people kept coming. For the food and for the company.

Enjoyed by unsuspecting humans and wolfans alike, Mabel's Diner was the heart of Maico. Mostly because of Mabel, a lively senior who sported a red beehive hairdo and resuscitated bright sky-blue eyeshadow that should've been left to rot in the eighties. Treating everyone like family, she nosed into everyone's business, doling out advice and scolds as readily as she served good eats.

"He needed to release some pent-up energy," Lincoln said.

"So you volunteered to be his punching bag?" Angeline waved away the menu he offered after reading it. She'd known exactly what to get the moment he'd mentioned brunch.

"Better me than someone else." Fingers laced, he rested his hands on the table. "It was a friendly brawl. We're both fine."

"I'll hold off agreeing with you until after I've seen Damien." Though, she had to admit, Lincoln certainly seemed more relaxed and some of the weariness in his eyes had faded. "He's not in the hospital, is he?"

"I said he's fine."

"You always say you're fine and you're missing a leg,"

Angeline said. "Are Dogmen trained in the Black Knight mentality? ''Tis but a scratch… It's just a flesh wound…'" she said, imitating the movie character. "'I'm invincible.'"

Lincoln's laugh, deep, rich and masculine, wreaked mayhem on every feminine molecule in her body. She crossed her arms over her chest to rein in the hormonal circus.

"I wouldn't peg you as a Monty Python fan."

"I'm not. Tanner was."

"Oh." Lincoln's smile tightened at the corners of his mouth.

"Well, well." Mabel Whitcomb's heavy Southern twang pinged them from three tables away. "Angeline O'Brien, here for breakfast no less."

"Brunch," Angeline clarified. "It's almost noon."

"Doesn't matter." Mabel leaned over and gave Angeline a friendly hug. "Always good to see you, hon."

"Same here, Mabel."

"Who's this fella you got with ya?" Mable winked at Angeline, then turned to Lincoln. "Haven't seen you before."

"First time visiting Maico." Lincoln held out his hand to the vivacious, human restaurateur.

Accepting his handshake, Mabel whispered loudly to Angeline, "Make sure he stays."

Gracefully, Lincoln hid his smile.

"I bet you're military," Mabel continued in her nosy way. "You've got an air about you. One that says *Special Forces*," she said, flashing jazz hands.

"Thanks, but…" He lifted his pant leg to reveal his prosthetic leg.

"Oh, I'm sorry, hon." Sympathy dampened the tease in her eyes. "How did that happen?"

"I fell out of a two-story window. Shattered the knee and twisted the leg so bad nothing could've saved it." Lincoln spoke without attachment or emotion, as if the injury hadn't cost his career.

"I'm glad you came through it all right," Mabel said. "And happy you came with Angeline. It's always nice when her pretty face brightens up the place."

"She brightens a lot more than she realizes." Lincoln's gaze caressed Angeline's skin.

"Could I get a refill on the coffee?" Angeline asked, not wanting to add more fodder to the diner's gossip circle.

"Sure thing," Mabel said. "Do you want the Co-op's special to go with it?"

"Two, please." Lincoln handed Mabel the menu.

"Um, I'll have the stuffed French toast, a ham and cheese omelet, and an order of bacon." Angeline smiled sweetly at Lincoln.

"One Co-op special and one special order coming up," Mabel said.

"No," Lincoln said before Mabel walked away. "I'll have two orders of the Co-op special."

"Hon, that's a lot of food." Mabel looked him up and down. "Even for you."

Lincoln glanced at Angeline. "I've been in the resort's gym since six this morning and have another workout planned for this afternoon."

"All right. Two it is." Mabel waved to a nearby server before moseying into the kitchen. The young woman hurried over and refilled their mugs nearly to the rim before rushing off to the next table.

"So, Tanner…" Head slightly bowed over his coffee cup, Lincoln's troubled gaze lifted to Angeline. "The Dogman you called ancient history?"

"Yes."

"I'd like to know about him."

"We met in college." Angeline looked out the large glass window at the Wyatt's Automotive Services building across the street. "I thought he was so handsome, smart, and funny." Arrogant at times, and proud. "He believed in me, in my talent."

Or maybe he simply wanted her to have something to pursue when he left.

"The night we met, I had gone to a secluded spot on campus to play my guitar. Since no one was nearby I also sang my heart out. Tanner said the voice of an angel had led him to me." The chemistry between them had been instantaneous and undeniable.

And yet he still walked away, abandoning the life they could've had together. For what? To die before he'd really had a chance to live?

A masculine essence gently ebbed inside her, pulling her back from the edge of the dark hole on which she teetered. Lincoln's hands were molded around hers, keeping her anchored in the present. And although his beautiful silver-green eyes were brimming with tenderness and worry over her past, in them she saw a hope for the future.

"Maybe your history with him isn't so ancient," he said softly.

"It is." Angeline withdrew from his touch. "He made his choice and then he died. End of story."

"I think you skipped a lot of parts." Lincoln's gaze didn't waver. "It's okay to talk about the good times and the bad ones. I'll listen to whatever you want to say, whenever you need to say it. Always."

She believed he would, too.

"Music is an important part of my life. It helped me heal after the ordeal with Tanner. You've seen my guitar, but I also play the piano, a clarinet and a little on the fiddle."

"I'd love for you to play and sing a song for me." A devilish grin spread across Lincoln's face.

"Oh, no, you wouldn't." Surprisingly, Angeline's laugh felt like it sounded. Lighthearted and genuine. "Tanner was tone deaf. I sound like a banshee being strangled by a troll."

"Didn't know they existed." Lincoln laughed.

"According to Connor, they do. He once suggested that my vocal cords be removed to avoid attracting the murderous creatures to our treehouse."

Deep peals of laughter caused Lincoln's shoulders to shake.

"It's not that funny." Angeline rested her arms on the table.

"Easy, Angel." Eyes twinkling and mouth broadened with a generous smile, Lincoln reached over and patted her arm. "No one is perfect, but you are close enough for me."

All the irritation building inside her immediately turned warm and gooey, and a dopey smile took control of her mouth.

"What's your imperfection? And don't say your missing leg, because that is definitely not one."

Lincoln's expression blanked, and he sat back in the seat.

"Come on. Confession is good for the soul."

"I don't like spiders," he finally said.

"That's not a deep, dark secret. You can do better."

"No," he said, growing visibly uncomfortable. "It really is spiders." Eyes wide and rounded, Lincoln stared at her without blinking, and his mouth folded down into a flat curve so tight that the edges of his lips turned white.

She lowered her voice. "You're really afraid of spiders?"

He shook off a hard shiver and wiped his palm over his face. "Can't stand them."

The thought of a big bad Dogman afraid of a little bitty arachnid was comical, but Angeline didn't dare laugh. Lincoln had shared a deeply personal tidbit and she would not make him regret it.

"What happened?" Most phobias, she figured, were rooted in bad experiences.

"I had just learned to shift and my parents took me to the woods for my first run. They were so proud of me pouncing and tracking by pure instinct until a Texas brown tarantula dropped on me. I felt it scurrying through my fur." Lincoln rolled his shoulders. "I thought it would kill me. I howled and cried and my parents thought I was a coward for panicking over a spider.

Angeline's heart tweaked for him. Wahyas were fairly young when they developed the ability to shift.

"So, to teach me to be a brave wolf, they locked me in my room at night with a tarantula. Oh, and they took out the light bulb so I wouldn't sleep with the light on. Instead, I used my wolfan vision to watch it. I didn't sleep for three nights, sitting in the middle of the bed, worried the spider would bite me."

"What happened on the fourth night?"

"I spent it in the hospital. I had stopped eating and drinking because I couldn't stop worrying about that damn spider getting on me. I became dehydrated and delirious from sleep deprivation. To make matters worse, I refused to go home until our pack Alpha swore he'd personally check my room and tell my parents not to bring any more spiders into the house."

"Lincoln." Angeline rubbed her chest bone to loosen the tightness. "What your parents did was wrong on so many levels."

He let out a long breath. "They actually thought it would help."

Bobbie Sue stopped at the table and unloaded a tray of food. "Let me know if you need anything," she said, then hurried back to the kitchen.

"After that story, are you sure all that food will settle well in your stomach?" Angeline pointed at the double

serving of eggs, pancakes, grits, biscuits with sausage gravy, ham and bacon.

Lincoln glanced around the restaurant. "No spiders, so I'm good."

Head down, face set in firm determination, he dug into his meal with gusto.

Angeline smiled, cutting into her French toast stuffed with strawberry cream cheese. Lincoln had trusted her with a deeply personal secret simply because she had asked. At the very least, she needed to reciprocate.

"The National Music Awards are on tomorrow night." She paused. "Interested in watching them with me?"

If he comes, I'll tell him. If he doesn't, I won't.

Lincoln's unreadable gaze lifted to hers and he took his time chewing the food in his mouth.

A sudden, large dose of anxiety caused her stomach to plunge. "Um, I just remembered that I have something else to do. I'll set the DVR and watch it later."

"I'll be home if you change your mind."

She wouldn't. If her family couldn't see the value in her musical talent, how could a hot-bloodied, near feral Dogman?

Chapter 18

"What's up with the flowers, Slick?" Angeline stepped back, welcoming Tristan inside the apartment. "You usually show up with sweets."

She closed the door before the cold air leeched the heat from the living room.

"The National Music Awards are tomorrow night." Tristan handed her the lovely rainbow carnation arrangement. "Congratulations on your nominations."

"Thanks, but you usually don't give me flowers for the occasion." Since he had, Angeline appreciated that they came in a vase because she didn't own one.

She placed them on the kitchen counter. The sweet, floral scent filled the apartment and the bright colors balanced the muted shades of the decor.

"Because I'm usually celebrating with you on the night of the ceremony, but I can't this time." Tristan's apologetic expression tugged at Angeline's heart.

"I completely understand. You have a mate, and she's

going to pop out your baby any day now." Angeline gave
him a tight, friendly hug. "Me and you, we're good."

Looking like some of the weight on his shoulders had
lifted, Tristan sat in the sofa chair. "Writing a new song?"
He tipped his head at the scatter of papers on the coffee
table.

"Yeah." Moving aside the guitar, she sat on the couch.
"It's different from what I normally write."

"Meaning, it's about finding love instead of losing it?"

Angeline nodded. "Definitely not my bread-and-butter
market, but it's exhausting to keep revisiting the emotions
of the breakup with Tanner and his death."

"You've found new inspiration. Is it Lincoln?" Tristan's
brow dipped over his woried dark brown eyes.

She could always depend on him to have her back.

Angeline drew her socked feet beneath her legs. "I
started experimenting with a new style before Lincoln
came to town. But my muse has been more cooperative
lately."

"He hasn't mentioned extending the sublet beyond the
end of the month," Tristan said. "Do you think he'll stay?"

"He has some things to take care of at the Dogman
headquarters but said he'll come back when his retirement
paperwork is processed." She paused, mentally and physically taking a steadying breath. "Lincoln and I sense the
mate-bond." There, she'd said it. With much more convic-
tion than she'd practiced.

Fingers laced, Tristan leaned forward, resting his fore-
arms on his knees. "I don't want you to get hurt again."

"Neither do I." Angeline's heart smiled at her friend.
"We aren't jumping into a mateship. I need time to really
trust him and Lincoln needs time to process how dramatically his life is changing."

"That's smart." Tristan relaxed in the chair. "With the

accidental claiming, Nel and I didn't have the getting-to-know-each-other period before beginning a mateship."

"She loves you, Tristan. And I know you love her."

"I do." His eyelids pressed closed and his jaw tightened. "Once the baby comes, we'll have very little time for just us."

"Make the time," Angeline said. "When you and Nel need a few hours, a night or a weekend alone, call me. Aunt Ange will always be happy to babysit her." She studied Tristan's neutral expression. "Or him." Still nothing.

"Oh, come on." She tossed a pillow at Tristan. "Are you actually going to make me wait until Nel delivers to find out?"

"We don't know, either." Tristan grinned. "Nel and I didn't have a chance to explore the mysteries of each other before she became pregnant. So we wanted to share this one. It's been so much fun, guessing and planning for a baby, not a gender. We don't regret one moment of not knowing."

"That's really sweet." Tears stung Angeline's eyes. "You're going to be a great dad."

"I hope so." Worry dimmed the joy in Tristan's expression. "I didn't have the best role model."

"Lead with your heart, like you always have, and you'll be getting those World's Greatest Dad gifts before you know it."

"Thanks." A charming grin erased the tension in Tristan's face. "In case I've never mentioned it, I'm glad we're friends. You helped me through some rough times."

"That river runs both ways." Angeline offered a smile. "I know things have changed between us and will continue to change. We'll adapt. We always do."

Tristan's eyes narrowed at her. "You're not going to turn this into a song, are you?"

She answered by slinging another pillow at him, which he easily caught.

"I'm proud of you," Tristan said, turning serious. "Of your talent, your success. And I really hope your songs win tomorrow night." He gave her the "but" face. "I wish you wouldn't hide it from your father. Give him a chance to be as proud of you as I am."

Angeline shook her head. "Someday, maybe. Tomorrow is way too soon."

"So you're gonna hole up in here and watch the ceremony all alone?"

"I invited Lincoln."

"Have you told him your top-secret identity?"

"I'm not a spy," she laughed. "I'm a songwriter."

"With how many awards?"

A closet full.

And a bank account that didn't need padding from a waitressing job at her uncle's restaurant.

Tristan shook his head. "I get why you don't want to tell your dad, but you shouldn't keep who you really are a secret from Lincoln, especially if a mate-bond is involved."

"I'll tell him when I'm ready."

"You said the same about your dad. How long has it been?"

Nearly fifteen years. And the way things were going, it could be fifteen more before she felt ready to endure his censure.

"It'll be different with Lincoln." She wanted to share her music with him. And when the time felt right, she would.

"Hey, Angel." The sudden rush of excitement that filled Lincoln upon opening the door tanked. "What's wrong?"

Tight-lipped and clenching her teeth, Angeline stood

rigid in the doorway. Her laser-intense gaze bore straight through him.

"Damien!" Anger and fear strained her voice.

Lincoln glanced over his shoulder at the young man seated at the kitchen bar, a homemade beef empanada paused halfway between his plate and mouth.

"You bastard!" Balling her hands, Angeline stormed past Lincoln.

"Marquez? What did you do?"

"I need a little context." Slowly lowering his hand, Damien laid the empanada on his plate. His spine stiffened and his demeanor slipped from relaxed to ready.

"Zach is just a kid!" Shaking, Angeline stood in front of Damien.

"Ah." A cocky smile slid mockingly into place. Damien looked Angeline up and down. "I guess he signed the contract."

"What's going on?" Edging close behind Angeline, Lincoln slipped his hands around her waist, hoping his nearness would calm her distress.

She pointed her index finger an inch from Damien's nose. "He bullied Zach into signing his life away to the Program."

Damn!

When Lincoln had talked to Angeline's cousin last night after leaving the bar, Zach had already made up his mind to join the Program but he was worried about his family. Lincoln briefly spoke about the personal sacrifices the Program required and asked him to wait until after his college graduation before completing the paperwork. His family needed the time to prepare for the inevitable.

Angeline pushed away from Lincoln. The anger twisting her lovely face immediately morphed into a look of betrayal.

"You knew he planned to do this?" Angeline's furious, frightened voice shrieked in Lincoln's mind.

Suddenly the situation had turned from bad to worse. If she could sense his thoughts and he could hear hers, then a mate-bond was forming faster than expected.

He'd be more excited about the ethereal connection syncing them, body and mind, heart and soul, if he wasn't going back on active duty soon. But the distraction of sensing her turbulent emotions while trying to extract Dayax could get them killed.

"Sweetheart, wait!" He reached for her hand to stop her from storming off.

"I'm not your sweetheart," she hissed, jerking free.

The slamming door as she left rattled Lincoln to the very core of his soul.

"I'm beginning to sense that your *angel* really doesn't care for Dogmen." Damien snorted. "She does know that you are one, or did you keep that a secret, too?"

Lincoln ignored the question. "What, exactly, did you say to Zach?"

"Dogmen are born knowing their path. There is no hem-hawing." Damien resumed eating. "I'm surprised, actually. I didn't think he had the balls to commit."

Swallowing a mouthful of curses, Lincoln dug the cell phone from his pocket.

"Lincoln!" Zach cheerfully answered the call. "Have you heard the news?"

"Please tell me that you haven't emailed the docs to the recruiter."

"Not yet. I promised my folks that I would have Brice read over the contract."

"Smart idea." Lincoln breathed easier. "If you don't mind, I would like to be there, too."

"You're still on my side, right? I have enough people against me right now."

"Yeah, Zach. I'm on your side," Lincoln said. "When are you meeting with Brice?"

"Tomorrow afternoon. Hey, I'm celebrating with some friends tonight. Wanna come?"

"Not this time." Lincoln needed to do some damage control with Angeline. "I'll see you tomorrow."

Disconnecting the call, he turned to Damien, who had resumed eating. "You should've stayed out of this mess."

Damien gave a halfhearted shrugged. "Bunch of hill-billies. I don't know why everyone is upset. Becoming a Dogman is an honor and privilege."

"For *us*," Lincoln snarled. "Not for Zach's family, who he will have to turn his back on once he earns his tags."

"Either they support him or they don't. Either way, his life. His choice."

"It's not that simple." Not for close-knit families or their packs. They needed time to process, even time to grieve, because when the time came for Zach to say goodbye, in all likelihood, it would be the last time they'd see him.

Lincoln packed the food he'd made in plastic containers and headed to the door. "Whatever you do tonight, don't make this situation worse."

Damien raised his drink. *"No problema."*

Reaching Angeline's apartment Lincoln didn't hesi-tate. He walked in without knocking. "I brought supper. Made it myself."

"I'm not hungry." She stood, staring through the bal-cony sliders, her arms wrapped around her middle. "I don't want you here."

If that were true, she would've locked the door.

He left the food on the kitchen counter and walked to her. Standing close, but not quite touching, he leaned over her shoulder and waited.

It wasn't a long one.

"I've known Zach his entire life. I changed his poopy

diapers, taught him to throw a snowball and helped him with homework. I even let him borrow my car for prom." Her voice broke. "I don't want him to be scarred or maimed. And I don't want him to die, Lincoln."

Cupping Angeline's arms, Lincoln turned her around and wrapped her in a giant hug. She trembled against him, and he felt the hot sting of her tears splash against his heart even though his shirt absorbed the actual moisture.

"Aunt Miriam and Uncle Jimmy are devastated, and they haven't told Lucy. Roslyn, Sierra and the boys will be heartbroken. Zach is like a brother to them, too."

"Zach is lucky to have so many people who love him." Lincoln swallowed, trying to dislodge the stubborn lump in his throat. "I can't imagine how difficult this is for you and your family, but it's hard on Zach, too. Can you imagine how scared and lonely it is for him to make this decision, knowing everyone he loves is against it?"

"I can, actually."

"What?" Lincoln hooked his finger beneath Angeline's chin and tipped up her face.

"We aren't talking about my decisions right now. This is about Zach." Emotion contorted her face. "How could you be a party to convincing him when…?"

"When what?"

"Tanner died." Turbulent emotions darkened Angeline's eyes. "I don't want anything to happen to Zach."

Lincoln cradled Angeline's face, gently brushing away straggling tears from her cheeks. "Zach's decision isn't about you, Angel. It's about him."

"No one should have to go through what I did."

"If anything happens to Zach, your family will be there for each other. Just like they were when you lost Tanner."

Angeline slowly shook her head. "They never knew about him."

"Why?"

"His rejection nearly broke me. My father raised us to be strong, to not be vulnerable. How could I tell him how weak I was?"

"You aren't weak, Angel." Lincoln saw in her an inner strength that had called to him, comforted him and saved him from the brink too many times to count.

"You didn't see me when I felt Tanner die. I thought I would die, too. If not for Tristan, I might have."

"I thought you and Tristan…"

"We were never more than really good friends."

"I'm glad," Lincoln said, holding her tightly. "Glad he was here for you back then. But I want to be the man for you now. I will never intentionally hurt you."

"But?"

"I've talked to Zach. His heart is set on the Program. He needs everyone's support now because the next few months will be what he carries with him. Don't let it be full of arguments, because that's what he'll dwell on during those long, lonely deployments."

"Tanner and I argued the last time I saw him."

"I'm sure he knew how much you must've loved him."

"I did love him," Angeline said. "And I had put all this behind me, but you came into my life and now this situation with Zach has stirred it up again. I don't want to lose him, and I don't want to lose you."

"Me?" Lincoln rubbed his hand down her back, infusing his strength into her spirit.

"Until your retirement papers are finalized, you are still a Dogman. What if I lose you, just like I lost Tanner?"

"You won't lose me." Now that he'd found her, not even the devil himself would keep Lincoln from Angeline for long. "I'm like a boomerang. I will always find my way back to you. I promise."

And Lincoln never made a promise he couldn't keep.

Chapter 19

"The situation with Zach escalated quickly," Brice said, watching Lincoln come into the Alpha-in-waiting's official office inside the Walker's Run Resort. "The whole damn pack thinks you and Damien are recruiting for the Program."

"We're not recruiters. And Zach told me that he's been planning to do this for quite some time. His parents really shouldn't be surprised."

"They're scared and upset. Walker's Run is family-centric. Conflict is not a conscious reality for the people here."

"And yet you're upgrading the security system, employing surveillance tactics and expanding the pack's sentinel program," Lincoln said, taking a seat.

Brice tipped his head.

"I didn't come to help you talk Zach out of his decision. However, I do want to give him a truer picture of how one becomes a Dogman, the sacrifices and the realities of living with the consequences 24/7."

"I expect no less." Brice pushed back from the desk. "It takes a special kind of wolfan to do what you do, Lincoln. When bullets started flying in Romania, you didn't hesitate. Even after catching one in the shoulder meant for me, you continued to mobilize your team and eliminated the threat. It was damn amazing."

"It's what we're trained to do. Being a Dogman isn't about us, it's about being a shield. We're expendable. Those we protect are not."

"Do you think Zach has what it takes to succeed in the Program?"

"He has the heart and motivation," Lincoln said. "But he'll have to endure grueling physical training, learn to take orders and follow without question and pass an intensive psychological evaluation. Realistically, less than a quarter of the recruits make it past the first six months of drills."

"Seventy-five-percent failure rate. That's steep."

"That's only the first round. Half of those who begin the second six months will successfully complete the endurance training program. After that, another third are eliminated with the final psych profile." Lincoln shrugged. "In the end, the Program is about service, not egos."

"Are you ready to take the final readiness test for active duty?"

Lincoln nodded.

"And if you don't make it?"

"That's not an option. Dayax is depending on me." Lincoln folded his hands over his stomach. "I will find him, and then we're coming here because I plan to claim Angeline as my mate."

"Is she in agreement?"

"Yeah." Lincoln felt his smile broaden. "Well, at the moment, she isn't too happy with me because of the situation with Zach. But we're starting to bond." And Lincoln damn sure wouldn't make the same mistake as Tanner Phillips.

The rich, buttery scent of fresh popcorn filled the air. In the comfort of her home, Angeline stooped in front of the microwave, watching the expanding bag and listening to the rapid eruption of the kernels. Usually, her nerves weren't jittery until the category and song titles were announced.

However, two hours ago her stomach had started doing low-impact flip-flops. More so because tonight, she had no moral support.

If she'd gone to LA to participate in the awards show, at least her agent, Sandra Lively, would've accompanied her. Win or lose, there would've been someone to share the moment with her.

After last night's meltdown, Angeline wasn't sure if Lincoln would show up. He'd remained levelheaded when fear had caused her emotions to overload. Like a pro, he'd helped her see that Zach's choices were his to make, and family supported each other, no matter what.

Helping Miriam and Jimmy accept Zach's decision? Lincoln proved to be good at that, too.

In the end, everyone realized how much becoming a Dogman meant to Zach. Including Angeline.

He had chosen to follow his heart. How could she not support him? Especially knowing how it felt to not have her family's support.

And she didn't want Zach to disappear into the Program believing his family had turned against him.

Angeline didn't like his choice, but it was his to make.

The microwave dinged. From the cupboard over the sink, she pulled down a large plastic bowl and filled it with the popcorn. Tucking a handful of napkins beneath her arm, she carted a cup of hot chocolate and the snack bowl into the living room, placed the items on the coffee table then settled comfortably on the couch with her drink.

Lincoln opened the front door and walked in. "Hey, Angel."

"What are you doing here?" Happily surprised, she didn't mind that he hadn't knocked.

"You invited me, remember?"

"I didn't realize you accepted the invitation, but I'm glad you did."

"Did I miss anything?"

"Nope. It should start after the next few commercials. Oh, there's beer in the fridge or hot chocolate in the electric kettle."

Lincoln detoured to the kitchen and poured a cup of hot chocolate before joining her in the living room. He sat close to her. He smelled of winter, clean and crisp.

"Has it started snowing again?" she asked.

"A few flurries. Nothing to worry about." He picked up the popcorn bowl and propped his foot on the coffee table.

"Oh, the show is starting." She took the sound off mute and got up to turn down the lights.

Returning to the couch, she snuggled against Lincoln. He tilted his head toward her so they touched. Cozy and comfortable, in that moment, she was the most content she'd been in a long time.

He watched the opening number raptly and laughed at the emcee's joke. She filled him in on tidbits about the nominees and added a little trivia.

"How did you learn so much about country music?" he asked during a commercial.

"Well," she said, "I do play a little guitar."

"And sing." Lincoln grinned.

"Not according to Connor."

"I'm a man who can make up his own mind." Lincoln laughed. "Even if your brother is right, any song you sing to me will be beautiful."

"Careful, Dogman." Angeline playfully bumped his shoulder. "You're starting to turn sappy."

He flicked a piece of popcorn at her. It glanced off her nose and tumbled down her chest, landing between her breasts.

"If I didn't know better, I'd think you did that on purpose." She plucked the popcorn from her cleavage and popped it into her mouth.

Lincoln winked. "Skill is making something look like an accident."

"Oh, really?" She grabbed a handful of popcorn and a fight ensued, quickly turning into a tickling fest with Angeline succumbing to giggles. And then they were kissing.

Long, deep, soul-bending kisses that nearly made her forget why the television was on.

"Wait!" She pushed against Lincoln's chest. "They're about to announce best song of the year."

Lincoln eased back into his seat with only a muffled groan in protest. Angeline sat up, increased the volume and perched on the edge of the couch. Her folded hands pressed against her mouth.

"And the winner is…" The camera panned from the announcer's face to her hand opening the envelope.

The air in Angeline's lungs stilled. No matter the dozen or so awards stashed in her closet, she always awaited the announcement with bated breath.

"'Heartache Lane.'"

"Yes!" A joyous howl erupted as Angeline jumped up

to dance her happy jig. Each win felt like the first and she took none for granted. Every musical note and lyric she had imbued with pure emotion. Recognition of her talent and knowing how loved her songs were nearly burst her heart.

Typically, Tristan joined the celebratory dance. However, Lincoln remained on the couch. A warm smile took the chill off his piercing silvery-green gaze tracing her every move.

The air whooshed out of her inflated excitement.

"I, uh…" She sat on the couch. Hands pressed together between her knees, she fixed her attention on the television. Jolene McKenzie, the woman who'd lent her voice to the words and lyrics Angeline had written, finished the acceptance speech. She would take home the award for the vocals, Angeline's gold-color statue would come in the mail.

"I really like that song," Angeline said, feeling the heat from Lincoln's gaze sizzle her skin.

"It's a memorable tune," Lincoln said. "I've heard it a few times on the radio. That Jolene girl who sings it doesn't look old enough to have endured that kind of heartbreak.

"Really?" Angeline had been a few years younger than Jolene's current age when Tanner had left her. "I didn't think there was an age restriction on when a woman could have her heart broken."

"Maybe it's her eyes. They don't reflect the deep pain that the song is about." Lincoln tapped Angeline's leg, drawing her gaze. "But yours do."

Awkward silence strained the space between them.

"The announcer said the songwriter was A. R. O'Brien. Any relation?"

Angeline's stomach clenched. Lincoln was opening the proverbial bag and her secret was the infamous cat. She could either allow the truth to escape or leave it muffled inside the bag.

"What gave me away? The dance?"

"The song." Lincoln squinted at her. "When I heard it on the radio after you mentioned the ancient history with a Dogman, all I could picture was you. I didn't think you'd wrote it, though. Until that little dance of yours. Come on." He laughed. "What was that?"

The tension broke as Angeline laughed with him.

"That was my happy dance."

"Kinda looked like an octopus on ice skates," he said playfully. "Arms and legs flailing in all different directions."

"Hey, that's my signature move."

"Anyone else seen it?"

"Just Tristan, and he's sworn to secrecy. He'll never admit to it."

"Is the secret just about the dance?"

"No." Angeline took a breath, for courage. "Come with me."

Without looking back, she led Lincoln into the bedroom and opened her closet. A waist-high cabinet provided a divider between her winter clothes and all the rest. The cabinet shelves displayed the trophies awarded for her music. She stepped back so that Lincoln could see.

"No one except Tristan knows that I'm a professional songwriter."

Lincoln's silence weighted the room. He knelt on one leg and seemed to read the inscription on each statuette.

"You've got amazing talent, Angel. Why don't you want anyone to know?" Concern laced his curious gaze.

"You've met my dad. How well do you think this would go over with him?"

"He should be damn proud of you."

"He would be ashamed that I allowed my heart to be so easily broken."

"Then he doesn't understand the nature of love," Lincoln said quietly. "It's a gamble. Sometimes it pays off, sometimes it doesn't. But I believe it's worth the risk."

On the other side of a once broken heart, Angeline wasn't sure she quite agreed.

Chapter 20

Lincoln eased over to the bed where Angeline had sat. "Are you still hurting over the past?"

"No," she said without hesitation. "When I wrote those songs, I had to put myself back into the heartbroken woman I used to be. It's exhausting."

"Why do you keep doing it?"

She gave him a quizzical look. "Have you seen what's in my closet?"

"Is the payoff worth the torture?"

"Not so much anymore." Angeline sighed. "I've been talking with Jolene—"

"Jolene McKenzie?" During his last deployment, Lincoln had seen the popular country-pop recording artist performing at a USO holiday function. "The woman who gave the acceptance speech, you know her?"

"Yes." Angeline gave him a funny look. "I know quite a few recording artists. It's my job to write songs for them."

"I didn't realize... Never mind. So, you were talking with Jolene?"

"She's young and doesn't want to get typecast as only singing one type of song. She wants to expand her repertoire and so do I. We've been brainstorming ideas and I've given her a few sample pieces."

"And?"

"She likes them." Angeline smiled. "And I like writing them. It was hard at first. My brain kept defaulting to all the hurt and turmoil I've lived. After a while, though, writing more upbeat music and lyrics became easier."

Lincoln grazed his knuckles over the skin of her cheek. Such a delicate appearance she had. Fine-boned and slender, she looked almost fragile. All the years he'd carried her photo, he'd thought of her as an ethereal beauty. One that might shatter at the touch.

But Angeline wasn't like that at all. Sass fired her soul and though she might look breakable, she had a will of steel.

Lincoln leaned in, brushing his lips against her mouth. She opened for him to deepen the kiss. She tasted of popcorn, chocolate and hope.

Her fingers slid past his ear to cup the back of his head and he felt her essence ebb inside him. His inner wolf howled in tandem with his heart's declaration. *Mine, mine, mine.*

Both admitting to the mate-bond growing between them made courtship easier. But Lincoln wanted to be careful. Mate-bonds didn't guarantee a conflict-free relationship. And he didn't want to rush getting to know Angeline. Really knowing her. The preconceived notions that he'd had needed to be unscripted so that he could see the real woman, not the fantasy.

Most important, he never wanted to cause her the pain

that she drew upon to write those haunting, achingly beautiful songs.

Without breaking their long, deep, sweet kiss, she drew him down to the bed with her.

Desire had been coursing through his veins prior to the kiss and his body was already hot and ready for coupling. Settling over her body would be a bit tricky. Though he could never be totally unaware of his prosthetic, most of the time he could ignore the feeling of the artificial limb cupped to his stump.

However, in the current situation, he found the prosthetic distracting him from a pleasurable experience.

"What's wrong?" Angeline whispered against his lips as her eyes fluttered open.

She had been straightforward and honest with him, he could do no less.

"I should probably take off my leg," he said.

"Okay." Her hands fell away, allowing him to change positions.

"This will be the first time…since losing my leg."

"Um, are you forgetting the full moon?" She playfully poked his arm.

"I was standing. This is different." Rubbing his hand against his jean-clad thighs, he felt the upper edge of the prosthetic cup snuggled high on his stump. "Things might get awkward."

"No, it won't. We'll figure this out, together."

Lincoln bent down to untie the laces, then pulled off his shoes.

"That's so cute," she said, looking at his feet. "You have a sock on your prosthetic."

"I feel weird wearing only one sock."

Obediently, he lifted his arms for her to pull off his shirt. Next, she straddled his lap and kissed him, possessing his mouth as her fingers laid claim to his shoulders and glided down his chest to his jeans. Deftly, she undid the button and inched down the zipper, then she slid her hand inside his boxers to stroke his shaft. His body ached as much as it hummed from her touch.

She urged him to lie back on the bed. Though his vision clouded with lust-laden lashes, he couldn't take his gaze off the sparkle in her eyes or the soft, genuine smile curving her luscious mouth. She was his. Not because some instinct demanded her to be but because she'd made the active choice to follow where the instinct led.

As she eased off his lap, her fingers curled around the waistband of his pants. Adjusting his weight, Lincoln lifted his hips, allowing her to slide down his jeans and boxers in one swoop.

"My God, Lincoln. How many times have you been hurt?" Her gaze seemed to bounce from one scar to another. Not counting the ones on his stump, he had twenty-seven.

"That's really not what a man wants to hear when he's naked in front of the woman he wants to have sex with."

"It's startling." An apology shimmered in her eyes. "I mean, I got a glimpse before, but I really didn't comprehend…"

"I've been a Dogman a long time." Lincoln pushed up on his elbows. "Battle wounds are par for the course."

Her bright blue eyes blinked back tears. She hurt for him—he could see the pain twisting her features.

"These scars aren't worth your sorrow, Angel. They healed and I'm still living." He sat up. "I don't regret any of it." Especially because the path he'd chosen had led him to her.

He clasped the cup of his prosthetic. "Should I take this off? Or get dressed?"

Angeline took his face in her hands. "I'm not put off by your scars. And I want you. Very much." She kissed him hard and passionately, breaking away to remove her sweater and yoga pants. The black lace bra and panties against her pale skin made his mouth water even as his throat dried.

"Your turn." She pointed a slender finger at his leg.

Carefully, he worked off the prosthetic.

"Can I hold it?" Angeline held out her open hands.

Gently, he entrusted her with the state-of-the-art limb.

"Wow! It's—"

"Expensive," he interrupted.

"I was going to say heavy." She carried the prosthetic to the dresser and propped it against the drawers.

"It shouldn't weigh more than my natural leg would."

"Have you seen your leg?" She sashayed toward him. "Tree trunk size and solid muscle."

He scooted farther onto the bed as she stalked up his body, then straddled him. Her sizzling kiss short-circuited the higher functions in his brain, reducing his ability to talk to a series of grunts and groans and growls.

Her lips trailed down his throat. The floral scent of her hair was as feminine and intoxicating as her touch. She kissed each and every scar on his chest and arms, making them more than worth the pain he'd suffered obtaining the wound.

Following the dark line of hair below his belly button, she licked, nibbled and kissed his skin all the way down to his groin. Never in all the nights he'd been alone had he dared to hope for a moment like this with her.

Maybe he had died in that explosion and been found worthy of a little piece of heaven.

The tip of her tongue traced the seam of his sack to the top of his cock. The anticipatory tension inside his groin coiled tighter, making it difficult to breathe normally. His pants sounded as ragged as a man dying from thirst yet inching his way toward a lush, beautiful oasis.

That was what she was to him. Hope. Soft and wonderful and incredibly beautiful.

Taking him into her mouth, she laved her tongue over his slit and down his shaft. His mind turned into a quagmire of images and instinct, all driving him toward claiming his mate.

"Mine," Lincoln said in a harsh, hoarse whisper.

Angeline ignored the declaration in favor of savoring the salty, masculine taste of him. Beneath her hand, the taut skin of his stomach trembled.

He was close, so close, and she took pleasure knowing she had brought him to the pinnacle of agony and ecstasy. She wanted him to teeter there a little longer, to share the experience of aching and clenching with need.

Men, always in a rush to the finish line, often missed the softer nuances of coupling that a woman wanted.

Slowly, she eased his shaft from her mouth and kissed a trail from his belly button to the hollow spot at the base of his throat. A sigh drifted on his long, drawn-out breath.

Though his lashes fluttered, his eyes did not open. Large, calloused hands gripped her hips and the contact unleashed a flood of hormones in her body already raging with feminine desire.

She looked down Lincoln's body, his bronzed skin marred with scars but no less beautiful. His loss of a leg didn't diminish his vitality or lessen her want of him.

His long, thick shaft pressed intimately against her lacy panties. She rocked back and forth, teasing him.

"Angeline." It sounded like a croak.

She did it again and again until his eyelids lifted and he seared her with his molten gaze.

"Now that you're awake…"

He growled, menacing, with a slight undertone of desperation.

Reaching behind her, Angeline unhooked her bra then took her time drawing her arms out of the straps before lowering the cups to expose her breasts. Lincoln seemed to stop breathing. His chest stilled completely and not one muscle in his body flickered.

Slowly, she leaned over him and softly touched her lips to his mouth. As they kissed, Lincoln slid her panties down her hips. Easily, she maneuvered out of the undergarment one leg at a time. Completely naked and straddling him, she watched his gaze follow his hands over every curve.

He brought her forward to take her breast into his mouth. Her growl competed with his as he fast-flicked his tongue over her nipple. With his arms wrapped securely around her middle, she couldn't escape the unbearable pleasure.

Though his hold did not lessen, she felt his hand move down the curve of her ass and his fingers caressed her inner thigh before teasing and sliding against her folds.

"So wet," he panted against the valley between her breasts as his mouth moved from one to the other.

The response on her tongue became a deep feminine groan as his finger traced her opening before pushing inside. Dropping her head, she rested her forehead against his shoulder as every muscle in her body went slack except for those in her lower belly. Those grew tighter and tighter, coiled and primed for release.

Lincoln grinned, damn him. Though he had every right. Turnabout was fair play and she had teased him to the point of ecstasy. Only she'd stopped at the pinnacle, hoping to prolong the moment. From the rhythm and pressure of his pistoning fingers, he had a different agenda.

Each time she tried to call his name, a passionate groan escaped. With her muscles refusing to cooperate, she simply indulged in the pleasure each stroke provided.

"Oh, God." The words were a chant in her mind.

"Want me to stop, Angel?"

"Do and die." She barely managed the thought before shattering in sheer ecstasy. Buoyed on the feeling, she barely noticed Lincoln rolling her onto the mattress.

He crouched over her; a wildness in his eyes she'd never seen made him all the sexier.

"Grab a pillow and put it under my leg," he said hoarsely.

It took a moment for her brain to process the words before her arm reached over to do as he'd asked. As soon as she did, some of the strain eased in Lincoln's shoulders.

Angeline molded her hand around his shaft and guided him inside her. Though it took a few positional adjustments for him to comfortably thrust, the trials and errors were worth the effort. They sighed in unison as he filled her.

His essence entangled with hers, heightening the sensation of completeness. She'd never expected to experience that feeling again, especially with another Dogman.

Lincoln had expressed his intent to retire from the Program and she found herself less afraid to open her heart to him. They had a long way to go, though, before they committed to a mateship but the getting to know each other part was rather fun.

"Mmm." His lips whispered along the curve of her neck, turning her insides giddy.

"No biting," she gasped.

A wolfan bite during sexual intercourse established a mate-claim and was binding until death. A mate-claim did not guarantee that a mate-bond would form. And some couples, like Tristan's parents, never became a cohesive pair after the claiming.

Lincoln licked a spot that instantly became her new favorite, causing her hips to arch and her fingers to dig into his back.

"Same goes for you, Angel." Lincoln's voice floated through her mind.

Peeking open her eyes, she realized how close her teeth were to his shoulder. Moving away from the danger zone, she captured his lips in a breath-stealing kiss that broke only when her head tipped back from the force of the orgasm pulsing through her body.

Wave after wave battered her senses, drowning her in an ocean of pleasure. Only Lincoln's strong, steady presence kept her from slipping into oblivion.

He shuddered against her and stilled, except for the rise and fall of his chest with each panted breath.

Her breaths easing, she brushed her fingers through his dark, wavy hair and tried to imagine how different the texture would feel if shorn in a military buzz cut.

Slowly, his eyelids fluttered open. "Hello, Angel," he softly growled. The gleam in his gaze was possessive and smugly satisfied.

Mine, mine, mine. Her heart thumped the declaration with every beat. Though neither had physically claimed the other, she sensed the power of the mate-bond stitching them together mind and body, heart and soul.

"That was fun." She kissed him lightly on the mouth.

"Fun?" His brow scrunched though humor lit his eyes. "Admit it, that was pretty amazing."

"I admit nothing." She made a turning-the-lock gesture over her lips.

"My training included techniques used to make people talk." Settling on his right side, he drew his left hand from her hip across her ribs and traced the curve of her breast, causing her to suck in a breath. "Shall I continue?"

"Please do."

He chuckled and Angeline reminded herself that unless she wanted Lincoln reading every thought that crossed her mind, she needed to remember to shield them from him.

Using the pad of his thumb, Lincoln strummed her nipple until it tightened into a sensitive bud. "Still not talking?" he teased and then lowered his head to suck her peak into his hot, moist mouth.

The comfortable ebb of satisfaction that had lulled her into a relaxed state suddenly churned with want and need and the knowledge that Lincoln could quench both.

Teasing and tormenting, his tongue flicked against her nipple a dozen times before he sucked it long and hard, driving her to near madness, and releasing it only to start the cycle again. On the fourth round, his hand slipped down her abdomen and between her legs, parted in welcome.

Gingerly, he fingered her folds. She wanted to stroke his shaft in tandem, but the way he was positioned prevented her from reaching his groin. Since his face was practically planted in her chest as he continued to lick and suck her breasts, she gripped the back of his neck, massaging the thick, corded muscles beneath her palm. A slight shiver rolled across his shoulders but didn't impede the attention he showered on two particular parts of her body.

Once more on the cusp of ecstasy, she arched her hips. A few more strokes would send her plunging over the edge. Only he stopped.

"Lincoln?" His name tore raggedly from her throat.

Silently, he cocked his head at the open bedroom door.

"Okay," she nearly panted, "I admit it. Sex with you is downright amazing. So, can we get back to it?"

"I need to answer my phone!" The urgency in his voice made her heart race.

They both sat up. He swung his leg over the edge of the bed and looked toward the dresser where his prosthetic rested.

"I'll get it." She scrambled off the bed and dashed into the living room, following the sound of the ring to the satellite phone on the coffee table. Someone from the Program was calling.

Her heart sinking into the pit of her stomach, she grabbed the device, rushed into the bedroom and handed it to Lincoln.

"Adams," he answered, his voice tight and his body rigid.

Angeline placed the prosthetic leg next to Lincoln on the bed. Then she quickly gathered her clothes and went to dress in the bathroom. Playtime had ended. And more than likely, her days with Lincoln were numbered. He'd warned her that he'd have to return to the Program for a while. She couldn't help but wonder if the Program would really let him go.

Chapter 21

Dayax is alive!

Lincoln's heart nearly cracked his chest with its furious beating. The adrenaline-laced blood rushing in his ears made it difficult for him to comprehend much of what had been said afterward.

All this time not knowing but hoping and praying. Refusing to believe any other outcome. To learn that the boy he loved like a son had been found, Lincoln came as close to tears as he'd ever been in his entire life.

"Are you orders clear, Captain?" The CO's crisp voice snapped Lincoln to attention.

"Yes, sir."

"Then I'll see you soon, Adams. Safe journey."

"Thank you, sir." A deluge of relief and determination rocked his body. The allied forces had eyes on Dayax and a group of children rounded up by the insurgents. But the wolfling wasn't safe yet.

Lincoln dropped the phone on the bed. Pocketing his

fist into his other palm, he pressed his hands against his mouth and clenched his eyes, sending a silent proclamation.

I'm coming, little wolf. Hold on for me a bit longer.

His senses returning to baseline after the adrenaline boost, Lincoln noticed the leg on the bed and Angeline's absence. A different set of emotions now churned inside his chest. Time with her had become extremely short and there were so many things he needed to explain.

He and Angeline might recognize the mate-bond drawing them together, but there was so much they didn't know about one another. Despite the warnings from the CO that the wolfling might not be cleared to leave the country, Lincoln had every intention of bringing Dayax home to Walker's Run.

But Angeline knew nothing about the wolfling and Lincoln had no idea if she wanted to be a mother. Or what he would do if she didn't.

"Angeline?" He sensed her in the apartment, but she neither answered nor returned to the bedroom.

Quickly and carefully, he secured his prosthetic and pulled on his boxers and pants, then put on his shoes. Strolling out of the bedroom, he stuffed his arms into his sweatshirt and yanked it down over his chest.

"Hey, we need to talk," he said, walking around the couch to stand in front of Angeline.

"Shh!" She flicked her open hand at him without looking up. "No, not you," she said into the phone. "Lincoln just walked in. Never mind about him. I'm on my way. I'll deal with your parents. Just get in there and help Nel deliver that baby!"

Angeline disconnected the call and looked at Lincoln, her face all aglow. "I'm going to be a godmother." Her happy shriek rolling into a squeal, she jumped up from the couch, her arms askew, and hopped around in a dance reminiscent of the one he'd seen earlier.

For someone with such musical talent, Angeline didn't have any rhythm when it came to dance moves. Still, he found her jerky, uncoordinated movements quite endearing.

"My purse!" She dashed into the bedroom.

Lincoln snagged his keys from the coffee table. Waiting at the door, he took her coat off the stand and picked up her boots.

"Here." She rushed to him, holding his Program-issued phone.

Now that he'd been notified about Dayax's whereabouts and received official orders, Lincoln doubted he'd receive any more calls from HQ tonight.

"Thanks, Angel." Dropping the device into his other pocket, he kissed Angeline's temple then passed her the boots.

"Sorry, I'm rushing off," she said, holding on to him with one hand while using the other to pull on her boots. "But the baby's coming. And I—" She looked around. "Have you seen my keys?"

"Are they in your purse?"

"Maybe." She glanced around the room. "Do you see it anywhere?"

"On your shoulder." He lightly tugged the strap.

"Duh," she said. "I don't know why I'm so scattered. I've been around babies. Five, in fact."

"Is this your first time being a godparent?"

"Yeah." Her face lit up with a huge grin and some of his worry faded.

He'd watched Angeline with her nieces and nephews. She was an absolute natural in handling them and they loved every minute spent in her company. Dayax would be lucky to have her as a mother—if she could accept a package deal.

Lincoln helped her into her coat then flipped up the hoodie on his sweatshirt as they stepped out while she locked the door.

"This was...fun." She offered a half shrug and a smile. "See you around?"

He didn't like the way that sounded. Was she brushing him off?

"You'll see me for the rest of the night," Lincoln said, walking her to the stairwell. "I'm taking you to the hospital."

Instead of arguing, she looked relieved. "Thanks. I didn't expect to be this nervous."

They started down the three flights of stairs.

"I wasn't asked to be involved with the births of my neice and nephews." Though Angeline's voice remained cheerful, Lincoln sensed the deep hurt the slight had caused. "Tristan and Nel have no siblings and Nel's parents were killed in a car accident when she was young. Tristan's parents—" she peeked at Lincoln "—well, you'll see for yourself."

"In case no one has ever told you," Lincoln said, "you're great with kids."

"You've mentioned it." She smiled. "After Sierra's party—which, by the way, she hasn't stopped talking about. I think she's your biggest fan."

"I was hoping her aunt would be."

Angeline laughed softly.

"Have you ever wondered about becoming a mother?"

Her steps faltered slightly. "When I was younger," she finally said. "But life happens and now I'm not sure that I want to do the whole pregnancy thing."

"There's always adoption," he said quietly.

She touched his arm as they reached the first-floor landing. "Do you want be a father?"

"I've started thinking about it," he said, dodging the question rather than providing a direct answer. If she was resistant to the idea of an instant family, then he didn't want to put pressure on her with the knowledge that he had realized how very much he wanted to be a dad.

"Gavin Walker is a big supporter of wolfan adoptions," Angeline said.

Good to know that about his future Alpha. Not all packs were keen to the idea.

"In fact," she continued, "his godson, Rafe, was adopted from another pack. I heard Gavin faced down the Woelfesenat when they challenged the transfer."

"They didn't want Rafe removed from his birth pack?" Lincoln had the same fear regarding Dayax.

"No, an illness wiped out his birth pack. The Woelfesenat objected because Rafe's adoptive father is human."

"I can see why they were concerned." The general human populace had no idea of the existence of Wahyas.

"They couldn't see past Doc being human. But Gavin knew him. Trusted him. And he fought to give a little wolfling a loving home and a son to a human who has dedicated his life to our pack."

"Brice once told me the backbone of the Walker's Run pack is family."

"It is. Even the dysfunctional ones, like mine."

With his hand gently pressed against her lower back, Lincoln led Angeline to his truck and helped her get settled in the seat.

"Thanks, again," she said as he slid behind the steering wheel.

"Anytime, Angel." He started the engine and adjusted the heater control so that she would be comfortable.

Even catching all of the red lights on the main road,

they made it to the hospital parking lot in less than ten minutes.

Angeline took his hand as they entered the emergency department and led him through the waiting room, past the check-in station and down a long corridor with locked double doors. She swiped her Co-op ID through the card reader mounted on the wall.

"Where are we going?" Warily, Lincoln watched the doors slowly swing open.

"The west wing," she said. "When the Co-op built the hospital, as a precaution, it was set up to keep injured and sick wolfans separated from human patients."

She held his hand as they walked. He liked the warmth that the physical contact produced. It made him feel as if she didn't want to let him go.

Very soon, she would have to do that very thing. But for now he wanted to stay connected to her for as long as possible.

"Jayson Nathaniel Durrance. What a fine name for such a handsome wolfling." Angeline lightly tapped the baby's little button nose. Yawning, he balled his hands and pointed his toes in a rigid, full-body stretch for about five seconds, then returned to a snuggly position in her arms.

Her heart nearly burst with love. She kissed his forehead, and he peeked at her beneath half-opened eyelids. His little mouth formed a cute little grin that reminded her of his father's trademark smile.

"Oh, you're gonna be a little charmer, just like your daddy." She glanced at Tristan, sitting next to his mate and holding her hand as she slept. The labor had been difficult, and Angeline was glad mother and son were doing well.

"So how does it feel to be a dad, Slick?"

"Terrifying," Tristan said in all seriousness. "The only time I've felt more afraid was when I thought I would lose

Nel." His fear in that situation had been justified. Nel had been at the mercy of a deranged wolfan. In the end, Tristan had been forced to put down his own blood-kin to protect her.

Angeline had no doubt he would do the same for his son. "You are going to be great at this."

"I will try my damnedest." Using his cell, he grabbed a snapshot of her holding Jayson.

"Text that to me," she said. "I have virtual scrapbooks of my nieces and nephews, and I want to start one for Jayson. I plan to make videos and make everyone watch them at important events, like graduation parties, rehearsal dinners. Whenever they think they're too old for their breeches, I'll be there to remind them they aren't."

"Done." Tristan laughed. "Where's your purse? I didn't hear your phone ding."

"I left it with Lincoln. He's in the waiting room."

"You brought Lincoln?" Tristan's demeanor changed slightly with the protective-brother gleam coming to light in his eyes.

"He brought me." The baby stretched his arm and his tiny fingers tangled in her hair. Cradling him with one arm, she carefully worked opened his hand and swept the errant strands over her shoulder. "I was too excited to drive. And he volunteered."

"Things are going good with you two?"

Angeline shrugged. "He got a call on that clunky phone. I'm pretty sure it was someone from the Program. Lincoln mentioned that he had a few things to take care of before his retirement papers are processed." But what if the Program decided he could continue? Would he make the same choice as Tanner?

Deep inside, she feared he would.

"Hey, Sassy." Tristan caught her attention. "If Lincoln told you that he's coming back, he will."

"Since when did you become a prognosticator?"

"I haven't been around him a lot. But when I have, and someone mentions you, he lights up like Mary Jane McAllister's house at Christmas."

Warmth rushed through her. "That much, huh?" Mary Jane, an elderly human woman whose homestead bordered the wolf sanctuary, put out so many lights and animated decorations that one needed sunglasses driving by her house, even at midnight.

"Lincoln's at a different place in his life than Tanner was, and so are you."

"It scares me sometimes, the mate-bond."

"Preaching to the choir, sister." Tristan's phone dinged, and he checked the message. "I think this is for you."

"Why? What does it say?"

"'You're a natural, Angel.' Oh! And there are three hearts and a kissy-face smiley emoji." Mischief lit Tristan's eyes. "I am never gonna let the Dogman live this down."

"Play nice," Angeline said. "Remember, he's licensed to kill."

"That's James Bond, a fictional character. And there's no such thing as a license to kill."

"You sure about that?"

"I'm sure," Tristan said. "Fairly sure."

Scrunching his reddening face, Jayson squirmed in Angeline's arms and his mouth opened in an ear-piercing wail.

Tristan jumped up. "What's wrong with him?"

"He's either hungry or having his first poo. Neither of which I can help with." Angeline carefully stood with Jayson and walked to Tristan. "Time to go to daddy." She placed the crying infant in his father's arms.

"What am I supposed to do with him?"

"Bring him to me." Nel's soft voice sounded tired. "I think he's hungry."

"Okay, little one." Tristan kissed Jayson's balled hand. "Mama says it's time to eat."

The baby made loud sucking noises as Tristan laid him in Nel's arms.

"That's my cue to leave," Angeline said. The new family needed bonding time. "I'll come back later with Suzannah and Ruby."

Tristan's mother and aunt were a handful to deal with, which was why Angeline had promised to "handle" them.

"Thanks for everything," Tristan said.

"No thanks necessary." She slipped out of the room, her heart full and heavy at the same time. Her joy for the new family was immeasurable but the bubbly excitement concealed a heavy ache of uncertainty regarding her future.

She quietly entered the west wing waiting room. Shortly after she'd arrived last night, Tristan's parents had departed. Mostly because she'd demanded they leave since they wouldn't stop arguing. Accidentally mated nearly forty years ago and still they had never learned to get along.

Since she'd gone in to see Tristan and Nel's newborn son, dozens of pack members had arrived. Prominent among them was the Alpha- and Alphena-in-waiting, Brice and Cassie Walker, and their close companions, Rafe and Grace Wyatt, and Ronni and Bodie Gryffon. In their midst sat Lincoln. Her heart tweaked at how comfortable he seemed with them.

Although Tristan and Nel were part of the inner circle, Angeline had kept her distance.

"Well?" Brice's voice boomed across the open area.

Everyone fell silent. Expectantly, they looked at Angeline for the revelation of the pack's longest kept secret—the gender of Tristan and Nel's wolfling.

"I'm proud to announce the newest member of the Walker's Run pack is Jayson Nathaniel Durrance." She paused for the collective cheer, knowing it would've been the same enthusiastic cheer had Angeline announced a girl's name. "Mother and baby are fine. Dad is still a little green."

Everyone laughed and happy chatter followed.

She made her way to Lincoln, sitting comfortably among the cluster of Tristan's closest friends. Although Tristan was tight with the Alpha-in-waiting and his circle of companions, Angeline felt a little awkward in their midst. Mostly because they were a tight-knit group whose members trusted one another with their secrets, and she wasn't willing to do the same.

"Are they up for visitors?" Brice asked.

"Right now, Jayson is nursing. But as soon as he's done, I'm sure they'll be glad to see you." Angeline glanced around at the others in the room. "Maybe the rest should wait until later. Nel's pretty worn-out."

"You've been here all night," Cassie, Brice's mate, said with a friendly smile. "Why don't you go get some sleep?"

Good advice, especially since Angeline would need to come back later with Tristan's mother and aunt.

"Come on, Angel." Lincoln helped Angeline into her coat then whispered in her ear. "Let's get you home."

His presence made her feel all snugly. She did want to go home and go to sleep. The problem was she wanted Lincoln warming the spot next to her.

Chapter 22

Sweat glistening on his skin, Lincoln finished the last rep in his final set on the bench press and racked the bar. He performed a series of deep breathing exercises before sitting up and checking the time.

In the three hours he'd been working out at the Walker's Run Resort gym, he still had not figured out how to break the news to Angeline that he was returning to temporary active duty and that he would come back with custody of an eight-year-old boy.

She'd fallen asleep in the truck as they'd left the hospital. He'd hated having to wake her upon parking at the apartment building, but carrying her up three flights of stairs wasn't a smart idea. He hadn't practiced carrying more than seventy-five pounds going up and down steps and wouldn't risk stumbling with her in his arms.

Lincoln had walked Angeline to her door and made her promise to get some rest. Later, they'd have dinner and he would tell her everything and do his best to put her mind at ease.

"Quitting time already?" Zach Taylor racked his bar and sat up. Since announcing his recruitment, he'd joined Lincoln for daily training sessions in the hope of getting a jump start on his physical readiness.

It would take a while before Zach could handle the weight Lincoln did, but the new recruit would be able to hold his own during Basic.

"Yeah, we're good. You want to push your endurance, but not to the point of exhaustion or injury." Lincoln grabbed his hand towel and patted down his face, arms and bare chest.

Zach did the same. "Thanks for taking me seriously from the start. You're the only one who ever did."

"How are your mom and dad coping?" Angeline seemed to have come to terms with her cousin's decision, but most parents had a difficult time accepting that they were losing their child to the Program.

"They say they're proud of me," he said. "I know they're scared. But I told them that just because I got accepted into Basic doesn't mean I won't wash out before the end of the program."

True. A lot of recruits wanted to be Dogmen. Few had the tenacity and fortitude to endure the grueling training to the end.

"Washing out isn't a bad thing." Lincoln shoved his arms into the sleeves, then stuck his head through the neck of his sweatshirt. "It means your heart is somewhere else and you need to figure out where it is."

Zach pulled on his long-sleeved T-shirt. "I know exactly where mine is."

Lincoln knew where his heart was, too. With the ones he wanted to call family.

Zach's phone pinged and he dug the device out of his duffel bag. "Shane wants to grab an early dinner at Taylor's. Want to join us?"

"Thanks, but no."

"I'm in good with the owner." Zach grinned. "I can get ya a free meal."

"I have plans. Another time?"

"You got it." He stood, hooking the strap of his duffel over his shoulder.

Lincoln swiveled on the bench, swinging his good leg to the same side as his artificial one. He dropped his hand towel into his duffel and slung the bag over his shoulder as he stood.

"Come on, pup." Lincoln used a friendly tone. "I'll walk you out."

"I'm not a pup." Zach gave him a cross look.

"You're gonna get called that a lot. Get used to it."

They walked out of the resort gym and took the stairs up to the lobby.

"It's amazing," Zach said. "If I didn't know you, I'd never suspect that you have an artificial leg. It's not noticeable at all."

"I notice it." The stump sleeve and cup felt nothing like his real leg and he was keenly aware of each prosthetic step.

"What's it like? To lose a limb?" Zach gave him an honest, open look.

Awkward. Frustrating. Humbling.

"Life-changing." And in more ways than the obvious physical and emotion ramifications of adapting to having only one leg. Because of the injury, he'd been invited to Walker's Run. Although he'd searched for Angeline after Tanner's death, Lincoln likely never would've met her otherwise. "It helped me find a whole new world to explore."

They crossed the lobby and exited near the valet station. Lincoln greeted the car jockeys, recognizing two of them as sentinels who were at the bar a few nights ago.

"I have classes tomorrow," Zach said as they walked between two of the waiting vehicles. "But I'm out at three. Want to meet me here around four?"

Waiting on the median separating the incoming traffic from the outgoing traffic, Lincoln watched a car leaving the self-park lot and drive past them.

"Sounds like a—"

Boom!

Suddenly, Lincoln was standing on the second floor of that abandoned building in Somalia. Bits of glass and plaster and wood flew all around him in slow motion.

"Lila!" He yelled for his second-in-command, his voice loud, clear and panicked. But that was impossible because in his wolf form he couldn't speak.

His nostrils stung from the spontaneous fire and he could barely breathe because billows of black smoke gobbled up the oxygen. Sensing the percussive wave coming, he scrambled to latch onto something that would keep him from being swept out the window.

Heart pounding, he struggled against the invisible force grabbing and snatching at his chest. He had to get to Lila. Had to save her.

The more he fought to stay upright, the heavier his arms and legs became. He called desperately for Lila, praying she would answer, even though his training had taught him that no one survived an explosion at the point of origin.

Each gasp drew more of the thick black smoke into his lungs. He coughed, trying to get a clear breath. He felt himself slipping.

No! He would not go through that damn window. Not again.

* * *

"How is he?"

At the sound of Tristan's voice, Angeline turned from the hospital room window and smiled at him in the doorway.

"You should be with Nel."

"She wanted me to check on you and him. I wanted to, too." Hands in his pockets, he stepped into the room. "Brice and Cassie are with Nel and the baby. If she needs anything, they'll take care of her until I get back to the room."

"They just left here." Still hugging herself, Angeline sank into the chair beside the hospital bed.

"Brice said Lincoln had some sort of episode at the resort."

"Doc called it a traumatic flashback." She glanced at Lincoln, sleeping peacefully now, but it had taken a high dose of sedatives to calm him down. "Zach was with him. One of the resort guests drove by them in a car with a cherry-bomb exhaust and intentionally made it backfire. Apparently, it sounded like an explosion."

Angeline rubbed her shoulders. "Zach said Lincoln suddenly blanked out for second and then started yelling and turning around. The sentinels tried to help, but ended up having to take him down.

"Before they did, Lincoln had broken one man's nose and cracked another's ribs." She took a deep breath. "He could've killed them."

"But he didn't. And this isn't his fault."

"I know." She nodded.

"Why don't you grab a bite to eat in the cafeteria? I'll stay with him."

"I'm not hungry." If she tried to eat now, it would sit in her stomach like a rock. "Besides, Lincoln gets restless if I move too far from him."

"It's good he knows you're here."

"Will this keep him from joining the pack?" Brice had assured Angeline that it wouldn't, but she had a constant nagging in her gut that wouldn't go away. "What if Gavin thinks he's a danger to the pack?"

"No one thinks Lincoln is a threat," Tristan said. "I'm sure Doc is doing everything he can to help Lincoln."

"He is." Still, she couldn't help feeling that things were about to get worse. Like the universe had decided to play a sick joke on her because she'd fallen in love with another Dogman.

"I'm going to pick up some coffee from the cafeteria. Want some?"

"Sounds good."

"I won't be long," he said, heading out of the room.

"I'm not going anywhere." She reached between the bed rails and squeezed Lincoln's hand. He was still too sedated to respond.

Someone knocked at the door.

"Forget something?" She turned. "Oh! Damien."

"I came as soon as I heard. I was tagging along with some of the sentinels on patrol." He walked into the room and stood at the foot of the bed. "How is he?"

"Physically fine." His mental state had her worried. What if the episode had triggered some sort of psychosis and he couldn't find his way back to the real world?

"I guess you really are his guardian angel."

"What do you mean?"

"The picture of you he carries in his pocket. It goes everywhere he goes. He told us that you were his guardian angel and as long as you were with him, everything would be all right."

"What picture?"

"It's an old faded photo. I think you were sitting in a

café because you were holding a large foam coffee cup and there's a pastry on the plate in front of you."

"It couldn't be me. I didn't know Lincoln before he came to Walker's Run."

"Oh, it's you." Damien tucked his hands into his pockets. "If the team was here, they'd all agree."

"Your Dogman team?"

"Yep. In fact, a couple of times when we were pinned down by hostile fire, the lieutenant would ask Cap if his angel was still in his pocket." Damien laughed. "We did all kinds of crazy shit. Sometimes one of us caught a bullet or two, or some shrapnel, but nothing too serious. Until—" he shrugged "—the explosion."

It didn't make sense. "Where would Lincoln get an old picture of me?"

"Off a dead guy is what I heard."

Angeline's heart froze, but her stomach churned nauseous waves. The man couldn't have been Tanner. What were the odds?

Why hadn't Lincoln told her? About the picture? About the man?

"How long is he going to be out?" Damien tapped the bottom of Lincoln's foot.

Lincoln showed no sign of waking up.

"He'll probably sleep through the night." At least, that was what Doc had said.

"I'm going to meet up with some of the sentinels for dinner. I'll check on him later."

Damien nodded his goodbye and Angeline was glad for him to leave. She'd always felt a sense of unease around him and he hadn't earned any brownie points with his revelation.

Quietly, she closed the door and then searched through Lincoln's things. She found no photo in his pants' pockets or duffel bag, so she opened his wallet. Three photos were stuffed in the card slots.

One was of an adorable little boy with a short crop of Afro-textured hair. His face radiated with pure joy as Lincoln, kneeling on one knee, gave him a tight hug. One of the sweetest things Angeline had ever seen, the tender moment tugged at her heart.

Dogmen did not claim mates while in the Program, so the child obviously could not be Lincoln's biological son. But even in the photo, Angeline could see the two were bonded. It must've broken Lincoln's heart to have left him behind. It broke hers just thinking about it.

The second photo was a group picture of Lincoln and five others standing in front of a tank. All were dressed in camouflage pants and T-shirts, wearing mirrored sunglasses, bulletproof vests and holding assault rifles. His team. As in the photo with the boy, Angeline could see the bond between the soldiers.

She didn't see Damien in the group, but Lincoln stood next to a woman with his arm casually draped across her shoulder. *Lila?*

More petite and not at all how Angeline had pictured her, the woman had to be Lila. Lincoln had mentioned she had been his best friend. And according to Zach, she had been the one Lincoln had called out for several times during his traumatic flashback.

Jealousy nipped at Angeline's heart but she ignored the feeling in favor of the empathy she had for Lincoln losing two important people in his life.

Removing the third photo, Angeline dropped the wallet. Her hand flew to her mouth to silence the gasps.

Tanner had taken the snapshot on their first date at the café on campus.

Tears stung her eyes. She'd assumed when Tanner had left her for the Program that he'd gotten rid of any reminders of her and the time they'd spent together. But if Damien was right and Lincoln had taken the photo from a dead man, then he must've been with Tanner when he died.

Heart hurting, she walked to Lincoln's bedside. "Why didn't you tell me?"

Whatever his reason to hide the truth, when he woke up, Angeline expected answers.

Chapter 23

Suddenly awake, Lincoln tried to get a bearing on his surroundings. The smell of antiseptic lingered in the air. A droning beep behind him and to the right sounded at regular intervals. He lay in some sort of bed, covered in a white sheet. Window blinds were closed but a soft light lit the room.

He tried to sit up, but something held him down. "What the hell?"

"Glad to see you're awake." A voice drifted from the dark corner.

"Brice? What's going on?" Lincoln forcibly blinked to sharpen his vision.

Brice stepped forward. "How are you feeling?"

A bit panicked at the moment. "Why am I tied down? What's going on?"

"Easy. You were combative when they brought you in." Brice placed a calming hand on Lincoln's shoulder. "Do you remember what happened yesterday?"

"Yesterday is relative." Lincoln tried to force the fog from his brain. "What day is today?"

"Friday." Brice worked his way around the bed, unfastening the restraints.

"I remember leaving the hospital with Angeline after Tristan's baby was born. Oh, God. Did we get into an accident?" Lincoln's stomach clenched and he struggled to sit up. "Where's Angeline?"

"She's fine. Cassie took her to the cafeteria."

"What happened? Why am I here?"

"Doc thinks you suffered a traumatic flashback. Do you remember being at the resort with Zach yesterday?"

Lincoln concentrated on mentally retracing his steps, but nothing came into focus. "I'm blank after Angeline and I left here. How did this happen?"

"A car with a modified muffler backfired as you and Zach were leaving the resort. Zach said you stopped talking in the middle of a sentence and had a faraway look. When he touched you, suddenly you began yelling for someone name Lila. The sentinels had to subdue you."

Lincoln's gut fisted. "Did I hurt anyone?"

"A broken nose and some cracked ribs, but the guys are not too sore about it. They can claim bragging rights with those injuries."

The sentinels might not be too upset, but the news thoroughly horrified Lincoln. "I must've been acting out my nightmare and didn't see them as a threat."

"Has this ever happened?"

"I have nightmares most nights, but never acted on one while awake." A flashback like that could screw up everything. "Yesterday, I got the call from my CO. They want me back at HQ and are putting me on a flight from Atlanta Saturday evening.

"They found Dayax in a rebel camp. He's being held with about a dozen other kids, and he isn't the only wolfling the insurgents grabbed. HQ wants me to go in with ground forces for hostage extraction. If they find out about this flashback, they could scrap me from the mission."

"Doc wants a psychologist to see you. If she says you're okay, then our lips are sealed. But if she thinks you're unstable, there's no way I'm letting you board a plane to HQ alone."

"I'm not unstable." Lincoln felt fine, except for his dislike of hospitals and the worry beading in his gut because he hadn't had time to tell Angeline that he had to leave. "If it makes you feel better, I'm sure Damien wouldn't mind flying back with me."

"About Damien." The grim line of Brice's mouth made an unhappy curl downward.

"Has the pup done something wrong?" Young Dogmen were often brash, egotistical and a little bullish at times.

"Did he mention to you that he suffered a traumatic brain injury in the explosion in Somalia?"

"He mentioned smacking his head but didn't say anything to me about a brain injury. How bad is it?"

"I don't know the specifics, but my understanding is that his neuropsychological evaluation revealed some significant concerns. He was suspended from active duty, pending further evaluation."

Damien had told Lincoln that after his med leave expired, he would be deployed with a new team. But he hadn't mentioned how long that leave would be. "When is his next eval?"

"There isn't one." Brice's gaze seemed to inspect every inch of Lincoln's face and Lincoln wondered if Brice was looking for signs of instability in him. "Damien suffered a violent breakdown when HQ advised him of the medical suspension from active duty. Once he stabilized, he was discharged from the Program."

Lincoln sucked in his breath as if he'd been punched in the gut. Dogmen lived and breathed the Program. Getting tossed out was a fate worse than death.

He'd gone through significant denial and anger upon learning of his own medical discharge. But Lincoln had found Angeline. No longer resentful, he looked forward to his discharge and starting a new life.

"Damien hasn't mentioned any of this to me. How long have you known?"

"Councilman Bartolomew called this morning. He'd heard that two Dogmen were here and wanted to confirm that Damien had come here to see you.

"He also knew Dayax had been found. Before the Woelfesenat started the paperwork to get the wolfling out of Somalia, he wanted to know if Walker's Run would accept a refugee into the pack, even if something happened to you on the mission."

Lincoln's heartbeat paused and he didn't dare to breathe.

"Of course we will. We would never turn away a child." Brice offered a small smile. "My best friend was an orphan from another pack and he's become an invaluable member of Walker's Run. I'm sure Dayax will, too."

The air in Lincoln's lungs rushed out. "I plan to be on that return plane with him."

"I have no doubt about that." Brice's grim expression returned. "What concerns me is Damien."

"You thought I knew?"

Brice nodded. "It would almost be better if you did, although I would've been disappointed that you kept the information from me."

"I only keep secrets that I'm required to by the Program. That would not have been one of them." Except he hadn't told Angeline of his plans.

Tonight, he would, although it would be a watered-

down version because he did not want to cause her unnecessary worry.

"Good to know." Some of the strain in Brice's expression eased. "Is Damien wanting to settle in Walker's Run?"

"Honestly, I don't know. He showed up, said he had
nowhere to go and wanted to stay with me until his deployment."

"It's my understanding that Damien needs ongoing
treatment. If he wants to remain in Walker's Run, he'll
be required to be compliant with the Program's recommendations. Neither my father nor I will put the pack or
our human neighbors at risk."

"I'll talk to him." Lincoln didn't want anyone to get
hurt, either.

"I trust that you will." Brice's demeanor became less
formal and his expression turned friendly.

Lincoln had seen the same transformation in Romania
when Brice had switched modes between a hard-hitting
negotiator dealing with hostile, warring Alphas and an
easygoing nightly campfire companion telling Lincoln
stories of Walker's Run. Stories that had made his heart
ache for a home and family of his own.

"I noticed that you and Angeline have become quite
close. Does she know of your plans to return to Somalia?"

"I told her that I have some things to wrap up before
my retirement is finalized."

Bound by a mate-bond, he had faith she would understand. Once Lincoln returned with Dayax, he would claim
Angeline as his mate and they would become the family
he'd always wanted.

A simple plan, really. What could go wrong?

Lifting a cup of fresh coffee to her lips, Angeline inhaled the robust aroma and forced herself to relax as the
rich, bold flavor laced with hazelnut slid down her throat.

She glanced at the digital clock on the wall behind the registration desk in the waiting room.

Ten forty-five.

Great! She'd been waiting an entire fifteen minutes. The psychologist said she'd be with Lincoln for at least an hour.

Between having breakfast with Cassie in the cafeteria and the nurse kicking her out of the room for Lincoln's psych consult, Angeline had barely had five minutes alone with Lincoln since he'd woken up this morning. Maybe it was for the best. The hospital wasn't the place for the conversation they needed to have.

Reaching for her purse, Angeline fumbled through the contents for her phone then dialed Miriam's number.

"Good morning, dear," her aunt answered on the first ring. "How's Lincoln?"

"Awake and alert." Angeline slouched in the chair. "He's with a specialist now. If all goes well, Lincoln will come home today."

"A specialist? That sounds serious."

"Just a precaution." At least, that was how Doc had explained it.

"And how are you?"

"Better now that Lincoln is awake."

"If you need tonight off, I'll call Ginger to come in."

"That won't be necessary," Angeline said. "She covered for me when I left early on Valentine's Day. I'm not going to ask her to give up another Friday night." If Lincoln came home, he'd need to rest. If he didn't, Angeline would need to keep herself busy.

"Jimmy and I don't need to be at the restaurant for a while. Do you want us to come to the hospital and wait with you?"

"No." She glared at the clock's red LED display, announcing the time as ten fifty. When had a morning ever passed more slowly? "How's Zach?"

"He's fine. A little shaken to have had a front-row view of a Dogman's meltdown."

"Lincoln didn't have a meltdown," Angeline said defensively. "He suffered a traumatic flashback and relived the most horrific moment of his life. He didn't lose just his leg in the explosion, he also lost his best friend."

"I didn't mean to upset you, dear."

"I know. I'm just edgy."

"Everything will work out." Always positive, Miriam truly believed her mantra.

Life had taught Angeline that although everything eventually did work itself out, it wasn't always the way she expected.

"I'll see you at Taylor's later."

After her aunt said goodbye, Angeline pulled up Solitaire on her phone. Though not particularly challenging, the card game allowed her mind to vegetate rather than race.

When the nurse called her name, more than an hour had passed.

"Yes?" Angeline put away the phone.

"Lincoln is asking for you." Carmen smiled pleasantly.

"Thanks." Angeline tossed her empty coffee cup into the nearest garbage can.

"I bet it's exciting," Carmen said, grinning. "Dating a Dogman."

"To me, he's just Lincoln." Angeline had once imagined Dogmen as narcissistic, coldhearted bastards but being with Lincoln had helped her see past her own prejudice.

"Aww." Carmen laid her hand over her heart. "That is so sweet."

"I'm gonna go check on him." Angeline collected her

jacket and purse then walked down the corridor to Lincoln's room.

The door was partially closed, so she knocked before easing into the room.

"Hey, Angel." Lincoln's smile warmed her inside and out. "Come to break me out of this place?"

"That depends on whether or not you've been cleared for discharge," she said, watching him put on his prosthetic leg.

"Where's your sense of adventure?" He winked. "Mind handing me my pants?"

Angeline doubted he would be in a playful mood if the doctors had wanted to keep him longer for observation.

She retrieved his clothes from the small corner closet and laid them on the bed. "Mind telling me what the psychologist said?"

Lincoln put on his jeans. "I'm okay, but she wants me to get counseling to help me cope with what happened."

"Do you plan to follow through?"

Lincoln shoved his arms down the sleeves of a black sweatshirt, poked his head through the neck and tugged it down over his scarred, muscular chest. "I agreed to a few sessions because I don't want to snap and hurt you or anyone else."

Angeline's heart melted. She hadn't expected him to admit that counseling might be beneficial. Her father and brothers would've flat out refused.

Lincoln closed the distance between them, then drew her into his arms and held her snugly against his chest. Although warm and safe in his embrace, she sensed a cold chasm emerging between them. One she hoped to close once she learned the meaning of the photo.

After the nurse brought by the discharge papers, Lincoln held Angeline's hand as they left the hospital.

He seemed his regular self, yet Angeline knew he was keeping secrets.

A Dogman and their missions were often top secret. Those secrets, she wouldn't demand to know. But the one concerning *her*...absolutely.

They made a quick stop to pick up sandwiches for lunch before returning to the apartment. Lincoln blocked the wind nipping at her back as she unlocked the door and hustled inside. Dropping the sandwich bag on the coffee table, she shucked off her coat and tossed it onto the sofa chair before plopping on the couch.

Lincoln took his time removing his coat and laid it carefully across the back of the couch. His movements were always deliberate, as if he had mentally calculated every possible move and chosen the most direct and efficient one to employ. She appreciated that he wasn't reactive or impulsive. Simply strong, steady. Solid.

Still, he kept secrets and, if they were going to be mates, Angeline needed to know that she could trust him and show that he could trust her.

"Lincoln, there's something I need to tell you."

He met her gaze and worry troubled his eyes. "Same here, Angel."

"Damien told me about the old photograph of me and I went through your wallet to find it."

Lincoln sat next to her, then curled his fingers around her hand.

"Tanner took that picture on our first date. How did you get it?"

"He gave it to me," Lincoln said quietly. "Right before he died."

"You were with him?" Tears stung Angeline's eyes, and a caustic knot rose in her throat.

"Yes."

Suddenly, Angeline felt as if all the strength had drained

from her body. Although sitting, she swayed from the dizzying assault.

Lincoln pulled her close, tucking her beneath his arm, and she rested her cheek on his shoulder.

"My first deployment," Lincoln began, "the team I was on got sent overseas to replace Tanner's team. There was an overlap so they could bring us up to speed on the protocols and mission plans. We were doing a ride-along with the human forces when Tanner's Humvee ran over an IED. The convoy took heavy fire. By the time I reached him, there was nothing I could do."

"Was he in a lot of pain?" The words were barely a whisper because her throat had tightened.

"No," Lincoln said after a pause. "He was clutching your picture and told me if he had a second chance, he'd choose you."

Angeline wanted to cry, but so many tears had already been shed that no more were left to fall. All this time she'd believed that Tanner had abandoned her without a second thought. Knowing he hadn't filled her with a genuine sense of peace.

Lincoln took out his wallet and gave Angeline the picture. "I asked HQ to find you, but no one from Tanner's pack knew you."

"He was in his senior year in college when we started dating. I never met his family or pack." Angeline turned the photo over. On the back, Tanner had written her name, but over time the ink had worn off and only the first few letters—Angel—were readable.

"I couldn't bring myself to throw away an angel, so I've kept her with me ever since. Sometimes, knowing that one day I had to find this woman is what kept me going." Lincoln stared hard at the picture in her hands and she knew it was much more than a photo to him.

"I want you to keep it." She handed him the photo. "For good luck."

"She certainly is." Lincoln's finger lightly traced the woman in the picture. His gaze lifted to Angeline. "But you are so much more to me."

Cupping Angeline's face, Lincoln pressed his lips against her mouth and kissed her so sweetly, her heart ached because in that moment she absolutely knew that Lincoln was already planning to leave.

Chapter 24

"Do you want to talk about what's bothering you?" Lincoln asked, watching Angeline shove her barely touched sandwich into the refrigerator. He couldn't pinpoint exactly when her mood shifted but it had definitely worsened during lunch.

"You're leaving. I can feel the inevitability of it coming much sooner than later." Uncertainty shimmering in her eyes, she flattened her hands on the kitchen counter. "How much time do we have?"

Lincoln's lunch suddenly felt like lead in his stomach. He'd wanted to break the news to her gently and with a lot of reassurances. Instead, he'd have to blurt it all out and hope for the best.

"I'm waiting for HQ to finalize the return flight to Munich. I expect it will be sometime Saturday evening."

"I see." She tensed, her muscles tightening to the point of rigidity.

"I don't think you do." He gathered the paper his sandwich had been wrapped in and his empty glass, then joined her in the kitchen. "I mentioned there are a few things I have to take care of before my retirement papers were processed."

"Is your retirement a lie?" She didn't meet his gaze.

"No." Lincoln placed his glass in the sink, disposed of the trash, then took the picture of Dayax out of his wallet and handed it Angeline. "I promised this little wolfling that when I left Somalia, I would take him with me. His parents were killed and his pack can't support him."

Tears filled Angeline's eyes as she traced the boy's outline in the photo, and a lump formed in Lincoln's throat.

"My final orders are to give him a home." His voice cracked. "Brice has been helping me with the adoption paperwork, but I have to be the one to go get him."

"What's his name?" Angeline's voice was barely a whisper.

"Dayax."

"Why didn't you tell me that you're going to be a dad?"

"I wasn't sure how you would feel about the situation." Lincoln's heart began to race. "Because if you accept me as your mate, then you become—"

"A mom!" Angeline slipped her arms around his neck and silently sighed against his body. Her essence touched his and he could feel the happiness bubbling inside her.

The tension balled in Lincoln's stomach eased. "Once HQ gets everything arranged, I'll pick up Dayax, sign a lot of paperwork and then we're flying home." An oversimplification of the truth, but he didn't want Angeline worrying. If her fears leaked into their strengthening mate-bond, he wouldn't be able to concentrate on the mission.

"So it's not dangerous?"

"No." Lincoln would swear to the lie as many times as it took for her to believe it.

He'd spent years holding on to her photo. Now that he'd

found the real woman, nothing would keep him from returning to her.

"Can I call you?" she asked.

"No, it's against regulations. Everything will be fine, Angel. I promise." So much had happened in such a short time, Lincoln looked forward to things slowing down once he officially retired. "We should get some rest."

Angeline's brow arched in a beautifully delicate curve. "By rest, you mean—"

"Rest," he said, despite his body's instant response to her unspoken suggestion.

"I don't want to sleep away what little time we have."

"We have a lifetime ahead of us." He hoped.

"Fine!" She clutched his hand and led him to the couch. "Take off your pants."

"Angeline." He growled soft and low, but it didn't have quite the warning he'd intended and didn't stop her nimble fingers from unfastening his belt.

Playfully, she tugged his zipper. "If you want me to stop…" Her beautiful blue eyes slowly gazed up at him. "Just say so."

An impossible feat considering his mouth had gone dry and his tongue felt so thick that forming the word seemed an impossible task, even for a Dogman.

Holding his gaze, she inched down his zipper, taking nearly an eternity to open the fly. A sexy smile widened her luscious mouth a second before her hand cupped his sack and lightly squeezed.

Already hard, his shaft strained against his boxers and his inner wolf prowled anxiously, eager to claim his mate. Lincoln drew a deep, deliberate breath into his lungs. There could be no claiming today. Otherwise he'd never be able to leave her and do what needed to be done to get Dayax back.

She stroked his shaft through his clothes. "Last chance

to say no." As she dragged out the last word, a very clear picture of her soft-looking lips taking him into her mouth formed in his mind. His entire body primed to receive the laving attention the vision promised.

If she wasn't a she-wolf, he might've expected to hear her purr as she slid his pants and boxers over his hips and down his legs. Instead, a possessive, feminine growl rumbled softly in her throat.

Oh, boy!

Slowly, Lincoln sat on the couch and clasped the prosthetic.

"You don't have to take that off," she said softly.

"I want to be comfortable and this—" he tapped the stump cup "—will only get in the way."

Angeline perched on the coffee table, giving him seductive smiles and searing glances as he removed the prosthetic and took off his other shoe.

"Mmm." Her gaze warmed his groin before lifting to his face. "Lose the top, too. I want you completely naked."

She didn't need to ask twice. Yanking the sweatshirt over his head, he dropped it behind the couch.

"Now, you." Lincoln cradle his sack with one hand and slowly stroked his shaft with the other.

Employing the same torturous speed she used to bring down his zipper, she unzipped her boots and tossed them aside.

Lincoln groaned. He'd never make it through the strip-tease.

After the second boot came off, she took her time inching up her sweater before pulling it off to reveal the lacy bra hugging her creamy breasts. Lincoln squeezed the base of his shaft, stalling the orgasm clamoring for release.

"Angeline." The menace in his growl warned that his control was waning.

She gave him a perfectly innocent look as she slowly

pushed down her leggings. Not once did she break eye contact. Stepping out of the leggings, she moved directly in front of Lincoln.

"I need a little help with the rest," she said, all breathy and sexy. She turned around and wiggled her lace-clad backside.

Lincoln grasped her waist and pulled her into his lap.

Startled, she let out a small gasp. Instead of pulling away, she relaxed against him.

His hands glided over her smooth abdomen and his fingers toyed with the waistband of her panties before delving beneath the lace to find her wet and wanting.

"Mmm." She arched and rocked her hips to match the rhythm of his strokes through her folds.

Lincoln smiled against her cheek then nosed her hair aside to pepper her jaw with wet kisses. The slightly salty taste of her skin made him hunger for so much more.

Dipping his finger into her opening caused her to quiver. She was close, so close, to ecstasy because of his touch. He wouldn't disappoint her.

Teasingly, he slipped two fingers inside her, alternating the rhythm of each stroke. She writhed against him, moaning incomprehensible words that grew louder and louder until her inner walls began to spasm and her body trembled.

Closing his eyes, Lincoln breathed in her scent, allowing her essence to invade to the depths of his soul. Never had he hoped to find such deep and utter contentment. Even becoming a Dogman hadn't filled him the way she did.

He belonged here with her, he knew that to the marrow of his being. Once he returned with Dayax, they would be a family and nothing would ever separate them again.

Limp as a wet noodle, Angeline forced her eyes to open. Lincoln's soft, rhythmic breathing replaced the hum in her ears. And his strong, muscled arms caged her in a way that made her feel safe and treasured.

"Wow," she sighed. "I needed that."

"I know you did, Angel." Lincoln's words whispered across her ear. Gently nuzzling her neck, he retraced the kisses he'd placed earlier.

She tilted her head, granting more access to his warm lips. Every touch, caress, stroke and kiss, she committed to memory. As much as she wanted to believe Lincoln would come back to her, part of her feared he wouldn't.

Blinking back unbidden tears, she pushed open his arms and stood in front of him. His gaze freely roamed her body, branding her skin along every inch where it lingered. When he lifted his face to hers, she slowly removed her bra and panties, then returned to straddle his lap.

Needing to be close to him for as long as possible, she held his face between her hands and kissed him deeply, drawing in his essence in the hope he would become a very present part of her soul. She probed the depths of his mouth, wanting to brand his taste on her tongue.

His rough but gentle hands kneaded her buttocks as he took control of the kiss, laying claim to every inch of her mouth before abruptly breaking away. Pulling her closer, he lifted her so that her breasts were but a hairbreadth from his face.

He flashed a wicked grin then blew a breath across her skin. Anticipatory chills ran down her spine and her nipples tightened into rosy buds. In an erotic game, he sucked one peak into his warm, wet mouth, flicked his tongue against the nipple until she squirmed and slowly released it with a noisy pop, only to do the same to the other one.

Angeline drove her fingers through Lincoln's thick black hair, clutching him to her chest. All the while, his hands roamed her body, warming, teasing, possessing. Claiming her with his touch.

No one had ever turned her into a quivering ball of need and want the way he did. She could think of nothing else but joining with him. Merging completely.

His hands caressed her shoulders then slid down her back until they fastened around her waist to lower her until they were face-to-face again. When he looked into her eyes, she felt the masculine touch of his essence fill her soul.

Trailing her hand down his muscled chest, she felt the warmth of his skin, the beat of his heart and the tremble of desire the closer she came to his groin. Dark and angry-looking, his erect shaft strained toward her open legs.

Gently molding her hand around the base, she rubbed the tip through her folds before guiding him inside her, inch by glorious inch, until he filled her completely.

His groan rolled into a possessive growl. One hand pressed against her lower back while the other snaked up her spine and cupped her neck. She clung to him as his hips lifted with each thrust and hers rocked in tandem.

Earlier, his fingers had teased her to the brink of ecstasy and kept her hovering there until she'd thought she might go mad with need before finally succumbing to orgasmic release. Now, there was no playful torment. Only a hard, fast pace, driving her onward until she shattered.

Ribbons of color dazzled her mind. Lost in the overwhelming sensation of wave upon wave of pleasure pulsing through her body, she would've drifted into oblivion if not for Lincoln's essence tethering her to him.

Groaning with his release, Lincoln tightened his steely arms around her as his hips stilled. His pants synced with hers and gradually eased to soft, even breaths.

"Still with me, Angel?" he said in a hoarse whisper.

"Uh-huh," was all she could manage to return.

He smiled smugly and she could almost hear him congratulate himself on giving her a bone-melting orgasm.

"Two." His voice whispered through her mind, a manifestation of their deepening mate-bond. *"I gave you two bone-melting orgasms."*

"I was faking," she answered in kind.

Lincoln laughed out loud. Deep, rich, satisfyingly male. And she loved every arrogant note.

Closing her eyes, she squeezed him tightly, knowing that soon they would say goodbye. "I don't want this to end."

"It won't, Angel." His deep, masculine voice was a soothing whisper.

Knees beginning to ache, she eased off his lap.

He clasped her hand before she had a chance to stand. "Lie with me for a while."

In his eyes, she saw that he wanted her as close as possible for as long as possible. Despite the affirmations that his trip to pick up Dayax would not be a long one, she saw a flicker of doubt.

He stretched out on the couch, turned onto his right side and hooked his arm beneath the sofa pillow. Then he urged Angeline to lie on her right side and snuggle into him. Once she settled, he rested his stump against her thigh and pulled the sofa blanket over them.

"This is nice." She relaxed in the heat of their bodies and the ebb and flow of their mingling essences.

Lincoln didn't say anything but she could feel him smile against her head. Angeline also sensed his thoughts turn inward, so she reached for the remote, turned on the television and lowered the volume. After flipping through the channels, she stopped on a home and family talk show.

A few minutes later, Angeline yawned. The lack of sleep over the last couple of days had caught up to her. She closed her eyes, waiting for the commercials to end.

"Hey." Lincoln nudged her.

Angeline glanced at the clock. Nearly three thirty. "Oh, no. I have to get ready for work."

She sat up and Lincoln caught her hand.

"I saw a commercial for the Academy of Country Music Awards. Is your song nominated?"

"Two are. Why?"

"You should tell your family and accept the award in person."

"Um, no." Angeline reached down to pick up her clothes. "There's no guarantee that my songs will win. Even if one did, my father and brothers would not be impressed."

"I am," Lincoln said quietly. "I'm proud of you and your talent. Your family deserves a chance to be proud, too."

Angeline kissed Lincoln lightly on the lips. "You're sweet to think so, but my dad won't be impressed."

"What about Miriam and Jimmy?"

"They don't need to know, either." Not sharing the musical side of her life with them tweaked Angeline's heart, but she couldn't tell them because it would be too hard to keep the news from her father and brothers. She was better off keeping that secret. Besides, her aunt and uncle would insist she quit working at Taylor's, and they needed her.

"I'm happy with the way things are."

No, not really. But the secret had gone on so long that to let it out now might do more harm than good.

Chapter 25

"¿Dónde has estado?" Lincoln used the remote to turn off the television. He'd been texting Damien to call or come home ever since Angeline had left for work.

"No estamos en servicio activo." Damien closed the front door. "I don't have to report to you."

"I'm an officer. And active duty or not, you would report to me if you were still a Dogman."

Damien's face reddened and the jagged scar along his cheek turned a blackish-purple. "Don't get all high and mighty. You're on your way out of the Program, too."

"Not yet."

"Oh, Somalia." Damien waggled his hands. "Do you really think the Program is going to put you in a hot zone? They're jerking you around, man."

"I'm headed to Munich tomorrow night. My orders say I'm going back to Somalia."

"Who at HQ fucked up?" Damien dropped into the living room chair. "You're missing a goddamn leg!"

"This one works fine." Lincoln tapped his knuckles against the stump cup.

"You're going back for that kid, aren't you?"

"I won't leave him behind."

The muscles in Damien's jaw flexed. "How did you convince HQ to actually put you back in?"

"Brice has connections to the Woelfesenat. And I asked him to put in a good word for me."

"He's got that much sway?"

"I guess someone on the Council owed him a favor." Lincoln knew Damien well enough to know the wheels were already turning in his mind. "Brice won't help you get reinstated."

"You know that for a fact, do you?"

"He's the one who told me that you were discharged and why."

"There's nothing wrong with me," Damien snarled. "They had no right to kick me out."

"You suffered a head injury and refused treatment. If you can't prove mental and physical fitness for duty, you get booted."

"HQ is letting you back in and you're missing a leg."

"I have to take the physical readiness test." Lincoln hoped the training he'd been doing would pay off. Otherwise he'd be sidelined and it would be a crapshoot as to whether or not Dayax trusted an unfamiliar extraction team enough to go with them rather than going wolf and running away. "I'm flying out of Atlanta tomorrow afternoon. I'd like you to come with me."

"For what?"

"HQ is better equipped to help you deal with your injuries."

"Then why didn't they fix my face?"

"I don't know. Maybe they would have if you'd undergone the psych treatment."

"My brain works fine. I'm not going to become one of their lab rats."

"So you'd rather leave the Program for good?"

"Yes." The flicker in Damien's eyes betrayed him.

"Why didn't you go home?"

"Yeah," he scoffed. "Going home a washout isn't high on my list of things to do this year."

"So you tracked me down for what? To reminisce about the good ol' days?"

"I thought—" Damien snapped his mouth shut and stared hard at Lincoln. "Doesn't matter now."

"You were looking for a place to fit in and, since I'm here, you thought Walker's Run might welcome you, too." Lincoln knew he'd guessed right by the surprised look on Damien's face. "They might, but if you want to stay, you'll have to get the counseling recommended by the Program."

"You're the one who had the meltdown yesterday." Damien shook his head. "Yet I'm the one who needs therapy."

"I met with a psychologist and I agreed to follow her recommendations because I don't want anyone to get hurt because of me."

"A little late for that, don't you think?" Damien snorted.

"Not a day goes by that I don't think about what happened. But I'm not entirely at fault. I gave a specific order. Lila, you and the rest of the team chose to ignore it. I can't undo my decision any more than you can undo yours."

Damien responded with silence.

"Once I return from Somalia, I'm retiring. I plan to make Walker's Run my home."

"Because of *her*?"

"If you're referring to Angeline, then yes."

"What is it about the she-wolf that has you so wrapped up in homesteading?"

"She's my true mate." From the moment Tanner had

given Lincoln the photograph, he unknowingly had been on a path leading him straight to her.

"And HQ thinks I'm the crazy one." Laughing harshly, Damien rolled his eyes. "You're a Dogman. How can you think of being anything but that?"

"Because after this mission, the Program doesn't want me and I've found someone who does." Not once in the last fifteen years did Lincoln have the courage to dream of a happy ending with the woman in the photo. To him, she had been as ethereal as an angel. And too good for the likes of him.

Then he'd met the real flesh-and-blood woman—strong, sassy and independent—and had fallen madly in love with her, not the photograph.

"What about me?" Damien's voice rose and bitterness laced his tone.

"Your whole life is ahead of you. You can go anywhere, do anything."

"The only thing I've ever wanted to be is a Dogman."

"Me, too." Lincoln's heart squeezed at the anguish in the young man's face.

"It isn't fair."

"No one ever said it was. But we're trained to adapt to any situation. This is no different, for either of us."

"So you're adapting by taking a mate and settling down?"

"Yeah."

"Lame, man. So lame. With your skills you could get contract work with any pack in the world."

"I'm settling in Walker's Run. It's time I learned a new set of skills." Such as how to be a good mate and father.

"Such a waste." Damien stood, his face twisted into a grotesque mask of disgust and despair. "I need some air."

"Hey," Lincoln called out before Damien reached the door, "I'm staying with Angeline tonight and leaving tomorrow afternoon. But Tristan doesn't mind if you squat here until you figure things out."

"Gee, thanks." Sarcasm weighted Damien's words.

"Walker's Run is a great place and you've made friends among the sentinels. Give some thought about staying. If you agree to follow a treatment plan, this could become your home, too. You could make a good life here."

Damien answered with a derisive snort and slight head shake. He left, closing the door with a quiet click, which unsettled Lincoln more than a resounding slam would have.

Lincoln started to go after Damien, but the kid had a lot to process and needed some space. If Lincoln had been sidelined so early in his career, he might not have reacted very well, either. Hopefully, Damien would see what lay before him as an opportunity rather than as a dead end. Because a Dogman with no options could quickly turn feral. And Lincoln didn't want to be forced into putting down one of his own.

I'm going to be a mother!

The roar of the Friday night crowd at Taylor's could not drown out that one singular thought in Angeline's mind.

Mixed emotions jumbled her nerves and caused her stomach to clench. She had no idea how to be a mother. Being a fantastic aunt was what she knew, and Angeline made a conscious effort to shower her nieces and nephews with as much love and attention as she could muster. But from her own experiences, she realized that an aunt was not the same as a mother. Miriam had been a strong and loving influence in Angeline's life and they had forged a close bond, but their relationship had never pinnacled that of a parent and child.

She wondered how the relationship between her and Dayax would evolve. Mother. Aunt. Or something else.

Regardless, she would do her best to help Lincoln raise him.

"Angeline!"

"Hmm?" She glanced at Avery, the bartender.

"Your drink order is ready." She pointed to the four tap beers and one specialty bottle on the bar.

"Thanks." Angeline began placing the drinks on the round tray in her hands.

"Are you okay?" Avery dropped ice cubes into two round glasses. "You haven't seemed yourself all night."

"I'm fine, just have a lot on my mind." With drink order in hand, Angeline squirmed through the swell of people around the bar and headed toward the tables.

"Here you go." She placed the glasses in front of the off-duty sentinels and the bottle in front of Reed. "Is Damien coming?"

Since his arrival, Damien seemed to have bonded with several of the sentinels who were close in age.

"He might come later," Shane said. "He's training with Zach."

"Why? Lincoln has been working with him." Angeline didn't like the idea of her younger cousin joining the Dogman program, but since he was dead-set on it, she trusted that Lincoln would help him prepare.

"Lincoln spazzed out. Zach got freaked. Can't say that I blame him," Shane said.

"Give Lincoln some slack," Reed snapped. "You have no idea what it's like to—" He sealed any further words behind firmly pressed lips, picked up his ale bottle and left the table.

The color in Shane's face faded and he stared hard at his glass. An awkward silence blanketed the table. Likely, they were all remembering that only a few months ago, Reed had faced his own mortality at the end of a poacher's shotgun. And he hadn't quite gotten over it yet.

"Shake it off, guys," Angeline said. "Lincoln and Reed need understanding, not pity. Besides, we all have things that get to us from time to time."

Lance, a newly deputized sentinel, raised a toast and the young men's spirits seemed to lift. Except for Shane, who picked up his glass and joined Reed at the bar.

"I'll check on you guys later." Angeline left to attend her other tables.

The rest of the evening went by in a blur, with the pace not slowing until closing.

Slumped in the booth she'd been cleaning, Angeline propped her feet on the opposite seat and closed her eyes, feeling like she could sleep for a week. Of course, she couldn't. Once she got home, she wanted to spend every waking second with Lincoln. Not that they had many left before he had to leave for Atlanta.

Though he promised not to be gone long, she had a nagging feeling things wouldn't go as smoothly as he predicted.

"Hon, why don't you go on home?" Jimmy squeezed her shoulder.

"I haven't finished cleaning my stations." She hid a yawn.

"We'll take care of it." Her uncle held out his hand to help her stand. "You all right to drive home?"

"I'm tired, not drunk. I just need some coffee."

"There might be a pot on in the kitchen." Jimmy picked up the cloth from the table and began wiping down the seats.

"Thanks." Angeline headed to the kitchen, swallowing the urge to ask for Saturday night off. She and Lincoln had discussed her accompanying him to the airport but he'd decided it would be too difficult to say goodbye at the terminal and preferred to make the near three-hour drive alone.

After pouring the last of the coffee into a large to-go cup, Angeline put on her coat, said good-night to the late-night staff, went out the back door and walked to her car. The chilly night air wasn't as cold as it had been last week, but it was still frosty enough for her to appreciate the car heater.

Sitting behind the steering wheel, she jabbed the key into the ignition and turned it, expecting the vehicle to roar to life. Sadly, it didn't.

She tried again and got the same result. "Damn battery."

At least she wasn't stranded. Jimmy and the others were still inside the restaurant.

Leaning across the middle console, she reached for her purse on the passenger side floorboard.

Rap, rap, rap!

A squeal accompanied Angeline's startled jump. Twisting in the seat, she saw Damien outside the car, his face peering in the window.

"Everything okay?"

Angeline took a calming breath. "The battery is dead."

"Want a lift?" Damien looked perfectly decent, but a creepy-crawly sensation rose from her clenched stomach. "I'm parked over there." He pointed to the car near the light.

"A jump would be better," she said. "I have cables in the trunk."

"I'll bring the car around." Damien jogged across the parking lot.

Guilt replaced the uneasy feeling she had. Damien had never actually done anything to warrant her distrust. Still, she remained inside, instead of climbing out to get the cables.

He parked in front of her vehicle and opened his hood. "Pop the trunk," he said, walking past her window.

Obediently, she pressed the button to unlock the trunk,

then pulled the lever to open the hood. Damien worked quietly and quickly. In only a few minutes he called out for her to crank the engine.

The car roared to life. Shortly afterward, he closed both hoods and returned the jumper cable to her trunk.

"I'll follow you out," he said, walking past her window without stopping.

"You really are a nice guy, Damien Marquez." Dismissing the annoying nag in her mind, Angeline waited for him to get into his car before backing out of the parking space and driving home.

Chapter 26

The first time Lincoln had knocked on Brice Walker's front door, his life had been in chaos. Now, only a few short weeks later, he knocked at the door again with a clear hope for the future.

He squeezed Angeline's hand, and she looked up at him. The fragile smile on her lips tugged his heart as much as the reticence in her eyes at attending a Saturday-morning brunch at the Alpha-in-waiting's home.

Brice opened the door. Almost immediately they were greeted with a high-pitched squeal and the fast patter of tiny feet headed toward them.

"Link-ed!" Arms wide-open, Brenna headed straight for him.

Brice swiped her up and gave her a stern look. "Manners."

"Puh-leez, comes in." Brenna waved her arm, motioning them inside the house.

Lincoln's hand gravitated to Angeline's lower back, guiding her to enter ahead of him.

Brenna tapped him on the shoulder and held out her arms with a happy grin on her slightly slobbery mouth. Brice handed her off and Lincoln held her in a tight hug.

"Good morning, Brenna."

Her chubby cheek pressed into his shoulder for barely a second before her attention turned to Angeline. "Who dat?"

"You don't remember me?" Angeline gave the child a playfully exaggerated frown and then pulled the knit cap off her head. "How about now, munchkin?"

"Ann-jeel!" Brenna clapped her hands and leaned toward Angeline to give her a kiss on the cheek.

"All right." Brice gently took his daughter from Lincoln and set her feet on the floor. "Go check on mama."

"Mmm, 'kay." The little girl darted down the hallway to hunt for her mother.

"She's growing so fast," Angeline said.

"Some days it's hard to believe she's almost two." Brice took their jackets and hung them on the coatrack inside his home office.

They followed him into the open living area, and the delicious smells of cinnamon rolls, ham and eggs made Lincoln's mouth water.

"Help yourself to some tea or coffee," Cassie said cheerfully, putting Brenna in her high chair.

"Juice?" Brenna lifted her sippy cup toward Angeline.

"Thanks, munchkin. But I'll stick with coffee." Angeline poured a cup for Lincoln and then one for herself.

"You two—" Cassie looked at Brice and Lincoln "—out!" She shooed her hands at them. Although the kitchen was large and open, with two wolfan males, two females and a child in a high chair, space was in short supply.

Lincoln hesitated long enough to see that Angeline had settled next to Brenna and the two of them were engaged in some imaginary game. A rush of pride caused his heart to swell. Not only would Angeline be a fine mate, she would be a terrific mother. Of that, he had no doubt.

Turning from the heartwarming domestic scene, he followed Brice into the living room. While Brice sat in the recliner without the footrest engaged, Lincoln chose the nearby love seat.

"Are you ready to go back on active duty?" Brice rested his right ankle on his left knee and massaged his calf.

"Yes," Lincoln said without hesitation.

"How about becoming a father?"

That made Lincoln's heart skip a beat or two. "I never imagined becoming a father, so I don't know if I'm ready. But I'll never rest easy if he's not in my care."

"Will you return to your birth pack to raise him?"

"They are good people, but there's a lot of pressure to be the absolute best. I want Dayax to have a more balanced upbringing." Lincoln glanced toward the kitchen. Watching Angeline play with Brenna while talking to Cassie filled him with a great sense of contentment.

"I've decided to bring him to Walker's Run and make a family with Angeline. I just need to figure out how to support them." Though he'd have a sizable pension, Lincoln wanted to be useful and productive.

"The Co-op's revenues pay for housing, health care, education and provides startup money for business ventures. Once you join the pack, all those benefits will extend to you and Dayax."

"I'm a Dogman. I don't know how to be anything else."

"Talk to Tristan about joining the sentinels."

"I'm not sure that would be a good idea. I think it could become problematic within the ranks, and I don't want my presence to undermine the chain of command already established." Neither did Lincoln want to start over in an omega position doing grunt work.

"Would you be interested in becoming a personal sentinel to the Alpha family?"

If Lincoln had been in his wolf form, his ears would've perked.

"A bodyguard?"

Brice nodded.

"Is one necessary? Or are you tossing me a pity bone?"

"My father thinks one is necessary and Cassie would feel better if someone we trusted traveled with me whenever I'm away from home." Brice folded his hands across his waist and tented his index fingers. "Our pack is on the cusp of a vulnerable transition. My father will retire in a few years. According to tradition, the Alpha's firstborn becomes the Alpha-in-waiting. Technically, I'm second-born, but my brother was killed a few years ago, leaving me to inherit the Alphaship."

Brice glanced over at Cassie then back at Lincoln. "Brenna is my firstborn and it's her birthright to succeed me. Even though we're decades away from her stepping into that role, some packs have already expressed concerns not only with her gender, but that her mother is human, as was her paternal great-grandmother."

Lincoln easily understood Brice's concerns. Less progressive packs were likely already positioning themselves to overtake the Walker's Run pack if the opportunity arose.

"To make matters even more interesting, Cassie is pregnant. If we have a son, we could face pressure from the Woelfesenat to put him forth as the Alpha heir."

"But you have friends on the Council."

"Not enough. Yet." Brice's expression remained neutral, but Lincoln had no doubts of the weight his friend carried on his shoulders. "We have no intention of usurping Brenna's birthright. Nor will we allow anyone to pressure her into abdicating."

As the pieces of information began clicking into place,

Lincoln understood why the Walker's Run Co-operative had taken measures to create a legitimate police force, along with its own emergency services and establishment as a municipality.

He had to give Brice credit. A lawyer, trained by his uncle, the renowned Adam Foster, Brice had figured out how to use the full extent of human laws to protect his family and his pack.

"So." Brice's gaze—one blue eye, one green, both of equal intensity—pinned him. "Are you interested?"

And just like that, Brice called in the favor of his help for getting Lincoln returned to active duty.

"Yeah, I am."

A fierce negotiator, Brice went to extreme lengths to resolve issues peacefully, but as those scars on his throat could attest, he was also damn lethal when he had to be. And if the Walkers were gearing up for a dogfight, Lincoln sure as hell wanted to be the one standing with them, not against them.

Saturday afternoon, after using nearly half a bottle of eye drops and a cool compress, Angeline's eyes were no longer red and puffy.

All day, she'd held in tears so Lincoln wouldn't see her weakness, but the moment he'd left, the floodgates opened and unleashed the despicable waterworks. She was lucky if there was any moisture left in her body.

"You big baby," she said, scowling at her reflection.

There was comfort knowing Lincoln had promised to return. When she'd said goodbye to Tanner all those years ago, there had been no hope of ever seeing him again.

This time it's different, she told herself. Tanner had been at the beginning of his career. Lincoln's career was coming to an end and he wanted to start a new life with her and Dayax.

In a matter of weeks, she would unofficially become a parent. Most mothers had nine months to prepare for their newborn. Angeline had far fewer days to prepare for an eight-year-old she'd never met.

What if he didn't like her? Or worse, what if he *hated* her?

"I think I'm going to be sick." She hung her head over the sink and pressed a cool cloth to the back of her neck.

Immediately, a comforting masculine presence chased away her panic. Hugging herself, she promised to keep better control of her emotions. There was no need to worry Lincoln with her insecurities.

Dropping the cloth and the towel she'd used after showering into the laundry hamper, she padded into the bedroom. Crisply folded, Lincoln's sweatshirt lay on top of her pillow. Her heart melted.

He'd left a token, rich with his scent, to keep her company in his absence. Rubbing the soft fabric against her cheek, Angeline smiled, thinking about the surprise she'd tucked inside his duffel bag.

She draped the sweatshirt over her pillow and dressed for work. Staying busy would keep her mind occupied so she'd have less time to worry.

After putting on her coat, she grabbed her phone and purse and headed outside.

The sun was bright and the sky was clear, giving the false impression of a nice warm day. Still, it was decent enough for folks to enjoy Maico's Art and Craft Show, likely in full swing down at the town square. One day she would like to check out all the handmade crafts. Perhaps the one in the fall would be a fun activity that she, Lincoln and Dayax could go to as a family.

Angeline hurried carefully down the stairs and to her car, gritting her teeth against the cold nipping at her face and hands.

"Come on, baby. I need some heat." She shoved the key into the ignition. Something clicked. The engine made a straining noise then died. "I don't have time for this."

She counted to one hundred and tried again.

Nothing.

Spotting Damien's car in the near-empty parking lot, she got out of her vehicle and hurried upstairs. Cold and stiff, her knuckles hurt when she knocked on the door to Lincoln's apartment.

"Damien? It's Angeline."

A moment later she heard footsteps and the door opened. Dressed in camouflage pants and a dark sweatshirt, Damien peered curiously at her.

"What's up?"

"My car won't start again. Would you mind helping me out?"

"No problem." He put on a jacket, pulled a skullcap from his pocket and fit it snugly on his head, then followed her down the stairs.

"I appreciate your help. Come by Taylor's tonight. Dinner is on me."

"Thanks," Damien said. "But I have other plans."

"Some other time then."

"We'll see."

They crossed the parking lot to her car.

"Pop the hood." Damien turned up his collar, making him look like he had no neck.

Angeline sat behind the steering wheel and pulled the lever near the floorboard.

Damien propped up the hood. "How old is your battery?"

"A year." Same age as her car.

"Maybe you have a loose connection." From the sound of his tinkering, Damien seemed to be checking more than the battery.

Angeline checked the clock on her phone. Miriam and Jimmy wouldn't care if she came in a few minutes late, but Angeline hated to not be on time.

"How about another jump-start?" That would at least get her to work and she could ask Jimmy to give the battery a jump after her shift ended. She wouldn't need the car on Sunday. And Monday she could ask Damien for another jump to get her to the service station.

"You should take a look at this," Damien said grimly.

Angeline didn't relish the idea of standing in the cold while staring at engine parts that she knew nothing about, but she climbed out of the driver's seat and joined him at the front of the car.

"What are we looking at?"

"You've got a loose wire."

"Really? Where?"

"Right down there." Damien pointed behind the battery.

She leaned farther over the open hood to get a better view. "I don't see anything." Even though she'd sharpened her wolf vision because of the low light.

Damien stepped out of her way to give her a better view.

"Nope. Still don't—"

Damien's arm locked around her neck and his other hand pressed against the back of her skull, pushing her head forward. Even as she dug her nails into the fleshy part of his arm, her vision darkened until there was nothing but blackness.

Chapter 27

Ninety miles north of Atlanta, Lincoln began to feel antsy. The flow of traffic had been good and there hadn't been any delays, so he didn't know why he suddenly felt like he was about to crawl out of his skin.

A quick glance at the console showed the truck had just under a half tank of gas. After checking the rear and side mirrors, Lincoln eased the vehicle into the far right lane.

Taking the next exit, he drove to the nearest gas station. Climbing out of the driver's seat, he did a few stretches, filled up the tank and then walked inside the store. Not particularly hungry or thirsty, he purchased a package of chewing gum and a couple of magazines to read on the flight, then returned to the truck.

As he drove away from the pumps, his phone pinged with a text message, mostly likely from Angeline. He smiled because it felt really good to know someone actually missed him and eagerly anticipated his return.

Having had no contact with his parents since joining

the Program, he had no idea if they remembered having a son. Or if they would be interested in knowing that they would soon be grandparents.

Lincoln's parents were only children and he had no siblings. At least Dayax would grow up with cousins from Angeline's side of the family.

Family.

The word resonated in his being.

For the longest time he'd believed having a family was well beyond his reach. Now one was within his grasp, all because of a photograph and a little twist of fate.

Instead of pulling onto the road, he parked in a spot near the air pump and vacuum station and picked up his phone. The alert showed a text from Damien. Lincoln swiped the screen to open the message.

A picture of Angeline appeared on the screen and Lincoln's heart stopped. Lying on a dirty wooden floor, she appeared unconscious. A cloth had been stuffed into her mouth and silver-dipped zip ties bound her wrists and ankles. The silver collar fastened around her neck was attached to a long silver-coated wire connected to a nearby explosive device. When frightened and trapped, a wolfan's natural instinct was to shift. But if Angeline transformed into her wolf, the silver would act as a conduit for the shift energy and ignite the bomb.

Lincoln called Damien's phone. "Hurt her and I'll rip out your throat," he snarled.

"Whoa! Whoa!" Damien laughed. "Settle down, *Capitán.* If HQ knew you were threatening people, they might revisit your active duty status."

"Where is she?"

"I'm going to hazard a guess that you're asking about Angeline. Isn't she working at Taylor's tonight?"

"I'm not playing games with you, Marquez."

"That's too bad." All the humor in Damien's voice was

gone. "Because right about now, you're approximately halfway between Maico and Atlanta. Am I right?"

"Yes," Lincoln hissed between clenched teeth.

"So, you get to choose between two outcomes. If you board that plane in Atlanta, you'll save the boy and lose the girl. If you turn around and come back to Maico, you *might* save the girl, but will lose your chance to find the boy."

Lincoln's heart felt like it would split in two. How could he choose between Angeline and Dayax?

"Tick, tock. Tick, tock. You have two hours."

"When I find you, I will kill you," Lincoln shouted into the phone.

"I didn't figure you would abandon your promise to the boy so quickly." Damien's heartless laugh made Lincoln cringe. "Then again, if your guardian angel dies, what happens to you?"

The line went dead.

Lincoln's heart pounded furiously as fear unleashed a deluge of adrenaline into his system. His hands trembled so badly that he nearly dropped the phone while searching the contacts for Brice's number. It took three tries before he managed to hit the call button.

"Damien has Angeline," Lincoln shouted before his friend finished saying hello. "He's tied her to a bomb and I only have two hours to find her!"

"I'll mobilize the sentinels to track them," Brice said calmly. "Where are you?"

"On I-75. I'm ninety minutes away." Lincoln heard the panic in his own voice and some part of him believed this was all a dream. "He's making me choose between Angeline and Dayax. If I miss the plane, I won't make it to HQ in time to meet up with the team heading to Somalia. If I catch the plane, I'll lose Angeline."

Worse than the nightmare reliving the explosion inside the abandoned building in Somalia, this situation would likely kill him or some part of him. Because losing either Angeline or Dayax would leave a gaping wound in his soul.

"Do you know where he's holding her?" Brice's clear, level voice helped modulate Lincoln's rising panic.

"No, but he sent a picture."

"Text it to me. We'll start looking as soon as the sentinels are gathered."

"If they find her, tell them to not engage." Swallowing the caustic lump lodged in his throat, he forwarded Brice the picture. "I'm coming to get her."

He'd made the best decision in the midst of an awful circumstance, and it was the one he knew Damien expected him to make. Dogmen prioritized rescues based on the most eminent and immediate threat of danger. Angeline was tied to a bomb. Dayax had a hostage extraction team working to free him and the other children.

"I just received the picture. I'll keep you updated."

"Brice, get word to HQ. I'm not going to make the flight so the team will have to go without me. As soon as they make contact with Dayax, they need to tell him that they're bringing him to me. Or he'll run away at the first opportunity." And Lincoln would likely never find him.

"Will do."

Disconnecting the call, Lincoln focused his mind on the rote mantra he used to prepare for dangerous missions. Once all emotion had drained from his conscience, he slammed the gearshift into Drive and spun out of the parking lot with a singular thought.

Damien Marquez is a dead man.

Something hard and cold pressed against Angeline's cheek. Opening her eyes, she saw a black snake coiled in the wake of a parallel sunbeam about six feet away.

Her startled gasp never left her throat because of the

large wad of cottony material stuffed into her mouth and held in place with a strip of cloth tied around her head. Quickly, she visually scanned the room, at least what she could see from her angle, lying on the floor.

Neither seeing nor hearing Damien, Angeline tried to sit up. Since her wrists and ankles were bound behind her, it took several attempts before she was successful.

From the weight around her neck, she suspected Damien had collared her and the silver wire dangling down her chest and beneath her arm was some sort of leash.

Really?

She would've thought a Dogman would be more original in kidnapping a she-wolf. Her gaze followed the wire across the dusty floor to a strange device sitting in front of several gas cans.

Run!

Her instinct flew into panic mode. With her hands and feet tied, all Angeline could do was scoot away from what appeared to be a homemade bomb. The silver tether didn't allow her to get far.

Normally, shifting would be her first response. The energy from the transformation disintegrated any material touching her skin. Except silver.

Changing into her wolf form wouldn't free her but it certainly might kill her.

She tried to maneuver her legs and discovered that not only were her hands and feet tied behind her, they were also trussed together. Somehow, she had to find a way to get free.

A hidden knife inside her boot was the perfect solution. Too bad she'd scoffed at the idea when one of the human servers at Taylor's suggested it. Why carry a knife when she could shift into a wolf and use her razor-sharp teeth? At the time she'd never considered a scenario in which a

Dogman would kidnap her and chain her to an explosive device.

Think. Think. Think!

What would her father and brothers do?

Angeline huffed. They wouldn't have gotten themselves into this situation.

She'd broken the first rule: never let your guard down. People like Damien were the reason for the rule. He'd gained her trust and, *wham*, used the Sleeper Move to incapacitate her.

Unable to do anything else, Angeline studied the room. The dusty windows were boarded up with old planks on the outside. The walls and floor were wood, termite-infested and rotten, from the looks of the panels. The huge door appeared to be solid oak, with rusty iron hinges, a doorknob and slider lock.

A hole in the baseboard at the far right corner of the room, might've been where the snake had entered. Using her knees to scoot around, she saw an old stone fireplace. Black marks scored the bottom of the pit and up the flue.

From what she could tell, Damien had dumped her in an old abandoned antebellum but she had no idea where this particular house was located. There were several throughout the area and Tristan knew each and every one. But Angeline had no way of contacting him. Even if she could, she had no idea how long she'd been out. Damien could've driven her anywhere, including right out of the Walker's Run territory.

Damn! All the years she'd resented her father's drive to make her tough, to make her capable, to make her just as hard-boiled as her brothers, now she understood why.

She fought against the restraints. The thin silver ties bit sharply into her skin but there was no give, no matter how hard she pulled. Exasperated, she roughly rubbed her cheek against her shoulder until she worked the gag loose and spit out the cloth.

Sharp pain shot through her jaw as she closed her mouth, the muscles in her face and neck sore from being forced open for an unknown period of time. With no moisture in her mouth, dry-swallowing felt like sharp barbs sliding down her throat.

Creaking boards distracted her from the pain. She attuned her ears to follow the sound of movement. Booted footfalls seemed to echo from different directions inside the house, as if someone was moving back and forth between rooms. Then silence.

Angeline tried to quiet her breathing in the eerie quiet. The sunbeam warming the snake faded. Slowly lifting its head, it stuck out a forked tongue to scent the air for danger.

The footfalls began again. This time in a linear path that seemed headed toward the door to Angeline's prison. Her heart raced.

On her knees, with her hands and feet fastened together behind her back, she had no means of self-defense. She couldn't even count on the snake, a black racer without the tiniest bit of poisonous venom.

Booted steps stalled at the door. The iron lock wiggled then turned. Slowly, the door creaked open and Damien stepped inside the room.

"Untie me, right now!" Angeline's voice cracked from the dryness of her throat.

"I'm not in the business of taking orders." His cold, dark gaze flickered over her.

"You're a Dogman! You take orders all the time!"

Madness churned in the arctic depths of his fathomless eyes. "No and no. Not anymore." His precise enunciation sliced the chilly air.

"What does that mean? You're *not* a Dogman?" In her

current predicament, Angeline figured it was best to keep him talking. Maybe she could find a way to reason with him and convince him to let her go.

"HQ's quack doctors think I'm..." Damien tapped a finger against his temple. "I'm not. But they cut me from the Program anyway. So the answers to your questions are no and no."

Oh, Angeline begged to differ. Damien might not be a Dogman now, but he definitely needed professional intervention.

"I don't have any sway with the Program." She softened her voice, hoping to lure him closer. "Why do this to me?"

"I don't give a damn about the Program," he snarled. "Not anymore."

"Then what does this accomplish? Why have you rigged me to a bomb, Damien?"

He paced a wide berth around her. "Lincoln always believed in his guardian angel. The rest of us thought you were nothing more than one of those photo inserts found in new wallets. Turns out—" he shrugged "—you're real. And you're his true mate."

Damien stopped in front of her, but far enough away that she couldn't lunge forward to topple him. "That is why you're here, *Angel*. Dogmen don't have true mates."

"Lincoln isn't a Dogman anymore. He's retiring."

"Aww." Damien squatted so he was eye level with her. "Is that what he told you?" His toxic laughter made her flinch. "Here's the truth. Captain Lincoln Adams is part of a team headed to Somalia and his mission is to extract hostages from the rebels' camp."

"You're lying." Lincoln promised he wouldn't be in danger, promised he was only signing paperwork and then would bring Dayax home.

"I have no reason to lie," Damien said. "I already have

you here and my plan has been set in motion. Lying serves
me no purpose."

"Except to hurt me."

Damien's mouth twisted into a grotesque smile. "That's
what the bomb is for, *Angel*."

"Stop calling me that!"

"Never heard you object to Lincoln saying it."

"You're not Lincoln!"

Damien's creepy smile faded as he replaced her gag.
"And you're no angel. I checked." He waggled his hands.
"No wings."

What she was, was a pissed off she-wolf. And the moment she got loose, Angeline would show him how much
of an angel she wasn't, using nothing but her bared teeth.

Chapter 28

Dirty old snow flew past the windows. The truck jostled from the deep potholes on the unpaved road but Lincoln did not let up on the accelerator.

Within twenty minutes of his call to Brice, the Walker's Run sentinels had tracked Angeline's phone using a GPS tracker. Unfortunately the device and her jacket had been found down the embankment of the ravine where her crumpled car rested at the bottom.

No one believed she'd hit an ice patch and missed the curve at Wiggins Pass. The consensus was that the accident had been staged. Recovery crews hadn't found a body, but Lincoln knew they wouldn't because the mate-bond he shared with Angeline had not been severed.

Periodically, he could sense her during moments of strong emotional reactions. However, he intentionally blocked feeding his emotions back to her, because if Damien knew they were communicating through the mate-bond, he might escalate his plan before Lincoln arrived.

Which would be within minutes, thanks to Tristan.

After arriving home from the hospital with his mate and newborn son and getting them settled, Tristan had answered Brice's text with the picture Lincoln had forwarded.

Tristan recognized the room where Angeline was being held and had sent a handful of sentinel scouts to the abandoned MacGregor homestead.

As Lincoln barreled into town, his phone had pinged with photo confirmation that Damien had been sighted at that location and a message that they were still trying to get a visual on Angeline.

He had responded with a request to pull the sentinels back to at least a half-mile radius. If Damien got wind of any interference, he might simply level the house with Angeline inside.

Sharply jerking the steering wheel, Lincoln swung the truck onto the overgrown driveway dusted with melting snow. Despite the initial fishtailing of the back tires, he sped toward the dilapidated house overrun with thick ivy vines and hardy weeds.

Nearing the porch, he slammed on the brakes and cut the wheels to the left while engaging the emergency brake. The truck swung in a complete circle before stopping.

Lincoln jumped out of the truck and bounded up the porch steps. Not fooling with the lock, he planted his shoulder in the center of the large, double mahogany doors with their rusted hinges and gave a good, hard shove. A second shove with his full weight behind him brought the doors down.

Angeline's essence suddenly rushed him. Relief, worry, anger, fear—all of it a tidal wave of emotion that nearly knocked him off balance.

"I'm here, Angel." He stood in what once might have been an elegant entryway flanked on both sides by a

curved marble staircase leading to the second-floor bal-
cony, which looked like it might collapse at any moment.
The row of doors vaguely reminded him of the building in
Somalia where he'd been searching for Dayax. No surprise
that Damien had picked this place for whatever twisted
game he wanted to play.

"Lincoln! It's a trap."

"Don't worry, sweetheart. I know what I'm doing." Lincoln cautiously stepped around the jagged remains of a
glass chandelier. When this ordeal was over, if he never
stepped inside another abandoned building again, it would
be too soon.

"Are you hurt?" Lincoln focused internally, trusting
his instinct to lead him to his mate.

"I'm tied up, but okay."

Lincoln began walking down a corridor toward a door
on the left. Perhaps once a study or a cigar room off the
main floor.

"I don't know where Damien is."

"I'll find him once I get you out." Lincoln rapped his
knuckles against the door panel.

"Someone's knocking."

*"It's me. Do you see any wires running along the door
frame?"*

"No!"

Holding his breath, Lincoln slowly and carefully turned
the knob and opened the door. His heart dropped at the
sight of Angeline bound and gagged in the center of the
room.

After a quick visual inspection to determine there were
no trip wires, Lincoln darted to Angeline. Tears shimmered in her big, blue eyes.

"I will get you out of here." He pulled the gag from her
mouth and she spit out a wad of cloth. "Did he hurt you?"

She shook her head.

Lincoln lifted the silver-coated wire running from her neck collar to the explosive device. "Did he say anything about the collar? Can we take it off?"

"No," she said hoarsely. "He said the bomb would go off."

Lincoln carefully ran his finger along the inside of the collar. He didn't feel a second trigger but wouldn't tempt fate.

Pulling out a pocketknife, he sawed through the silver-coated zip ties fastening her hands to her feet. Angeline began to topple forward. Lincoln caught her shoulders and helped her maneuver into a position to maintain her balance.

"Hang tight." Lincoln slipped the blade beneath the ties at her ankles. "You'll be free in a minute."

Less than that with any luck.

"Lincoln! Look out!"

Damien's wolf slammed into Lincoln with enough force to knock him across the room and push Angeline to the floor.

Lincoln shook off the momentary surprise and saw the brindle-colored wolf crouch over Angeline with his teeth bared, growling a challenge.

"Damien," Lincoln said, knowing the wolf could understand him. "You're a Dogman. We don't hurt innocents."

The wolf's growl got louder.

"You're making it hard for me to believe that you don't want to hurt her." Lincoln slowly and carefully rose on his hands and knees. "Back away from her."

Mouth open, Damien swung his muzzle toward Angeline.

Lincoln sprang forward, shifting into his wolf at the same time Angeline thrust her knees into Damien's ribs.

As Damien fell back from her self-defense move, Lincoln knocked him clear.

Both wolves hit the floor and skidded into the wall as a tangled heap. Uninterested in a parlay of bites and scratches to gain dominance, Lincoln immediately lunged for Damien's neck.

His mouth filled with fur, but before Lincoln clamped down on the young Dogman's throat, Damien wrangled free.

"What the hell is wrong with you, Marquez?" Lincoln positioned himself between Damien and Angeline.

"I'm finally seeing things clearly," he snarled. *"I would've followed you anywhere. Hell, I did follow you and lost half of my face."*

"You're angry at me because you disobeyed my order and got disfigured in the process?"

"I would've worn this scar like a badge." The wolf shook his twisted muzzle. *"You and me? We could've worked together. Lots of packs would've taken us on contract. Hell, the one in Miami already made an offer. Do you know how much money we could've made? The fun we could've had?"*

"You kidnapped the woman I want to claim as my mate because you wanted us to be business partners?" Primal rage rustled in the deep, dark, dangerous recesses of Lincoln's being. But he needed to rely on his training to resolve the current conflict without unleashing the primitive beast within.

"I looked up to you," Damien snarled. *"Hell, I was happy that the Program put you back on active duty status. And then you said you were giving it all up for her."* Damien glared at Lincoln. *"Traitor!"*

Lincoln anticipated Damien's launch toward Angeline and intercepted. Both wolves crashed to the ground in a frenzy of gnashing teeth and slicing claws.

* * *

Never did Angeline imagine in all the times her brothers had tied her up when they were kids that the experience would one day come in handy.

Though her hands and feet were still bound, they were no longer tied to each other. Which meant she could wiggle around, working her hands below her feet and…voilà, her hands were now in front of her.

She sat up, saw the pocketknife Lincoln had dropped and scooted close enough to pick it up.

Angeline's bound hands made it awkward to use the knife to saw through the silver zip ties. Lincoln had cut through the first restraints effortlessly. Then again, his hands hadn't been tied together.

Lincoln's and Damien's growls were no longer warnings. She glanced up as they collided in the air, their bodies tangling as teeth gnashed and claws slashed with deadly intent.

Crashing to the floor, the wolves wasted no time scrambling to their feet. Lincoln continued to block Damien's advances. The problem was that once Angeline freed herself, she'd have nowhere to go because Damien was closest to the door.

She might've caught him unawares with a knee to the belly once, but doubted he'd give her a chance to do it again. Continuing to awkwardly saw at her restraints helped to keep her focused on not freaking out. Although she had no idea what to do once her arms and legs were free because the wire to the collar around her neck was connected to a freaking bomb.

Lincoln will figure it out, she told herself.

A blood-curdling howl of pain caused her to drop the knife. She jerked in the direction of the fight.

Missing part of an ear, Damien bled from a gaping shoulder wound and multiple bites and scratches. Lincoln had several deep scratches and two really bad bites, but still had both of his ears.

Neither wolf moved. Perhaps a temporary truce?

Angeline fumbled for the pocketknife and continued to work the blade through her wrist bindings.

Someone barked. Startled, Angeline jerked and the knife sliced across the back of her hand. She clamped down on the cry of pain before it passed her lips, afraid any noise from her would distract Lincoln, who was actively engaged with Damien again.

She forced her attention from the wolves ripping into each other with their teeth to her own wound. The cut bled freely, but when she wiped her hand against her shirt to clean away the blood, the wound looked shallow and had already started clotting. Holding her hands in front of her face, Angeline studied the marks on the zip ties. Her attempts had barely scratched through the silver coating.

If she couldn't get the bindings off, it would do no good to go wolf. Silver morphed in tandem with the shifter's body, which meant she'd still be bound in her wolf form.

Clearly, she understood why some animals chewed off a limb when caught in a trap. Sometimes it was the only alternative. However, she had not reached that point of desperation. Yet.

Picking up the knife, she wedged the handle between her teeth with the sharp edge of the blade safely protruding beyond her lips. Then she positioned her wrists on either side of the blade, pulling downward on the tie as she sawed backed and forth until the binding broke.

Yes!

She glanced at the wolves. Blood and spittle matted their coats, puddled on the floor and smeared along the walls.

Oh, God!

They would both bleed to death unless they stopped fighting soon.

Hands now free, Angeline feverishly attacked the binding around her ankles with the knife until they broke. She stretched her legs and wiggled her toes, trying to rush the feeling back into her feet.

In her peripheral vision, she saw a flicker of movement and looked up to see Lincoln's hind paw slide into a puddle of blood, causing him to lose his balance. Damien pounced, biting and swiping at Lincoln until he went down.

"Get the hell away from him!" she screamed.

Damien swung his muzzle around and his cold, dark, deadly gaze targeted her. She sensed the threat of attack before one muscle flexed to propel him in her direction.

Instinctively, she flipped the knife so that the handle pointed upward when she raised her hand, then threw it, just like her father had taught her to do.

The knife sailed toward Damien. The rotation could've been better but the weapon struck the target and stuck. Unfortunately, it didn't stop him. But it did make him angry.

Angeline's instinct screamed for her to shift.

Lincoln's wolf rose up behind Damien and slammed him to the ground. The force of the landing caused them to slide straight toward her.

There was no time to get out of the way. Upon impact, she flew in one direction, the two wolves in another.

Shaking off the daze from the hard landing, Angeline lifted her gaze. The silver wire dangling from the collar around her neck was no longer tethered to the explosive device.

"Run!" she screamed at Lincoln, who had Damien by the throat in a kill strike.

She shifted. Darting out of the room, she raced down the corridor, leaped over the broken glass on the foyer floor, bounded across the broken doors at the entryway, skidded across the porch, sailed over the steps and kept running.

Lincoln shadowed her, barking nonstop. Urging her to run faster.

Dammit! She was trying.

At one time, the meandering, oak-lined driveway might've been a delight, but covered in melting snow and petrified acorns, it was a bitch to run.

The first glimpse of the dirt road beyond the property gave her the adrenaline boost she needed. Her speed increased, and Lincoln kept pace.

They were going to make it. Surely they would.

Lincoln suddenly slammed into her. She landed in the deep ditch alongside the road with him on top of her.

The tremble in the cold, wet ground beneath them grew into a seismic force. Only then did she hear the percussive force of the house exploding along with the shatter of glass, the whoosh of debris sailing past and the thud when it dropped to the ground. It was over in seconds, but it felt like an eternity.

When all fell quiet, she felt the buzz of shift energy as Lincoln returned to his human form, naked and without his prosthetic. He eased his weight from her body.

"Baby, are you all right?" Uncertainty sharpened his voice as he removed the silver collar around her neck.

Angeline shifted. "I'm okay."

Bloody and dirty, Lincoln hauled her against him, his hands gliding over her nude body as if to make sure she spoke the truth. Seemingly satisfied, he let out a long breath.

"Do you think Damien made it out?" she whispered.

"No. He didn't want to make it out." Lincoln buried his face in the curve of Angeline's neck.

Even though the danger had passed, Angeline realized

she was shaking. Lincoln, however, was rock-steady and smiling against her bare shoulder.

His secret thoughts whispered through Angeline's mind. In that moment she knew. Damien hadn't lied to her.

But Lincoln had.

Chapter 29

Lincoln's plane to Munich was flying over the Atlantic and, instead of seeing blue skies and even bluer water, he stared up at the ceiling lights in the emergency bay at Maico General Hospital.

"Okay," Doc Habersham said. "That's the last stitch."

"Thanks." Lincoln sat up on the gurney and glanced at the new patchwork on his body. Then, he fingered the gauze covering some nasty gashes on the side of his neck that would definitely leave obvious scars when healed.

"You get used to them," Brice said. And he should know, having a similar reminder of when someone had tried to rip his throat out, too. He pushed up from the chair in the corner and handed Lincoln some clothes and shoes. "You look about my size, so I hope it all fits."

Lincoln was grateful for the hand-me-downs since his clothes were in the duffel bag in the passenger seat of the truck that had been destroyed in the explosion. Along with everything else he owned—which was very little.

Shoving his right foot into the pant leg, he had to roll to the left to pull the jeans over his hip, then roll to the right after putting his stump in the other pant leg. He appreciated that Brice didn't offer to help. Dressing wasn't the easiest task but it was one Lincoln could do independently, even covered in stitches.

Once he put on the long-sleeved shirt, sock and shoe, Lincoln felt somewhat normal again, except for the missing prosthetic. HQ would not be happy that his bionic limb had been destroyed.

Hell, they probably wouldn't even issue a wooden replacement now. Crutches might be his only available means of ambulation for a while.

"I'm going to need a new place to stay," he said quietly. "Without my prosthetic, three flights of stairs will be problematic."

And that wasn't his only worry. Through the mate-bond, he felt Angeline distancing herself from him and he sensed the real possibility that she would reject a mate-ship with him.

"Have you decided not to return to Somalia?"

"I missed the last flight that would put me at HQ in time to take the physical readiness exam and join the team before they leave."

"After what you just went through to save Angeline, no one at HQ will doubt your readiness."

"I appreciate the vote of confidence, but I don't see how I could make it to Munich before the team leaves."

"I happen to know that Councilman Bartolomew is leaving Atlanta for Munich on a private jet tonight," Brice said. "There's a seat reserved for you, as well."

"A member of the Woelfesenat just happens to be going to Munich. Tonight?"

"I believe he said there was some paperwork at HQ regarding the transfer of a minor wolfling that required his personal attention."

Lincoln rubbed his temple. "Exactly how many favors does the Woelfesenat owe you?"

Brice smiled but said nothing.

A nurse came in with a pair of crutches for Lincoln. "Doc said he put through your discharge papers. You're all set to go, but he wants to see you in ten days to check your stitches."

Though he politely nodded his agreement, Lincoln expected to be gone a lot longer than ten days if he could wrangle HQ into giving him a new prosthetic in time to rendezvous with the team going to Somalia. "How's Angeline?"

"A little dehydrated. Doc has her on IV fluids. She should be ready to go home soon." The nurse handed him some paperwork and left the room.

Using the crutches, Lincoln got up from the bed. "I want to see her before I leave."

"I'll wait for you in the lobby," Brice said.

Lincoln carefully maneuvered down the hallway, his instinct leading him to Angeline's room. She looked so fragile sleeping in the hospital bed that he couldn't believe she was the same woman who'd stood up to a deranged Dogman, freed herself from captivity and escaped a deadly bomb.

It was difficult to be quiet, easing into her room on clumsy crutches.

Opening her eyes, she smiled at him, but it was brittle and stiff.

"Hey, baby." He leaned down, giving her a soft kiss. "The nurse said you can go home soon."

"What about you?"

"They've already kicked me out." He curled his hands around her fingers resting on the bed. "I don't have much time, Angel. Brice arranged for me to hitch a ride to Munich with Councilman Bartolomew."

Her body went rigid. "Damien said your medical retirement was rescinded and you're back on active duty. You're not just signing paperwork, you're going into a war zone. How could you lie to me?"

"You've been lying to your family for years because you're afraid of telling them the truth." As soon as the words finished spilling from his mouth, Lincoln regretted them.

"How dare you!" She jabbed her finger in the direction of the door. "Get out!"

"Angeline, I'm leaving and I don't know how long I'll be gone. The last words you say to me will be the ones written in my heart when I go into Somalia."

Tears glistened in her eyes. "Just go," she whispered.

Lincoln had hoped that Angeline would put her faith in him. But on the heels of everything that had happened, she simply didn't have the courage to do it.

Leaning over her, Lincoln kissed her sweetly on the mouth. "In case these are the last words you hear from me, I want you to know that I love you and I believe in you."

In silent agony, Angeline had watched Lincoln leave. After his profession of love, a vacuum had opened in her chest, crushing her heart and stealing her breath.

She'd gone through this with Tanner. He had loved her, too. But not enough to choose her over the Program.

What a fool she'd been to fantasize about a mateship with another Dogman and motherhood. Now her heart was doubly broken. And the only thing Angeline could tell herself was that she should've known better.

"Angeline?" Her father stood in the doorway, holding a bag of her clothes and personal items to wear home after discharge. "Are you all right?"

"I'm okay," she said, noticing the worry lines creasing his forehead. "Doc said I can go home once I've finished the IV fluids."

The strain on her father's face didn't ease as he sat in the bedside chair and reached for her hand. His gaze swept her head to toe and back again before the stiffness in his posture faded. "Coming in, I met Lincoln leaving. He said a curious thing."

I bet he did.

Her emotions raw and ragged from allowing herself to end up in the same devastating position she knew she needed to avoid, Angeline didn't want to deal with the impending inquiry. Especially because Lincoln was right. She had been hiding the truth from her father for most of her adult life because she was afraid of his ridicule and rejection.

"What is this whole other side of you that he mentioned I should get to know?"

Continuing to keep the truth from her father would only prolong the inevitable. The time had come to face the music.

Figuring the beginning was the best place to start, Angeline told him all about pursuing music instead of a business degree. About falling in love with Tanner and how much his rejection had hurt when he'd chosen being a Dogman instead of her, and how she'd channeled those difficult emotions into writing award-winning songs.

When she finished unfolding the details of her secret life, Angeline waited for her father's response.

And waited. And waited.

"Are you going to say something?" she finally asked.

"Why did you wait so long to tell me?" Her father's disappointed gaze searched her face.

Angeline folded her hands in her lap. "You never approved of my musical interest. Instead, I had to take karate classes to make me tough. How could I tell you that I'm earning a living writing songs about getting my heart broken?"

"Don't you think I understand heartache? Your mother was everything to me. Those first few months, even a year or two after she died, I was so lost that I didn't know what to do." Her father swiped his hand across his jaw. "I regret giving away her things, but at the time I couldn't tolerate the reminders."

"Is that why you cut off my hair? I've always thought it was because I looked like mom."

"I was a single father with three young kids and no time to primp and curl a little girl's hair."

"What about the music lessons? Aunt Miriam paid for them because you wouldn't."

"I thought you were going through a phase and I didn't want to waste money." His sigh sounded sad and tired. "Until now, you've never explained to me how much music meant to you."

"Would it have mattered?"

"I wouldn't have been happy to learn that you wanted to write songs for a living. A career like that is a risk. I would rather know that my children have a solid foundation for their future."

"Is that why you're always badgering me during Sunday dinners to join the family business?"

"I thought you were floundering. You don't have a mate and I'd hoped you would eventually have higher aspirations than being a part-time server at your aunt and uncle's restaurant."

"There's nothing wrong with waiting tables for a living."

"No, there isn't. But I was right. You did want more for yourself. I just wished you hadn't kept your talent a secret.

Songwriting isn't a job I would pick for you, but I'm proud of you, no matter what you do for a living."

"One of my songs is nominated for an Academy of Country Music Award. The event will be televised live from Las Vegas in April. Maybe we can get everyone together to watch."

"How about we go there instead?" her dad said in earnest.

The heaviness in Angeline's chest gave way to an effervescent joy. "I'd love it!"

Her father stood, then leaned over and kissed her forehead. "Lincoln should join us, too."

Some of Angeline's happiness dimmed. "He's a Dogman, Dad. He isn't coming back."

"That's not what Lincoln told me." Her father squeezed her hand. "What's this about a new grandson?"

Angeline's heart paused while her brain processed her father's words, then it kicked into overdrive as a jumble of emotions fought for dominance. "What did he say exactly?"

"He's going to get his boy and they're both coming home to Walker's Run, if you'll have them."

"I need your phone!"

Clasping the device her father handed to her, Angeline dialed Lincoln's number. Her heart, which seemed to have climbed into her throat, tumbled into her stomach when the recording announced incoming calls were no longer accepted.

All she could do was pour all of her love and support into the mate-bond and trust that her intentions were getting through because she did not want her last words to Lincoln to haunt him the way they did her.

Chapter 30

Gunfire echoed in every direction, though no one on the rescue team had fired a single shot. Still, they took advantage of the confusion and advanced on the insurgents' compound.

Waiting for the team leader's next signal, Lincoln sensed a gentle feminine essence graze his spirit. Always nonintrusive, Angeline had reached out to him through their mate-bond on a daily basis for the three and a half weeks he'd been on active duty.

More than once he'd been tempted to respond, but encouraging the connection was a Program violation and could distract him at an inopportune time and devastate her if something terrible happened. Though touched by her expressions of support, especially after the way they had parted, Lincoln closed her out of his thoughts and senses.

Redirecting his focus to the rebels who kidnapped children and forced them to become soldiers in their militia, he watched two adult males with rifles slung over their shoulders walk within a few feet of his hiding spot. The urge to rip them to pieces for their parts in the atrocity grew as they passed him on their rounds. But the task to take out the foot patrols fell to someone else.

Lincoln was on point for first contact with the kids. When the time came, he would have to maneuver through the enemy compound to the building the reconnaissance scouts had identified as the children's barracks. Nearly midnight, all should be asleep in the common quarters, making it easier for Lincoln to get them in one swoop.

He glanced around the compound, his wolfan vision unhindered by the suffocating darkness. The cloak of ominous clouds provided an additional layer of coverage to the team, already dressed head to toe in black clothing and wearing camouflage paint on their faces. Lincoln hoped his appearance didn't frighten the children. He needed their trust to get them out alive.

The gunfire ceased one minute and twelve seconds after it started, just like the last five times. Too patterned to be actual gunplay, he suspected the rebels were brainwashing the children into believing their captors were protecting them. Depending on how long the ploy had been in use, the children could be affected by Stockholm syndrome. Whatever their condition, Lincoln prayed that Dayax would recognize that he was not the enemy.

"All clear." The CO's voice whispered through Lincoln's earpiece. "Go, go, go!"

Immediately, Lincoln sprang forward and ran. His temporary prosthetic didn't have the versatility the previous one had, but it fit comfortably and provided solid, steady support.

With his heart practically in his throat, he reached one of the trucks the rebels used to gather and transport children after a raid. Hunkered down, he glanced around to ensure he'd not been seen. Then, he slipped a tactical knife from the sheath fastened around his good leg and jabbed it into the back tire. Jerking the weapon free, he heard the hiss of escaping air.

Carefully, he eased along the driver's side, the body of the vehicle shielding him from the view of any foot patrols. After puncturing the front tire, Lincoln broke radio silence.

"The mongoose is in the pocket."

"The mongoose is in the first pocket. Hawks stay frosty." The CO's whispered instruction went out to the entire team.

One obstacle down, five more to go.

Random foot patrols slowed the team's progress and their standing orders were not to engage unless discovered. In that event, hand-to-hand combat was preferred. No one wanted to alert the rebels of their presence. The likelihood of successfully escaping with all twelve children unharmed dropped dramatically if all hell broke loose.

Still, every team member had been equipped with an M16A4, just in case.

Finally reaching the barracks, Lincoln dispatched the unsuspecting lone guard, then pressed his ear against the door. Not hearing any suspicious movement, he carefully entered the single-room building. Thirteen children were sleeping on small mats strewn on the floor.

Damn!

The recon team had only counted twelve.

Lincoln broke radio silence. "The mongoose is in the ring with a baker's dozen. Repeat, *baker's* dozen."

In the ensuing radio silence, he scanned the room, his gaze settling on Dayax's small form. Lincoln's heart nearly leaped from his chest. After nearly thirteen weeks of separation and worry, he'd found his wolfling.

Lincoln swallowed the gasps of joy and relief rising in

his chest. Danger surrounded them, and he had a lot to do before allowing himself to celebrate.

The team had five escorts—three of whom were Lincoln's former teammates—assigned to whisk two children at a time to safety, with Lincoln providing cover as they retreated. Either someone would have a trio to wrangle through the woods and protect, or he would have to keep number thirteen with him.

The CO made the call for the latter.

Quietly, Lincoln woke up Dayax first.

The boy's dark eyes widened. "Lincoln!" He threw his thin arms around Lincoln's neck. "I knew you'd come."

Lincoln's throat closed around a sharp, ragged breath that he had to clear before he could speak. "Shh. We must be quiet." He held the boy tightly, his heart pounding so hard, he thought his ribs might break. Since the wolfling had gone missing, Lincoln had hoped and prayed for a moment just like this one.

But they weren't out of danger, not yet.

Lincoln gently pulled back, gritting his teeth against the painful resistance of every muscle. "I need you to help me explain to the others. We're taking them home." Although Lincoln could speak Somali, he knew the children were more likely to trust one of their own than a stranger.

With Dayax's help, they quickly and quietly woke up the remaining twelve. Lincoln paired up the six oldest children with the younger ones, leaving Dayax as the solitary spare.

Lincoln checked the perimeter and radioed the CO.

Once he received instruction to begin the evacuation, he sent them two by two to the first spotter stationed less than thirty feet from the building, who then sent them to the second spotter, and so on and so forth until each had two children they would escort through the woods to the rendezvous point. Once the final pair made it safely to the last spotter, Lincoln knelt in front of Dayax.

"Do exactly what I say when I say it. Don't think, just do it. Okay?"

Dayax nodded.

Lincoln shouldered his weapon and eased out of the barracks. Almost immediately, his senses tingled.

Drawing the tactical knife from its sheath, he spun to the left and threw the weapon at the guard racing toward them. The target dropped silently to his knees, clawing at the knife lodged in his throat.

Clutching Dayax's hand, Lincoln quickly followed the path the other children had taken. Shouts went up behind them. From the sound of the chatter, someone had found the guard Lincoln had dispatched.

Lincoln and Dayax stayed their course. When gunshots rang out and bullets whizzed past Lincoln's head, he pulled Dayax behind the nearest tree, readied his weapon and returned fire.

Above the commotion, he heard the rebels' shouts and their advancing steps. Outgunned and outmanned, their capture was certain if they remained where they were.

He hadn't come this far to end up dead.

Lincoln grabbed Dayax's arm. "Run!"

The boy dropped to his hands and knees, shifted into his wolf and bolted through the woods. Lincoln did the same, only he was much faster. On the fly, he picked up the wolfling by the nape of the neck and ran like the devil had lit his paws on fire.

Chapter 31

Sitting in a large auditorium filled with famous faces, Angeline twisted the note card in her hands.

"Don't be nervous." Sandra—Angeline's longtime agent—squeezed Angeline's hand. "You've got this."

I hope so!

However, Angeline's reasons for wanting to win the Songwriter of the Year Award were likely entirely different from her agent's reasons.

Angeline had not heard a peep from Lincoln in over a month, despite flooding the mate-bond with love and positive vibes at random times throughout the days and nights.

She firmly believed that he remained unharmed and that he had successfully rescued Dayax. If the opposite were true, she would know.

The performing act finished their routine, and Angeline joined the audience in giving applause. The emcee appeared on the opposite corner of the stage, gave the introduction to the next category and then called out the names of the nominees.

"And the Song of the Year goes to—"

Angeline held her breath, but the emcee had trouble opening the envelope. She nearly passed out from lack of oxygen before the song title was announced along with the name of the songwriter. Generous applause erupted.

At home, she would do her happy dance in front of the television. But in the auditorium with a stage and lights and cameras, Angeline froze.

Anonymous for so long, she wasn't as prepared for the spotlight as she'd hoped.

"Come on, hon." Taking Angeline's arm, Sandra helped her stand.

Clutching a handwritten speech, Angeline made her way to the stage. A young man wearing a tuxedo escorted her up the steps and across the stage to the podium where she was handed a small statuette of a golden hat.

The bright lights prevented her from seeing the audience, which she decided was a good thing. As applause died down, she opened the note card in her hand.

"Thank you for this wonderful honor. Usually, I'm at home watching the awards ceremony on the television. But it is a privilege to be here with you tonight and, for the first time, to share this special moment with my family, who are somewhere in the audience."

She paused. "Until recently, they didn't know that I was a songwriter. Despite any previous awards or accolades and songs that reached number one on the charts, part of me felt that my talent wouldn't measure up in their eyes."

Angeline wished she could see her family's faces right now. Too many opportunities to share her life with them had been lost because of the fear of their rejection. "But really, I was reflecting my own insecurities onto them. And I'm so very thankful to Lincoln Adams for coming into my life and teaching me how to have faith in myself, in my loved ones and in him. He's the reason I came tonight, because he's out there somewhere, working hard to make the world a better place. And before he left, I didn't take the opportunity to tell him how much I love him. So I'm doing it now."

She thought of his smile, his larger-than-life presence, but mostly she thought of his unwavering loyalty. "Lincoln, wherever you are, whatever you are doing, know that I love you with all of my heart. I believe in you. Thank you for teaching me to believe in myself. I miss you, and I'll leave the light on so you can find your way home."

Tears rolling down her cheeks, Angeline stepped away from the podium to the sound of thunderous applause. Though a weight lifted from her shoulders, her heart remained heavy.

An escort led her backstage, where she walked a gauntlet of flashing cameras and big fat microphones being shoved in her face for impromptu interviews. Of course, Sandra steered her safely through them.

When her splotchy vision returned to normal, she saw a young wolfling approaching with a red rose. His big brown eyes, flawless bronze skin and dark, tight, curly hair cropped close to his head caused an unusual beat in her heart. He flashed a gloriously beautiful smile. "A rose for an angel," he said with an accent.

"Thank you, sweetie." Accepting the flower, she knelt in front of him. Prickly tears threatened to blur her vision again. "Are you—"

"Dayax Adams," he announced proudly. "Lincoln signed papers to be my *aabbe*. The tall man on the plane said it's not 'ficial, yet. But I can say he is."

"Come here." Angeline hugged him tightly. "I'm so happy to meet you."

"You smell good," he said, sniffing her hair.

"Already taking after your dad." She laughed. "Speaking of Lincoln, where is he?"

Grinning, Dayax took her hand.

Angeline had to step quickly to match his pace. All the while her heart raced as the wolfling led her straight to a man wearing a black tuxedo and surrounded by her entire family.

He turned and stepped from their midst.

Lincoln!

Her heart couldn't decide whether to race, furiously pound or flutter with happiness. She forgot to breathe and her knees threatened to buckle.

"Hello, Angel." Lincoln opened his arms, and she melted into his embrace. "I'm so proud of you."

Her family echoed his words.

"I missed you," she said, pressing her face into the curve of his neck and inhaling his clean, masculine scent.

"I missed you, too." He kissed the crown of her head and a feeling of rightness spread through her body, all the way down to the tips of her freshly polished toes.

"Why didn't you call me after you found Dayax? Or reach out through the mate-bond?"

"I couldn't make any calls. We left Somalia immediately following Dayax's extraction and flew to Germany on a transport. Once we got to HQ, we went through extensive debriefing and then I had to be fitted with a new prosthetic. Since I didn't know when we would get back to the states, I asked Councilman Bartolomew to get word to you. But he cut through the red tape and flew us here in a private jet."

Lincoln grazed her cheek with the back of his hand. "As for the mate-bond, you don't know how much I wanted to reach out to you. But it's against protocol and I didn't want to risk screwing up the adoption or my retirement plans. It's scary what the Program can do. But that's all behind us now, baby."

Her heart settling comfortably in her chest, Angeline took her first easy breath since Lincoln had left. "Did you see any of the show?"

"Enough." He smiled that wonderful smile of his. "I love you, too, baby."

"Angel?" Dayax tugged her arm, then presented to her a tiny box. Inside, she found a beautiful marquis diamond ring.

"I choose you, Angeline O'Brien, to be mine for now and always." Lincoln slid the ring onto her finger. "And I promise to love you until my last breath, and beyond."

"That's an awfully long time, Dogman. Are you sure you're up to the challenge?"

"Retired Dogman." Lincoln gathered Angeline close and held Dayax's hand. "And I've been preparing for this my whole life."

* * * * *